VENGEANCE SERIES

KAYLEA CROSS

STEALING VENGEANCE

Copyright © 2019
by Kaylea Cross

* * * * *

Cover Art and Print Formatting:
Sweet 'N Spicy Designs
Developmental edits: Deborah Nemeth
Line Edits: Joan Nichols
Digital Formatting: LK Campbell

* * * * *

ISBN: 978-1095080573

Dedication

For Big Weasel. Love you to infinity. Thanks for the plot bunny on this one.

Mom xo

Author's Note

Welcome to the start of my series about the Valkyries! I've been pondering a series for these badass ladies for several years now. Given the state of things today, I felt the need to unleash these strong, talented women on the world. I hope you enjoy the ride.

Happy reading!

Kaylea Cross

Prologue

Trinity Durant tucked the package safely into the bodice of her cocktail dress and walked out of the guest suite into the top floor hallway of the posh hotel like she owned the place. Black and simple, the dress was sexy and short enough in front to allow her full range of motion of her legs should a quick getaway become necessary.

Not that she anticipated having to make a run for it tonight. But she was always prepared for the unexpected.

She smiled at a couple she passed and headed for the stairs. Her target—a man with important CIA contacts and a past to hide—was currently down the hall screwing his mistress in another suite, allowing Trinity plenty of time to slip in and retrieve what she'd needed from the safe in the closet. As an added bonus, it would also allow her team to send an explicit video link of the couple to his new, young socialite wife later on.

Sometimes blackmail was the best currency to get what you needed.

Trinity hoped the footage got splashed all over every social media outlet out there. The slimy bastard and all his corrupt government buddies deserved public ridicule and humiliation once their dirty deeds were exposed.

Down on the second floor in the large, adjoining ballrooms, the party was in full swing. A ritzy gala supporting a children's charity, featuring a guest list made up of celebrities, politicians and government officials. Anyone and everyone who had power and money in Washington. By morning the package tucked into her bodice would have several of them panicking—especially the man upstairs.

She bypassed the party and headed for the main entrance, struck by how easy this was compared to the jobs she used to take on. So many times she had been forced to take the place of the mistress in the upstairs suite right now, using the powers of seduction she'd been trained with to get what she needed. And sometimes, the job ended only when she'd added another kill to her body count.

That was then. Now she had a new life. One where she called the shots, and only took on assignments she was comfortable with. Best of all, she had a wonderful man to share that new life with.

Her left thumb went unerringly to her bare third finger, startlingly naked without the weight of her diamond engagement ring. Pushing the nagging worry about it from her mind, she stepped outside.

Warm night air surrounded her as she exited the air-conditioned building. A few steps from the curb, the burner phone in her evening bag rang. She pulled it out and answered without looking at the display. Only one person had the number.

"Did you get it?" the familiar male voice asked.

"Of course I got it," she said, feigning insult. On a difficulty and risk scale of one-to-ten, tonight's op had been a zero-point-five on both counts. And yet it had hopefully been one of the most important of her career.

"Good. I'll pick you up at the rendezvous point."

Which they should have set up a few blocks closer, she decided as she tucked the phone away. Easy for him to set the RV point earlier—he wasn't the one walking three blocks in freaking four-inch heels. Heels that concealed stiletto blades in them. Because a girl could never have too many weapons on her.

By the time she reached the appointed intersection her feet were killing her, but her steps never faltered and her gait didn't change. A Valkyrie never showed pain or weakness on a job—not even a former one.

She folded her arms and shot a mock glare through the BMW's tinted windows as it pulled to the curb in front of her. The lock popped up and the passenger door swung open.

Her boss, Alex Rycroft, leaned across the front seat, silver eyes gleaming as he grinned at her. He was "retired" and happily married with a toddler at home, but took on certain things as a consultant from time to time. "You look gorgeous."

"Flatterer," she muttered, fighting a smile as she slid into the passenger seat and shut the door.

He smoothly pulled out into the evening D.C. traffic and headed toward the river. "How was the party?"

"Scintillating."

He grinned. "I'll bet. Here." He handed her the transmitting device.

She pulled the tube of lipstick from the bodice of her dress, unscrewed the base and pulled out the copy she'd made of the hard drive. The flash drive slid easily into the device. After entering the code she hit send, and the piece of electronic wizardry did its thing. "Who are we sending this to, anyway?"

"Two people I trust, and you know both of them. Whoever cracks the encryption first, wins."

"Then let's hope I got what we need this time."

He'd been frustratingly vague about what it was they were after, but for him to have taken this on in the first place meant it was important, and he'd approached her specifically, saying she had a vested interest that would be revealed in time. This was her third op of the mission, all involving stolen, encrypted files he wanted recovered. The first one had been in San Fran. The second in New York City. Now this.

"Third time's the charm, right?" he said.

"That's what they say." Trinity reached up and removed her long brown wig, then breathed a sigh of relief as she slid off the sadistic heels. The shoes were sexy as hell, but horrible to wear. Invented by a man. "Oh, *God*, that feels good." She leaned back in the seat, watching the lights and traffic out the window, relaxed but alert, and simmering with impatience to find out what was going on. "Wherever you're taking me, there had better be wine and cheesecake."

"I'll order you some from room service," Rycroft promised, a smile in his voice.

He was a good man. A hard man with a legendary reputation both in Special Forces and with the NSA. But he was fair. If you were motivated and dependable and delivered results, there was never a problem. Given some of the people Trinity had worked for in the past, that was a revelation.

They rode in comfortable silence until they reached a hotel and he turned into the underground parking garage. She didn't bother asking him where they were going because he wouldn't answer, and because she trusted him. She followed him into the elevator and down the hall to a room, which he unlocked with a key card.

"After you," he said, his silver eyes full of secrets.

Not sure what to expect, Trinity stepped inside. She drew up short, barely concealing her shock when she saw they weren't alone.

4

The two women waiting for them both jumped up to greet her, big grins on their faces. "Surprise," they chorused.

She laughed and reached for the slender, dusky-skinned brunette first. "Wow, a reunion." These two women were the closest thing she had ever had to sisters. And they had been through a lot together.

Briar DeLuca returned the hug a little stiffly, though so much less awkward about it than the former sniper would have been a few years ago. "Yep. Not sure what Rycroft's got up his sleeve, but I know it's gotta be good."

Georgia was there to hug her next, blond hair cut to her shoulders, her pale blue eyes bright with excitement. "Nice to see you."

"You too. Where's your mysterious husband at, anyway?"

"He's around," her friend answered evasively, and they both grinned.

"So, wine and cheesecake all round?" Rycroft said from behind them.

Trinity faced him and arched an eyebrow. "What's going on?" If he'd brought them all together for a secret meeting, then something big was up and she wanted details.

He gestured to the chairs in front of the flat screen TV. "Sit and I'll fill you all in."

When everyone was settled he leaned back against the desk and folded his arms across his chest, still broad and hard with muscle even though he was now in his mid-fifties. "I have confirmation that the Valkyrie Program was still operating up until several weeks ago."

Stunned silence met his words, and the mood turned dark. Trinity exchanged shocked glances with her fellow former Valkyries before focusing back on Rycroft. "That's impossible," she rasped out. It had been shut down for a long time.

He shook his head. "You three and the others who trained with you were part of phase one. But there was a phase two as well, initiated a few years later, and it kept going even after Balducci and the others were brought down."

Will Balducci—a former trainer and would-be senator who had betrayed them all for money and influence several years ago. He had put hits out on Briar's and Georgia's handlers. Then he'd tried to kill both Valkyries to cover his tracks.

Happily, he was rotting behind bars right now. But according to this latest twist, the apparent decay within the CIA and the intelligence community went even deeper than she or anyone else had realized.

"They changed the official name and buried everything deeper," Rycroft continued. "I'd just been informed about it and authorized an off-the-books investigation, then the trail went cold. Everything stopped, almost overnight. Then I found out why."

He pulled out his phone, typed in something and held it out so they could see the picture on the screen. It showed a young woman maybe in her twenties, her face bluish, eyes closed on top of an autopsy table. "Her name was Stacey. And she had a very interesting mark on her left hip." He swiped to the next photo, showing a symbol they were all intimately familiar with.

It was about the size of a silver dollar, positioned on her left hip. A black crow with a sword clutched in its talons, and the word *Valkyrja* written inside a stylized scroll beneath it. Each Valkyrie received it upon graduating from the program.

"Her death was reported to U.S. intelligence a few weeks ago. She was poisoned with a quick-acting isotope used exclusively by Chinese operatives. Investigators found her in a back alley dumpster in Shanghai."

Trinity shifted her gaze from the phone to him. His

expression was somber. As somber as she'd ever seen it, and a warning tingle started up in the pit of her stomach. Alex Rycroft had seen and done it all. If this situation had brought him out of retirement, it was huge.

"Her name and picture were sent to a Chinese mobster one day before her death," he continued.

"By who?" Trinity asked.

"That's what we need to find out. Because Stacey is just one of four dead Valkyries who have turned up over the past month—ever since the media got wind of the program during the fallout from the Balducci trial. Each operative was murdered in a foreign city after completing a job there. So far, all the evidence points to them being killed by the organizations they'd previously targeted."

Silence greeted his words as they all absorbed the gravity of the statement. Valkyries were notoriously difficult targets. Nearly impossible to find, and hard to kill. They were trained to be ghosts, and only a few people knew their true identities and locations.

Until now.

A cold wave of anger spread through her. Someone had deliberately leaked the operatives' names and locations once the public had gotten wind of the program. A program that to her and everyone else's knowledge had been shut down permanently.

Rycroft regarded all three of them in turn before continuing. "Here's what I know. Whoever leaked these files is involved with the program, and they're no longer with the CIA. They're likely a talented hacker, because it would take an electronic wizard to get hold of those classified files that were all destroyed. Whoever they are, our target is operating alone from the outside, and I'm currently analyzing anyone who might be involved. Whoever this is potentially has files on all former and current operatives, and is selling them off piece by piece to our enemies."

"To kill us off one by one," Briar finished.

He nodded. "That's how it looks right now. And that's why I'm asking for your help to stop the bleeding before it gets any worse. Nobody knows better than you three what needs to happen. The clock is ticking. We're in a race to find the hacker, mitigate the damage, and then bring the at-risk Valkyries in before they're captured or killed."

"I'm in," Trinity said without hesitating, rubbing her thumb over her bare ring finger. Brody would understand. Wouldn't he?

Rycroft nodded at her, then looked at Briar. "You're a new mom, so I'm not asking you to do field work. But are you willing to work logistics with a small, hand-picked team I'm putting together?"

"Yeah, of course, I'm in," Briar answered, her espresso-brown eyes burning with determination.

"What about you?" Rycroft asked Georgia.

"I'm in too. Whatever you need."

"Good." He crossed one foot over the other. "We got one Valkyrie's name by complete accident, and we're trying to locate her right now." He swiped on his phone again, then held it up so they could see the new photo.

"This is Megan Smith," he said, showing a young Caucasian woman with hazel eyes and chestnut-brown hair. "She was last operating in western Europe, but went to ground when the Balducci case hit the airwaves. We have no idea where she is, but we need to find her, and fast, because her name was potentially leaked to a terrorist organization two days ago."

Trinity studied the picture, trying to place her. She was fairly certain she'd never met the woman. But Megan was a fellow Valkyrie, and Trinity was going to be the one to find her. "I'll go."

The meeting lasted another half hour while they went over logistics and a plan of attack. As soon as they got a hit on Megan Smith's location, Trinity would be on the next flight out of D.C.

Rycroft stopped her on her way out of the hotel room, searching her eyes. "Is Brody home?"

"He's due home tomorrow night." And he wasn't going to be too happy when he found out what she had just agreed to.

His smile was understanding. "Good luck."

On her way down the hall she rubbed her thumb over the bare spot on her left ring finger, thinking of her fiancé and then Megan.

Brody might not understand, but she had to do this. She *needed* to.

Holding Megan's image in her mind, she strode for the elevator.

Hold on, Megan. I'm coming for you.

Chapter One

S o this was what freedom tasted like.

Megan had imagined it for so long, had told herself it would never be as good as she envisioned it. And she'd been right.

It was better.

Perched high in the stirrups, she leaned forward in the saddle over the horse's neck. She maintained the pressure of her knees against its sides as they galloped along the winding path that cut through the gentle, rolling hills of some of the most gorgeous countryside in England.

Warm summer sunshine filtered through the green canopy of leaves above her, dappling the worn, earthen path with shadow and light. The fresh scent of green, growing things filled her nose, mixing with the sweet, dusty scent of the horse. A gorgeous morning to spend any way she wanted to.

Out here she didn't have to constantly look over her shoulder, and there was no warning tingle at the back of her neck. Out here there was nothing but two-hundred acres of rolling countryside...and hidden targets to hit.

Her friend Marcus had been out hours earlier, still up before dawn every day despite having been medically retired from the military for the past two years. As was his custom he'd moved the targets around on the course, to test her. She'd found his note on the kitchen table this morning.

Let's see how you do this time, hotshot.

Megan had never been able to pass up a challenge. One of her many flaws. Here, however, none of her flaws could harm her.

Excitement pumped through her veins at the coming challenge but she automatically quelled it, letting the calm take over as it always did when she was about to fire on a target.

Except these days she shot plywood and straw rather than bad people.

The bay gelding raced along, neck outstretched, enjoying the chance to stretch his legs. He would stay on this path unless Megan turned him, his gait smooth and familiar.

As the scenery flew past, Megan spotted a target set off to the right in the distance, tucked up into the spreading branches of an ancient oak. Balancing her weight on the balls of her feet, she lowered the reins and reached back with her right hand for an arrow from the quiver on her back. She raised the bow in her left hand, knocked the arrow with her right and drew it back until her fingers touched her jaw, her gaze riveted on the target.

Her heart rate slowed. Beating in between the rhythmic thud of the gelding's hooves on the hard-packed earth. She counted down the seconds along with the calculated distance. Thirty yards. Twenty.

She let her breath out slowly, just as she'd been trained to do when firing a rifle.

Ten yards.

Her body poised motionless to counteract the horse's gait, Megan loosed the arrow. It sailed through the warm, clear air, striking the edge of the red center bull's eye.

One down.

Immediately she took up the reins and searched for her next target. Marcus had made it nearly impossible to spot them, the sneaky bastard. God, she loved that about him. How he constantly challenged and supported her, keeping her sharp in case her past caught up with her and she had to go off grid at any moment.

Eighteen targets and arrows later, the test was over. She shifted her weight back into the saddle and drew back on the reins a bit, slowing the gelding to an easy canter.

In the distance up ahead, a familiar figure stood leaning against the old stone wall that marked the end of the course, a brown-and-white Anatolian Shepherd beside him. He straightened as she approached, picking up his cane from the wall to steady himself with it.

"Ay up," she called out.

"Ay up." He glanced at his watch, lifted a taunting, dark eyebrow that pulled at the scars on the left side of his face. "Bit slow today, weren't you?" he asked in his endearing Yorkshire accent. He sounded just like Sean Bean. Short vowels, aitches missing from the start of words, and tees dropped all over the place.

"Nope. And I hit every one of your targets," she added with a smug grin.

The corners of his lips twitched in the hint of a smile. After what he'd been through, smiles from Marcus were a rare thing indeed. "Aye? Did you, now." He planted his cane, leaned some of his weight onto it to take the strain off his left leg. The dog, Karas, leaned into him, instinctively bracing him. "'ow many were there?"

"Eighteen."

He shook his dark head. "Nineteen."

What? She'd missed one? She stared at him, dismayed, and automatically blurted, "No there wasn't."

The tiny quirk of his lips told her he'd been teasing.

She relaxed and shot him a narrow-eyed look. *Jerk.* She stopped the horse, reached down to pat his neck.

"You're such a good boy, Rollo. So smooth and fast." Straightening, she focused on Marcus, the person she trusted most in the world.

Theirs was an unlikely friendship. At nearly forty-five he was twelve years her senior, and a reclusive bachelor. He'd served with the Royal Marines, then gone on to spend the majority of his career in the SAS before retiring on medical grounds.

She'd never been in the military. But thanks to her training she had a whole arsenal of skills and could kick serious ass.

Marcus was a quiet, serious bookworm who rarely left the house. She craved action, thrived on challenge, hated being cooped up, and preferred to be outside.

He liked Victorian poetry and classic movies. She liked action flicks and rock music, the more electric guitar the better.

Yet somehow, they clicked. Because they had more in common than anyone might guess. Their shared history had forged an unbreakable bond, so strong that when her life had been in danger and she was forced to go to ground almost two months ago, he'd risked his own neck by having her come here to stay with him in spite of the danger.

"So, what brings you all the way out here in the middle of the day? And don't say it was to time me," she added.

His dark-chocolate gaze was level, his expression giving nothing away. It still startled her sometimes, how hard he was to read. Even for her, a master at reading people while hiding her thoughts and emotions, he was an enigma. "We've got guests coming."

She frowned. Was he teasing again? She couldn't tell. "What kind of guests?"

"The last-minute kind."

She didn't like the sound of that. They never had visitors. Other than the occasional curious townsperson or lost tourist, no one ventured out here onto his land except the handful of loyal employees he kept, let alone near the main house. "Who is it?"

"Don't know them. But the woman knows you. And I already checked them out with a contact." His gaze was level. "Woman gave 'er name as Trinity Durant. Says she's with the NSA. Ring a bell?"

NSA? Honed from a lonely, frightening childhood and refined to a razor-sharp edge over her lifetime, her internal alarm began to blare. But there was no way Marcus would ever endanger her safety, or allow anyone onto the property if they posed a threat. He didn't seem concerned, so she relaxed a fraction. "No. How long do I have?"

He nodded at Rollo. "Just enough time t' get him back to the stable and brush him down."

More curious than worried, she nodded once. "Race you." She wheeled the gelding around and urged him into a flat-out gallop. When she glanced over her shoulder a moment later, Marcus was almost to his old Land Rover, Karas scampering behind him, white tail wagging.

While Marcus took the private road back, Megan chose another riding path she'd fallen in love with during her time here. She slowed Rollo for the final mile to let him cool down.

At the top of the next hill Megan drew in a deep breath and took a moment to admire the view, every bit as stunning as it had been the first time she'd seen it. The gentle Cotswold hills rolled out around her for miles in every direction like a green patchwork quilt.

Nestled between two of them in a small valley stood Laidlaw Hall. Built of the famous honey-toned Cotswold limestone in the early seventeenth century, the grand three-story manor house all but glowed in the morning sunlight.

Marcus's dark green Rover was already parked out

front in the circular driveway, and the mystery guests he'd been so evasive about hadn't arrived yet. She rode south of the main house and cut across the field to the stable. Marcus employed a small staff that included a stableman but they had to keep to strict schedules to protect her and Marcus's privacy, so she untacked and groomed Rollo by herself, then let him out into the paddock.

Pea gravel crunched under her riding boots as Megan walked through the formal garden and into the back entrance of the main house. The fresh, tangy scent of lemon oil greeted her, along with the sudden quiet, broken only by the ticking of the grandfather clock in the downstairs hall.

She let the sweet silence envelop her. Let it wrap around her with its comforting embrace. Quiet had been rare in her life. So had friendship and loyalty, and a bond with someone she could count on no matter what. Here, she had all of them.

Because of Marcus.

"We're back here," he called out from the direction of the library.

We? Frowning, she set her riding helmet and crop onto an occasional table in the hallway and started for the library, a telltale prickle of dread needling the base of her neck. With every step on the worn stone pavers, her senses became more acute, her body on alert.

The sweet smell of leather bindings and old paper hit her as she entered the open, carved mahogany doorway. A jolt of shock rippled through her when she saw the woman seated in the leather club chair beside the empty fireplace.

More than pretty. Verging on stunning. A bit older than Megan, maybe in her mid-to-late thirties. Fair skin. Shoulder-length black hair. Killer curves. An air of confidence so strong it was palpable. And deep blue eyes that saw right through her.

Megan stopped one step into the room, heart thudding as she stared at their guest. It bothered her that she hadn't realized anyone else was in the house. That she'd missed the signs. Because in her world, that kind of carelessness could get her killed.

The woman hadn't said anything, hadn't even moved, and yet Megan intuitively sensed she was in the presence of a lethal predator. Her subconscious recognized it, the truth of it humming inside her like the high frequency vibration of a tuning fork.

"Hello, Megan," the woman said softly. American. No hint of a regional accent that might give Megan a clue to where she was from.

Her unease went up another notch. She didn't move, holding that penetrating stare. "Who are you?" An operator. That much Megan was sure of.

"Trinity Durant."

The name still meant nothing to her, and her near photographic memory ensured she'd never seen that face before. "What do you want?" Why the hell had Marcus allowed her to come here?

"To talk to you. Alone."

Not happening. "Anything you have to say, you can say in front of him," she answered, nodding at Marcus without breaking eye contact with the woman. "Now. How do you know my name, and how the hell did you find me?"

Trinity didn't even blink. "That's a long story I'm looking forward to telling you soon. Suffice it to say, it wasn't easy. And as for the second part, I guess you could say I've got friends in high places."

High? Try highest in the intelligence world. Megan had gone off the grid a while ago. No one should have been able to find her. "I'm not going to ask again."

The woman's calm expression never changed, her body language gave nothing away. Not even a flicker of reaction in her eyes. "What I have to say is top secret. I'd rather have this conversation in private."

"Either Marcus hears it now, or I tell him later. I have no secrets from him." Behind his desk, Marcus leaned back in his chair with his hands linked across his stomach, his expression almost amused. Karas was curled up on her bed beside his desk.

He was *enjoying* this. Watching this bizarre scene unfold in his inner sanctum. Because he knew exactly what was happening, even if Megan didn't yet.

Trinity's eyebrows went up slightly at her response, the first hint of a reaction so far. "Really? Well, that's good to know," she murmured, her gaze far too penetrating. Too knowing. As if she could see *inside* Megan.

Megan folded her arms, raised her chin. "Well?"

Those sharp, deep blue eyes held hers for a long moment. "Your sisters are under attack. I need you to help me identify and locate the rest of them before they all wind up dead."

A sliver of cold threaded up her spine. "I don't have any sisters."

"Not by blood, maybe." Trinity uncrossed her shapely legs and stood, all lethal elegance and pinup curves, holding Megan's gaze the entire time. Without looking away she reached down to simultaneously pull up the side of her cherry-red top with one hand and eased the waistband of her jeans down with the other.

Stunned, Megan masked her disbelief at the small, all too familiar tat on the woman's left hip.

She flicked her eyes up to Trinity's, struggling to contain her shock. "Who are you?" she whispered, her heart thrumming in her throat.

Trinity concealed the tat once more, her expression unreadable. "A friend."

"I don't have friends." Except for Marcus, who she trusted with her life. She would do literally anything for him, including kill if necessary. Just as he would do the same for her.

"All right, then, consider me an ally in this war against our kind," Trinity said.

Our kind...

Megan's mind raced. It was astonishing to have another Valkyrie standing in front of her. Trinity was older than her, and therefore more experienced. For her to still be alive meant she was one of the deadliest and most skilled women on earth. And based on her physical appearance, Megan could already guess what Valkyrie category the woman fell into.

A seductress. An operative who killed her targets up close and personal—as up close as two people could get. "What did you mean, 'before they wind up dead'?"

"We're being hunted. Methodically. Surgically, taken out one by one. We need to find the others and bring them in to stop the bleeding."

More cold spread through her. "Who's hunting us?"

"We don't know. Until recently we thought the Valkyrie Program had been shut down a long time ago. We didn't know there were others out there, like you."

"Who's 'we'?" Megan asked.

"My team. You'll meet some of them soon."

She had to have some idea of who was hunting them, or she wouldn't be here. "Who else is with you?" Megan demanded, impatient to know what was really going on here.

"Your new partner."

Her eyes widened, partly in shock and partly in outrage. She let out a humorless laugh. "My *what*?"

Before Trinity could answer, the pit of Megan's stomach tingled in silent warning.

Quiet footsteps behind her on the old stone pavers made her whip around. Her spine jerked taut, all her muscles grabbing as the man's silhouette blocked the light filtering in from the windows at the front of the house.

Tall. Broad-shouldered. Powerfully built.

He came closer, his steps measured and purposeful, and she could feel the energy flowing from him. Patient. Focused.

The breath strangled in her lungs when he stepped into a beam of sunlight and his face came into view.

Chiseled features. Strong jaw. Light brown hair cut short. Slate blue eyes that missed nothing. Eyes she had never forgotten.

No. No, it can't be.

That familiar gaze wandered over her face for a long moment, almost in a kind of wonder. Then one side of that sexy mouth tipped upward and his deep, smooth voice rolled over her. "Hey, dimples. It's been a long time."

Chapter Two

Ty Bergstrom thought he'd been prepared to see her again. But the shock that ran through him told him otherwise. And judging by the surprise on her face, the sight of him was just as jarring for her.

He stood his ground, enjoying the disbelief in her hazel eyes. Those eyes were exactly the same as he remembered, intense and intelligent, framed by dark lashes.

The rest of her looked good too. Even better than the intriguing twenty-one-year-old he remembered. Her chestnut-brown hair was long now, falling past her shoulders in thick waves. Even though she'd filled out some too since he'd last seen her, her appearance still made her seem intensely feminine. Harmless.

He knew firsthand exactly how deceptive that last bit was. And from what he'd learned over the past week, the people she'd targeted over the years had no doubt learned that too late, and the hard way.

"What are you doing here?" she demanded, her posture rigid. Defensive.

He didn't blame her. They hadn't met under the most ideal circumstances all those years ago. And back then he hadn't understood what was really happening. "I was asked to help out an old acquaintance."

She studied him, mistrust clear in her eyes as her gaze bored into him. "An *acquaintance*? I barely knew you, and it's been over twelve years."

He inclined his head. She'd been twenty-one and he'd been a cocky twenty-five-year-old Army Ranger who thought he was The Shit. Looking back, the old him should have been embarrassed by all that he hadn't known. "I know." But he'd never forgotten her. Because forgetting someone like her was impossible, even when he hadn't known what she was.

A weapon. A deadly, secret weapon trained by the government, housed in a deceptively harmless-looking package.

"Meg. Come sit down and listen to what they 'ave to say," their host said in his northern English accent from behind the massive mahogany desk in a room that like the rest of this place, looked like it had come straight out of Downton Abbey. Marcus Laidlaw, combat wounded SAS veteran in his mid-forties, now lord of the manor. Ty wasn't sure how the guy fit into all this yet, but he was going to find out.

Megan eyed Ty for another long moment, then spun around and marched back into the study where she sat in the chair closest to Marcus and opposite Trinity. Ty followed her movements with a trained eye, no longer fooled by her misleading appearance. She still moved in that confident, purposeful way that had captured his attention all those years ago, though her matured curves gave her gait a slight sway that made it even sexier.

Of all the women he'd trained over the course of those fateful seven months, she was the one who stood out. Her quickness and determination. Her restless energy. Her complete lack of complaint when circumstances went from bad to shitty.

He'd been so impressed with her ability to compartmentalize and make the best of things. Then he'd gotten a taste of what she was truly capable of, and been blown away.

There were no more chairs left, so Ty leaned a shoulder against a bookcase stuffed with old, leather-bound volumes and waited, holding Megan's borderline-hostile stare.

"My team was looking for someone we could bring in from the inside," Trinity began, speaking to Megan. "One of them remembered Tyler and he remembered you, so we checked him out and vetted him thoroughly. He's well qualified for this mission—"

"What mission?" Megan demanded, staring at him.

"We'll get to that," Trinity answered calmly. "Tyler was Special Forces until his honorable discharge several years ago, and he's been a security contractor since. The head of our taskforce knows him personally and agreed we should bring him in."

Megan looked at her. "Who's that?"

"Alex Rycroft."

Megan stared at her for several seconds, and though her expression and body language gave nothing away, Ty sensed she recognized the name. Though it would have surprised him if she hadn't. Alex Rycroft had served in SF for the first part of his career before becoming one of the NSA's most celebrated agents. A nod from him amounted to the stamp of approval throughout the U.S. intelligence services, and Ty was honored to have it.

"When you met Tyler as a SERE instructor, he was filling in on a temporary basis before his unit rotated overseas to Afghanistan. Circumstances being what they were, he was completely unaware of the Valkyrie Program, or that you were a part of it," Trinity explained.

Megan glanced over at him again, skepticism clear in her gaze.

"It's true," he said, for what it was worth. Though his word probably didn't mean much to her. He hadn't even heard of the Valkyrie Program, and he certainly hadn't known it entailed taking orphaned girls and turning them into the most lethal female assassins walking the planet. "I'd never heard of the program until the whole story about Balducci broke in the media a few years ago."

She met his stare for a long moment before focusing back on Trinity. "So, what's this mission you're talking about, and what's his role?"

"Like I said, he's your partner."

Megan shook her head. "We work alone. Always. You know that."

"Not this time."

Megan opened her mouth to argue but Trinity didn't give her the chance. "We're trying to get a lead on who-ever leaked the identities of the other Valkyries, *and* bring all of them in before our enemies find them. Once we get a lead, you'll be sent to retrieve the target's files and bring him or her in. For that to work, you'll need backup, and since our hacker is intimately familiar with the Valkyries, going as a single woman just makes you more suspicious, and therefore a more likely target."

She paused before continuing. "Rycroft trusts Tyler, and so does a close Valkyrie friend of mine. That's good enough for me and will have to be for you as well. You'll conduct this mission together, and pose as a couple for your cover."

Megan sat up straighter, her eyes shooting sparks first at Trinity, then at Marcus. "You knew about this and you didn't say anything?" she said to him.

"I only 'eard it last night. And we'll talk later." They stared at one another, some kind of secret conversation going on that only they understood. It was eerie, and based on what he'd learned about Megan, Ty half-believed she could actually send telepathic messages.

"Rycroft and I asked Marcus to keep it secret," Trinity said, drawing Megan's attention back to her. "If he'd warned you, you would have been a flight risk. So any hostility you have should be directed at me. I'm a big girl, I can take it."

Megan drew a deep breath and settled back into her chair, her expression grudging but calm. "I've got no say in this?"

"Not about the partnership."

She turned her head to meet Ty's stare, and this time he could see the resentment burning there. "Not sure how much you know about us, but I'm not known for playing well with others."

"I'm aware," he said dryly. He'd seen it when he'd been an instructor for the survival portion of what he'd assumed was a normal SERE school. She'd stolen gear right out from under his nose, twice.

And then she'd shocked the hell out of him by showing up at his solitary camp in the middle of the night a week later, battered and bruised but defiant and proud, having escaped the enemy prison camp during the escape phase. He'd later learned from the cadre that she'd broken out of the bamboo cage they'd placed her in and snuck out of camp, without anyone noticing.

It was the first time it had ever happened. Everyone had been certain one of the instructors had helped her. But nope, it had been all her.

Ty had found it fascinating at the time. Now he wanted to get to know her, see what she could do firsthand, and somehow make up for any damage he'd unwittingly aided in all those years ago. He'd thought he'd been preparing her and the other students for life behind enemy lines. In reality, he'd been complicit in something much harsher.

Megan focused on Trinity again. "How many Valkyries have been killed?"

"Four so far that we know of, but we're not even sure who we're looking for yet because we only have partial personnel files. I recovered some on an op two days ago from a former CIA officer involved with the program, and your information was there. It took us until last night to locate you."

They shouldn't have been able to find her, though. That worried her. "How were the others killed?"

"Some were executed. Others were captured and tortured first."

Megan's expression never changed, but her eyes chilled. "Who do you think's behind it?"

"A hacker. An extremely skilled, elusive tracker."

"CIA? U.S. intelligence?"

"Possibly."

"Anything else?" Megan asked.

"That depends on you. Is there anything else you want to know?"

"Just when I'll be dismissed from this meeting."

Ty hid a grin, amused and intrigued by the fire in her. She might hate the idea of working with him on this, but she would do it, because the stakes were huge. The lives of the surviving Valkyries hung in the balance. Based on her background, he was pretty sure that was the only motivation she would need.

"As soon as you give me an answer on whether you're in or out," said Trinity.

"I'm in," Megan answered.

Trinity nodded once. "You can go."

Megan stood, aimed a loaded look at Marcus and turned for the door. She shot a warning glare at Ty as she swept past, leaving the scent of her fruity shampoo trailing in her wake.

The wooden door shut behind her with a thud. Not exactly a slam, but close.

For several seconds, no one moved or spoke.

"That went well, all things considered," Marcus said.

Trinity sighed. "Well, Tyler, you've got your work

cut out for you on this one."

"That's okay." He'd faced longer odds than winning over Megan Smith, or whatever her real name was. "Should I go after her?"

"No," Marcus said immediately. "Steer clear of 'er for tonight. I'll talk with 'er once she's cooled off. You can start trainin' together in the mornin'." He reached down to scratch the dog's ears. "Karas, go find our lass, eh?"

The dog got up and trotted to the door, ears up and tail wagging.

Tyler opened the door for it and stepped into the hall. This assignment should be interesting. But even if he was wrong and it turned out to be boring as hell, it sure felt good to be doing something he believed in again.

Chapter Three

Megan's fury had eased from a boil to a simmer by the time dusk fell and she started back across the fields to the house with Marcus's rescue dog trotting at her side. She'd left immediately after the "meeting" in the library, needing to get outside and burn off some steam before she'd exploded.

Though she wasn't in contact with any of them, it was sobering to know that she and the remaining Valkyries were being systematically exterminated. By who? And why?

The long run had helped burn off the worst of the emotional turmoil. Impulse control was something she'd struggled with when she was younger, and she'd had to learn to control her quick temper. Two of her many flaws, and none of her instructors or handlers over the years had been able to rid her of them.

Tyler freaking Bergstrom.

She shook her head, a wave of anger rising all over again. She'd liked him. Had liked him the best of any of her instructors during the entire course of the program, though she'd only been his student for a few weeks. Worse, she'd been attracted to him, and it had taken all of her formidable skill even back then to hide it, shove it down deep inside where no one, not even she could see it.

Right from the start she'd had no illusions about what her life as a Valkyrie would be like, and understood that there was no room for personal entanglements along the way. Nothing about those had changed.

Ahead in the distance, Laidlaw Hall came into view, warm rectangles of golden light spilling from some of its windows against the darkening sky. Overhead the sky was turning purple, a blanket of stars beginning to appear. Crickets and frogs sang all around her.

An unexpected pang of sadness hit her. She'd never had a home. Not a real one. She'd only been here a few months but somehow this place felt like home. It seemed weird to return to it now that other people were inside it. Like an invasion, or even a violation. A defilement of the private sanctuary Marcus had allowed her into, and yes, she was still annoyed with him.

She was no coward, however. She'd been tasked with helping save the remaining Valkyries, and she would do everything in her power to make it happen. *Loyal Unto Death.*

And sometimes, beyond it.

"Come on," she said to Karas, and quickened her strides. The dog broke into a lope, her tongue lolling out the side of her mouth in a grin. Not only because she had dinner waiting there, but because Marcus was there, and the animal literally worshipped him.

So did Megan, secretly.

She steeled herself for another confrontation with Trinity or Tyler but the house was still and quiet when she entered the lower floor. A bar of light came from beneath the closed study door. Marcus's most secluded domain.

She paused at it and knocked softly.

"Come in."

She pushed the door open. Karas rushed past her and headed straight for the desk where Marcus sat, her head down in a submissive posture, thick tail wagging in a blur of doggy euphoria.

"There's my good lass," Marcus said, his hard, battle-scarred face softening as he reached down to stroke the dog's head and neck. "You both had some energy to burn off, eh?"

Megan wasn't sure if he was talking to her or the dog, but she answered anyway. "Yeah. Where are the others?"

"Upstairs in their rooms sleepin' off the jetlag, I reckon."

Good. Megan didn't want to see either of them tonight. She needed a few more hours to come to grips with her situation. She planted her hands on her hips and faced Marcus across the expanse of his desk. "So? Why'd you set me up like that?"

Rather than answer he leaned back in his seat and turned it slightly, the hint of a wince contorting his face as he raised his left leg to rest his foot on the footstool. The surgeons had done their best to reconstruct his shattered hip joint, but he would never again walk without pain.

"I didn't set you up," he said in a tone so reasonable it set her teeth on edge. When he talked to her like that she felt like a damn child. "Rycroft called me himself and explained everythin'. Trinity was right, if I'd told you, you likely would've run off."

Her chin came up. "I'm not a coward."

His dark eyes sliced to her. "No one said you were. And I think I know better than anyone just how brave you are."

Mollified, she lost the defensive edge and let her hands drop to her sides.

"And there's another reason," he added.

"What?"

He reached across the desk and gestured for her to give him her hand.

Sighing, she put her right hand in his. "You gonna read my palm or something?"

"Your fingers," he answered, bending her wrist up slightly to show the mess around her nail beds where she'd picked all the skin away until she'd bled. "They've been like this a lot lately."

She pulled her hand away, embarrassed. "It's just a stupid habit." She wasn't even aware when she did it.

"Which you only do when you're anxious or bored out of your mind, and these days, lass, you're both." He settled back against his seat to regard her with knowing, dark eyes. "You've been goin' crazy cos you've got no direction. You're restless—more than usual—and you can't sit still. You're fidgety. Because you needed a purpose again."

He wasn't wrong. Part of her was psyched at the prospect of going on another op. The other part hated the idea of being saddled with a partner, let alone a man who instead of helping her, had delivered her back into the sadistic hands of her other trainers. "I keep busy."

"Trainin' and shootin' targets and ridin', aye. You're not fulfilled, though. There's a difference." He shook his head. "You think I haven't seen it? Or that I don't know 'ow that feels? I feel it every day and will for the rest of my life. But you don't have to. With this you'll be helpin' save the others. I reckon you need this."

Marcus was the only living soul outside of the program who she'd told about her past and her training. About the Valkyries and what she had been made into. The highs and lows, the rush of it and the extreme terror. He'd been an accomplice to Trinity and Rycroft because he cared about her. And she'd reacted by being a bitch.

The knowledge made her squirm inside. "How much do you know about Tyler?"

"I know 'e was one of your SERE instructors."

She set her jaw. "The enemy camp was situated miles

from any water, and I hadn't eaten in three days. I tracked him to his camp deep in the forest because I knew the area where he'd be, and because I knew he'd have supplies."

"Aye, I don't doubt you relieved 'im of those without his knowledge," Marcus said with an amused twitch of his lips.

"I was starving, and dehydrated after spending three days in the cage they put me in. So I did what I had to do." She let out an annoyed breath. "I don't see what the big deal was. The entire point of SERE school was to teach us how to survive any situation and escape the enemy. Which I did."

One side of his mouth tugged upward and he shook his head, pure admiration lighting his eyes. "I would've paid a lot to see you break out of there, and see their reaction."

She shrugged. "They didn't contain me well enough. That's on them. But when I found Tyler's camp, do you know what he did?"

"He gave you food 'n water and access to his first aid supplies."

"Yeah. And then he tied me up and radioed the cadre at the enemy camp to come get me." Outrage and something far too close to hurt pricked her. It had been a dozen years, and it still felt like yesterday. "They dragged me back there, beat me until I passed out, then made me finish the rest of my time in a pit." They'd broken two of her ribs during the initial beating upon her return, the bastards.

The amusement on his face faded, something cold and hard taking its place, the shadows of his own past visible in his gaze for a brief moment. "He didn't know they were Valkyrie trainers. He didn't even know your kind existed, let alone about the program."

"That's not the point. The point is, he betrayed me. And now I'm supposed to just accept him as my partner for this op?"

"He didn't betray you, because he didn't realize what was really happenin'. It was his job to prepare you for the worst. I might not've admitted this until recently, but I'm damn glad he did give you back to the other cadre, because if he hadn't, I wouldn't be here."

His words slammed into her with the force of an invisible sledgehammer, and Megan found herself at a rare loss for words. Memories cascaded through her mind, from that awful night in Aleppo.

She almost hadn't gone back for Marcus; the volume of fire had been that great. But she couldn't leave him there. In the end, she'd risked everything to go back and pull him out.

He'd hated her for it initially. For weeks after his rescue Marcus had raged at her, cursing her for forcing him to live when all he'd wanted was to die. To see him finally okay with still being alive was the best gift she'd ever received.

"At any rate," Marcus continued, his face tightening briefly again as he shifted his bad leg and reached down to stroke Karas's fur, "he's 'ere because whether you want to believe it or not, he cares."

"He feels guilty," she corrected. He didn't care about her. He wanted to soothe his guilty conscience.

Marcus shrugged. "Does it matter? The lad's here. He volunteered when they approached him and told him what really 'appened. He's here to watch your back and help you accomplish your mission."

She would ask Tyler about that later. "I'd rather go with you."

He huffed out a harsh laugh. "A few years ago, I would've been the first to step forward. But I'd only slow you down now, and I won't be a liability that could get you killed. You... mean too much to me, lass," he finished gruffly, his eyes on the dog.

It felt like an invisible fist shoved through Megan's chest to crush her heart in its grip. She swallowed against the sudden tightness in her throat, unsure what to say. She'd never had a father. Not one she could remember, anyway. She'd never had anyone, until him.

"You're the only family I've ever had," she told him softly, her heart pounding at the sense of vulnerability the admission caused. She would never bare herself that way for anyone but him.

He stilled, his hand frozen on Karas's soft head. Then he cleared his throat, still avoiding her gaze. "You should get some sleep. Trainin' starts at oh-five-hundred. And once they find that hacker, you'll be in the air almost immediately, so you need to be ready."

She knew a dismissal when she heard one, and besides that, he was right. "All right. Good night."

"Night, lass."

She paused at the door to look back at him. He was still seated behind the desk, his bad leg stretched out, Karas at his side. And yet she could all but feel the loneliness surrounding him. The self-imposed isolation born of trauma and survivor's guilt. Once she left, he would have no one.

For so long she'd been taught not to feel, not to trust. But she did both of those things with him.

"Want me to bring you a cup of tea?" she asked.

His dark eyes slid to her, and warmth chased away the shadows there. "Aye, a proper brew would be grand."

All was forgiven, and any remaining awkwardness banished. "Back in a minute," she said, and headed for the kitchen.

She hadn't known jack shit about tea when she'd first come here, had thought the Brit fondness for it was something made up and perpetuated for TV and movies. Marcus loved it, though Yorkshire tea only, and gold if possible. Now she knew exactly how to make it the way he liked. Most evenings she'd make one for him while they sat in his study together, reading. They didn't need to talk. Just being in the same room was enough for the both of them.

After delivering Marcus his tea she crept upstairs. The lights were off when she started down the hallway to her room at the south side of the house, both guest room doors closed, the occupants presumably asleep—or pretending to be.

She closed her bedroom door and crossed to the quilt-covered, queen-size bed tucked under the dark, Tudor-era beams in the ceiling. As much as she loved Marcus and as welcome as he'd made her feel here, this wasn't her home, it was his. Once she left here, she would probably never come back.

The thought left an aching, hollow void in the center of her chest.

Chapter Four

She was being watched.

Amber kept her pace steady and looked straight ahead as she walked along Prague's cobbled streets back to the rental unit she'd just checked into. Whoever it was, they were good, because she hadn't spotted them yet.

But not as good as her.

She took a winding route through the historic city center, threading her way down narrow alleys and a crowd gathered for a summer farmer's market in a square. A few blocks after that, the tingling sensation at her nape diminished. She risked a glance behind her, searching her surroundings, but didn't spot anyone watching.

Someone was definitely out there, though, and they were persistent. She'd felt it during her final night in Kiev, and last night here in Prague. Maybe someone the U.S. government had sent to keep tabs on her.

Or maybe something far deadlier.

She didn't dwell on that. Death came for everyone eventually and she'd already surpassed the life expectancy for someone like her.

Satisfied that she'd lost her tenacious tail for now, she took the long way back to her rental unit. At the wrought iron gate she paused to ensure her anti-trespassing device was still intact. It appeared untouched and her custom-made app hadn't sent her an alert that someone had triggered it, so chances were no one had tried to enter this way. Still, she maintained her vigilance as she took the back stairs up to the third floor as dusk fell.

The nearly invisible wires she'd placed on the door were still in place. And when she cracked it open, the edge of it hit the stacked drinking glasses she'd set up before leaving.

She eased the door open enough to slip through and locked it behind her. Out of habit she reached back and curled her fingers around the grip of the pistol hidden in the waistband of her jeans while she swept the place, room by room. Everything was exactly as she'd left it, the blinds and curtains drawn.

Another reprieve. She wasn't counting on getting many more.

With her perimeter secure, she was as safe as she was going to get. She'd moved mostly at night recently, so she needed to change things up to avoid setting a pattern. Tomorrow she would wipe this place clean and move again—in the daytime. For now...

Time to get back to work.

In the bedroom she booted up one of her laptops, using a custom VPN she'd designed to conceal her IP address. It wouldn't allow her to hide forever, but a moving target was harder to hit and she never spent more than one night in the same location. As long as she kept moving, kept a step ahead of whoever was after her, she still had time to get the next part of her mission completed.

A quick search gave her the information she'd been hoping for, this time from a British news site.

Woman's body found in the Moskva River yesterday. Police say the unidentified female was weighed down by concrete slabs. Cause of death is unknown but an autopsy is underway, and the circumstances surrounding her death point to organized crime. The investigation is ongoing.

Triumph pulsed through her. A fitting end for Zoya, the mastermind of the plot that had almost cost Amber her life. One more traitorous Valkyrie down. Several more to go, and most of those wheels were already in motion.

She checked her most recent fake email account, smiled to herself when she saw the encrypted response from the people she'd contacted yesterday before leaving Kiev.

Awaiting further instruction.

They were ready to give her what she wanted, both in payment and end result.

Transfer 250,000 USD to the following account, she typed back.

Only once the full amount was received would she provide them the intel they wanted in return.

While she waited she monitored her security perimeter and continued searching the web for more talk about her latest victim. If this breaking news story was true, then she was almost halfway to her goal.

Five down. Six to go.

First this remaining Valkyrie operative who had sold her out and left her to die. Then the people responsible for the destruction of her and so many others' lives.

A soft ding interrupted the silence, alerting her to a new email. From the Bermudian bank she was using for the transfer.

She checked the account. The full amount was now in her offshore account, buried in a series of fake shell corporations that would take months for investigators to unravel—if they managed to ID her in the first place.

Second worst-case scenario, in a matter of weeks or months this mission would be over and she'd be living a new life somewhere on an island in Greece or Croatia.

Somewhere warm where she could blend in, on the other side of the world from the evil people who had created and betrayed her.

Worst case, she'd be dead before any of that happened. But until she drew her last breath, she was going after her own kind of vengeance.

Sifting through her files, she pulled up the personal information on her current target. A Valkyrie specializing in sabotage, who had recently infiltrated a criminal organization in Syria with both government and terrorist ties.

Using an encrypted program she'd designed, Amber sent her most recent customer the woman's name, image, and all the sensitive intel contained within the Valkyrie personnel files Amber had hacked from the program while the corrupt government officials responsible for it all scrambled to shut it down.

Staring hard at the woman's picture, resolve hardened inside her. Hannah Miller had been one of the Valkyries who had betrayed Amber on that op weeks ago. She deserved to die, and what better way to achieve that than to leak her top-secret files to the very people she'd been sent to destroy in Syria.

Amber hit send and immediately put Hannah out of her mind. As far as she was concerned, the traitor was already dead. It was just a matter of time now, and all Amber had to do was sit back and watch it happen.

Immediately she began plotting out her next task. Starting with identifying the people involved in the conception and inner workings of the Valkyrie Program.

Amber had suffered because of them. They all had.

Sacrifices had to be made, costs endured. She would see this through no matter what, even if it meant her own death. At least then she would die with a clear conscience.

For now... All that mattered now was making sure the people who had betrayed her paid for what they'd done.

****

"Too slow. You need to be quicker," Marcus chastised, shifting to the left and changing the position of the hand targets he held. Karas was snoozing over in the corner of the gym.

Megan bit back the retort she wanted to snap at him and dragged her forearm across her sweat-slick forehead, her boxing gloves held close to her face. She loved the way he spoke, the cadence of his speech and his endearing Yorkshire dialect, but right now he was seriously pissing her off.

She narrowed her focus to those targets, met every move they made with the full force of her body behind each punch.

"Better. Now add a spinnin' hook kick at the end."

She didn't answer, merely went back into fighting stance to await the next combination he called. Her body was tired, but revved. She craved this. The release of the pent up energy that always burned inside her. Marcus had been right last night. She'd needed purpose again. More than she'd realized or been willing to admit.

When they'd first started doing this soon after her arrival here, she'd been reluctant to train with him, and had taken it easy on him because of his leg. But Marcus was a proud, stubborn man and had quickly disabused her of any notion of him being hampered by his injury.

He'd put her on her ass time and time again, proving he was more than able to hold his own with her, bum leg or not. She respected his skill and his time, his dedication to helping her. He didn't owe her anything, no matter what he might think.

"Again," he commanded when she'd finished the next round.

He was hard on her, but nowhere near as hard as most

of her Valkyrie trainers had been. And unlike them, he was always fair. She loved that about him, because that quality had been rare in the people she'd known throughout her life.

Life isn't fair, Megan. You're a fucking Valkyrie. A weapon. Forget that for one moment, drop your guard even an inch, and you'll wind up dead.

They'd drilled that lesson into her head over and over again until it consumed her, helping turn her from an average trainee in the pipeline into exactly what they wanted—a finely honed weapon. A weapon with highly specific skills she'd shown an aptitude for early on.

She completed the series of punishing combinations until her muscles burned and she was panting as though she'd just sprinted for a mile.

"That's enough for you now," Marcus said, his tone almost frustrated as he lowered his hands.

It stung. Sure she wasn't at peak physical form like she'd been when they'd first met, but she was still in damn good shape and she hated the thought of him ever being disappointed in her. "No. Let's go again," she argued, struggling to catch her breath.

He regarded her with a doubtful expression, then shook his head and started to take off the hand targets. "That's enough for today."

"No, it's—"

"I'm up for some sparring if you want."

Her spine stiffened at the deep voice behind her.

Keeping her expression neutral, she turned around to face Tyler. He was in shorts and a black workout shirt that stretched across the muscles of his chest and shoulders. It annoyed her that she even noticed them. "You just get up?"

"No. Been up since dawn going over a few things with Trinity."

What things? She held the words back. She'd find

40

out what she needed to know later. "Spare gloves are in that trunk over there." She jerked her chin across the gym the previous owner had built in the old carriage house across the back courtyard from the main house.

"Good, because I'm starvin'," Marcus said, and walked off with Karas, his cane thudding against the floor with each step. He'd be in pain from what they'd just done, but he'd rather die than show or give into it. She loved that about him too. Marcus was an honest-to-God badass.

Megan used the few minutes it took for Tyler to wrap his hands and get his gloves on to let her heart rate recover. By the time he stepped onto the mats with her, she was ready to give her all again.

"How long have you been at it already?" he asked.

"An hour." More, but who was counting?

He reached his gloves out toward her. "Come on. Tap." He wiggled them, giving her what he probably thought was an adorable grin.

The grin might be adorable but *he* wasn't, because he sucked for what he'd done to her and she wasn't ready to forgive him for it. Even if in his mind he'd only been doing his job back then.

Resisting the urge to roll her eyes, she tapped and stepped back with her right foot, raising her gloves close to either side of her face as she tucked her chin in. "Let's go."

He started off slow. Insultingly slow, and with even more insulting gentleness, pulling his punches as if she couldn't handle him.

She used the next thirty minutes to show him otherwise, getting in several body shots and almost one to the side of his head when he wasn't quick enough to block it. He danced back, gave her an assessing look and came at her again, this time with more effort. She went on the attack, while he struggled to protect himself and keep up.

But she was tiring fast, her muscles depleted and aching. Growing weaker with each passing moment.

She moved too slow. Failed to block the quick jab he threw.

Her head snapped back with the impact, momentarily stunning her and sending her to her knees.

"Shit, sorry," he blurted, and immediately reached out to help her up.

More than failing to block the punch, his rush to rescue her triggered buried insecurities she'd kept locked down for years.

Gritting her teeth, Megan swept her top leg out and took his feet out from under him, satisfaction rolling through her when he toppled over and hit the floor.

He grinned. Freaking *grinned*.

They were both on their feet again in an instant, staring at one another and breathing hard.

She refused to be the first to look away. "Don't *ever* treat me as if I'm weaker than you just because I'm a female," she warned, heart pounding as she battled the age-old enemy of self-doubt.

You're weak because you're a woman. And you won't get special treatment here. You're nothing until you earn that mark. You hear me? Nothing.

The trainer's voice echoed in her mind, his snarling face crystal clear as he held her by the throat against the wall and forced her to watch while a Valkyrie graduate received her "mark" on her left hip. She blinked, forcing the memory away, and refocused on Tyler. She'd earned her mark and was damn proud to bear it. Why did she feel the need to prove herself to anyone?

Tyler's grin vanished. His jaw tightened, then he nodded once. "Fine."

"Fine."

"Am I interrupting?" a female voice said from the doorway.

They both turned to face Trinity, looking gorgeous in a snug, plum wrap-style summer dress and heels. Sweat trickled down Megan's face and between her breasts. "No," she muttered, taking off her gloves.

"Okay, then." Trinity glanced between them. "You want the good news or the bad news first?"

"Bad," Tyler said, ditching his own gloves.

"Our suspect struck again. Another Valkyrie was murdered, this time in Russia. Her body was found in the Moskva River, weighed down by concrete slabs. Russian mob's our best guess right now. We think she'd infiltrated their organization several months ago."

Dammit. That made five dead Valkyries. How many more were going to die before their team got a break and a solid piece of intel?

"So, what's the good news?" Megan asked, wiping the back of her wrapped hand across her forehead.

"We got a possible location on our suspect."

She stilled, hope and excitement spreading through her. "Where?"

"Prague. But it's going to be a tight window, and the trail might already have gone cold." That deep blue gaze swept over them both. "Ready or not, as of now we're all on the clock. Our flight leaves in forty minutes."

Chapter Five

Megan waited until after takeoff to make her move. She unbuckled her seatbelt and strode up the narrow aisle in the private jet she wasn't sure who was paying for, heading for Trinity, who was essentially Megan's handler for this mission.

Trinity glanced up from the intel reports she was reviewing. "Hi."

"Hey." Megan scooted past her and took the plush seat beside the window.

Trinity set the tablet in her lap and raised a coal-black eyebrow. "Something on your mind?"

"Yeah. How are you tracking the suspect?"

"Rycroft's got a couple of his best analysts monitoring chatter, watching money transfers and trying to match the Valkyries in our personnel files with facial recognition software. Once they get a possible hit they follow up with security footage from various places, sometimes satellites or even other countries' security databases. From there they narrow down possible target locations, and we hit the most promising ones."

She nodded. "The people working on this—they're good?"

"Yes. Rycroft considers one of them to be his honorary daughter, and another is my sister-in-law. They both have the security clearance and the know-how to get this done."

"Okay, then I'm going to be blunt." She'd learned to be forthright with people because her social skills sometimes weren't all that polished. Dancing around things for the sake of politeness was a complete waste of time that drove her nuts.

"Good, shoot."

"You were trained to be a seductress, weren't you?" Megan was pretty sure, but clarification never hurt.

Faint amusement showed in Trinity's eyes. "I was."

Knew it. Not only that, everything she knew about Trinity so far told her the woman had been exceptional at her job. How many in Trinity's position had lived long enough to retire from the field? "Then how come you're not heading up this operation? You'd be way better at posing as a couple with Tyler than me." That part of the situation made no sense to her.

Trinity laughed softly. "You're not getting out of this, sorry."

She pushed out a frustrated breath. "Why not? You pose as his other half to maintain the cover, and I'll break into the buildings and steal whatever you want." She was good at being unseen, blending into her surroundings. Alone. Being with Tyler for this whole mission made her skin itch. He was just one more complication that increased the risk against her and the mission.

"Because *reasons*."

Megan scowled in annoyance at the sucky answer. "Such as?"

Trinity gave her an almost pitying look, then leaned in. Not that Tyler could overhear them, seated on the opposite side a few rows back. "Because you two know each other. Because he's got what it takes. And, if you want the cold, hard truth, the couple ploy works because you've got chemistry."

Her eyes widened in outrage. "*Chemistry*?" Resentment and mistrust, maybe. Anyone thinking there was physical chemistry between them was dead wrong. "I spent less than a week with him during SERE school, and neither of us knew the first thing about each other." She'd been stupid and naïve about men, and had indulged in a little harmless fantasizing about him. It galled her now.

Trinity's eyes twinkled. "Yep. The moment you saw him in the study, it was there. Sparks. Lots of sparks."

I don't think so. He'd snuffed out any "sparks" the night he'd turned her in. But she wasn't going to argue with Trinity because A, it wouldn't get her anywhere, and B, it would only make her seem immature and petulant. Professionalism was a point of pride with her. "You want him to keep tabs on me, not to watch my back."

"He's responsible for both." Trinity's stare was steady. "We can't afford to have another Valkyrie disappear on us."

She snorted. "You think I couldn't ditch him if I wanted?"

"You could," Trinity acknowledged with a slight nod. "But we're hoping you won't."

Well, this conversation was pointless. Megan switched tactics and went for reason. "I'm a high-level thief. I've always worked alone, and I'm totally antisocial. Kind of comes with the territory, you know? I've never been partnered with anyone on an op before. I don't like this. It's too messy."

"You'll do great."

In other words, the discussion was over. And Megan was betting that there was more going on here than she realized. Trinity knew something she didn't. They'd chosen Tyler for this specifically, because of her. Why?

It wasn't easy for her to let this go, but at this point

what choice did she have? Part of her training had made her an expert at adapting to whatever was thrown at her. At compartmentalizing. She'd take this in stride and deal with it, even if she didn't like it.

She glanced at the tablet in Trinity's lap. "Anything new?"

"Just some SIGINT reports. Analysts are trying to narrow down which of these signals might have come from our suspect so we can narrow down another area to search."

"Those files you retrieved from the CIA officer. Is he dirty?"

"Let's just say he's under close investigation. And once we know exactly who we're dealing with and how they're involved in all of this, I have some pretty juicy blackmail material at our disposal if necessary."

Megan grinned. "Sex tapes?"

Trinity smiled back, smug as hell. "Sex tapes."

Ha, good. The people involved deserved to be brought down hard *and* humiliated before they had their lives blown up and went to jail. "We still hitting the first target when we arrive in Prague?"

"Yes. In the meantime, you might as well review everything again with your partner." She gave Megan a sweet smile. "You should spend some time together before we land, get your cover story nailed down."

Bah. She wasn't that good an actress. Not like Trinity and her kind were—since Megan worked alone out of view, she rarely had to interact with anyone. Faking being in love with a man she was still pissed at was a tall order.

Chemistry? She mentally snorted, embarrassed that Trinity or anyone else had picked up on her subconscious reaction to seeing Tyler yesterday. This whole thing was stupid, she thought sourly as she marched back down the aisle toward her fake boyfriend for the duration of the mission.

Tyler glanced up from his own tablet as she approached, and in spite of herself a rush of awareness slid through her. Grudge or not, something about him called to her on a primal level that she couldn't deny. She didn't like it, though. It made this entire charade even more complicated. And risky. For her, at least.

He moved a stack of papers over to make room for her on the seat next to him, watching her expectantly.

"We're supposed to go over our cover story together again," she informed him crisply, dropping into the seat beside him and taking the tablet from him, careful to make sure her shoulder and hip didn't touch his. "And I want to review the first op plan, too."

"Okay." Being this close to him was unsettling. It reminded her how big he was, over six feet, and muscular. He leaned over a little to get a better look at the folder she opened, and she caught his clean, soapy scent.

She cleared her throat, irritated that she'd even noticed how he smelled. So he was good looking and built and had good hygiene. Didn't mean she trusted him. Or liked him.

"Not sure what kind of security the target location has, but probably not much. If the suspect's been moving around a lot, then he or she wouldn't have time to set up anything good anyway. So, once I disable any exterior cameras, I'll go in through the basement. I'll know what we're dealing with once I get inside." She tapped the screen to bring up the schematics of the building she was going to infiltrate.

A big, bronzed hand landed in the middle of the screen and pushed it downward.

Her gaze snapped to his with a frown. "What?" It was irritatingly disconcerting, being this close to him. Close enough for her to smell him and see the blue and gray flecks in his eyes. As well as the shape of his lips amidst the few days of light brown stubble on his face.

"You've really never worked with anyone on an op before, have you?" he asked incredulously.

She shrugged. "We work alone. Always." Well, she did, anyway. And most of the others did too, only teaming up with another Valkyrie when absolutely necessary. "Easier that way. And then we don't have to worry about anyone else screwing something up, or, you know, screwing us over." She couldn't resist adding the barb.

He kept his hand flat on the tablet now resting on her lap, and his body heat radiated along her side. His steady stare delved into hers, his expression serious. "I didn't know what was really going on back when we met. When I turned you over to the other instructors that night, I thought they'd just make you complete that portion of the course with the other students, and that would be it."

Surprised he'd brought it up, she made a huffing sound and pushed his hand out of the way, lifting the tablet again. "Let's just focus on this." Nothing would change the past. They had to figure out a way to work together now.

"No." He pushed the tablet flat into her lap again, bringing her gaze back to his—this time in exasperation. "We're supposed to be a couple. We need to get past this and start fresh if we're going to be convincing."

She narrowed her eyes. "Maybe we're going through a rough patch," she said, an edge to her voice. "Maybe we fight a lot."

"We're on vacation together in one of the most beautiful cities in Europe. We're new and in love. We won't be fighting. Yet. And if we did have an argument, I'm sure we'd make up really fast." There was a teasing gleam in his eyes.

She jerked the tablet out from under his hand, tamping down her irritation. "Maybe my background is old school Italian and I hold grudges."

He grinned. "Are you?"

"No idea. But I could be."

"Well, I wouldn't let you stay mad at me for long." He leaned back in his seat, his expression sobering as he regarded her. "I'm sorry I turned you over to them."

The stark apology took her off guard. She wished he'd just let it go already, she was getting embarrassed. Her stupid face was starting to heat up. "Just...whatever. Can we get back to this now?"

"In a minute." He reached out and took her chin in his hand, stunning her into stillness. She rarely let anyone touch her intimately. But what disturbed her far more than his touch was the weird curling sensation it caused low in her abdomen.

His hand was large and powerful, his skin warm. Yet he cradled her chin gently with his fingers, holding her gaze. She was too proud to shove his hand aside, or be the first to look away. So she sat there and endured it, refusing to acknowledge the sudden jump in her pulse or the tingles skittering outward from his touch.

"You caught me off guard when you showed up at my campsite that night," he said. "I turned you over because it was my job as an instructor to make sure you finished the course. Whether you believe me or not, I had no idea they were going to be so hard on you for it."

Hard on her. Yeah, they sure as hell had been.

"If I'd known that—or even half of what I know now, I wouldn't have turned you in."

She studied his face. She was good at reading people. Not as good as the more intimate operatives like Trinity had to be, but still pretty good. And based on Tyler's expression and body language, he seemed like he was telling the truth. Although considering the effort it was taking to ignore what was happening to her body, maybe she wasn't reading him well at the moment. "What *would* you have done?" she countered.

"Help you escape."

That was ridiculous. Because they would have caught her eventually. And then she and Tyler would both have been punished. He'd been a Ranger. It might have ruined his career and prevented him from earning the coveted Green Beret later.

She pulled out of his grasp and studied him in suspicion. "Did Trinity or Rycroft put you up to this?" In her experience, guys didn't apologize for shit they did.

His teeth flashed in another grin. As though he got a kick out of her. At least she'd given him a real one this morning, hard enough that he wouldn't forget it. "So suspicious," he murmured. "And no. I've wondered what ever happened to you for years. After Rycroft and Trinity filled me in, I wanted the chance to apologize to you in person."

Megan wasn't sure what to do with that, or whether she could trust it. She lowered her gaze, wanting to get back to work. "Fine. Apology accepted."

"That didn't sound very convincing."

She shot him a look. "Can we move on now?"

"All right. Cover story. Do you have a family?"

The question shouldn't have snuck under her armor, but it did. Hitting a tiny, secret part of her that had yearned for a sense of belonging all her life. "Seriously?"

He blinked. "What? If we're a couple, then it stands to reason I'd know about your family."

What was this BS, and what did it matter for this mission? He had to know she was an orphan. That all Valkyries were. Because it was way easier for the government to recruit and train young girls the way they did if the candidates didn't have ties to anyone. "That's overkill. We don't need to go that far."

Thankfully he let it go. "Then how long have we been together?"

"A month."

"Where did we meet?"

51

She considered that for a second. "At a library. We were both in the military history section looking for a book. You saw the one I picked and told me you'd just read it." She'd read that same meet cute in one of her favorite romance novels and it had always stuck with her as sigh-worthy. Finding a man who shared the same interests as her seemed like an unattainable dream.

He raised his eyebrows. "Do you read military history?"

"Yeah. Don't you?"

"Once in a while."

"Okay, well, you're an...engineer, and I'm a consultant in the tech industry."

The side of his mouth went up. "Fine. So we hit it off, and things got hot and heavy from the get go."

"Nope. We both travel a lot for work. It's been a long-distance thing, and this is our first trip together to see how things go." She arched an eyebrow. "A trial period, you could say." It worked. And it also gave them the perfect excuse if something awkward should happen between them while anyone was watching.

He chuckled softly. "I can work with that."

She liked his laugh. It was one of the things she'd remembered about him all those years ago. He was quick to smile, wasn't harsh or austere like some of the robotic, programmed instructors she'd had during her training. And the way he'd smiled at her, with admiration and respect... No wonder he'd gotten under her skin.

Megan looked away. Concealing her feelings—even from herself—was something she'd learned to do at a young age. She hadn't completely mastered it, though. If she had, she wouldn't feel lonely or secretly wonder about her parents, the extended family she must have had at one point. Still, she was curious about Tyler. "Do you have a real family?"

He nodded. "My parents live in Michigan."

"Any brothers or sisters?"

"I…had an older sister. She died when I was fourteen."

She was surprised he'd told her. The slight hesitation made it clear the loss still haunted him.

Now she felt bad for asking. She floundered for something to say. She wasn't good at this sort of thing. "I'm sorry," she finally said.

He nodded once. "Thanks. I'm still close with my parents. And I've got aunts and uncles and cousins back home, too."

That actually sounded…kind of nice. Having a network of people you were linked to. "Do you have Christmas dinner together and everything?" The idea captivated her. She'd always wondered what that would be like. To be in a room full of people you belonged with, a decorated tree, presents, everyone gathered around the table together for a big meal. Like on TV.

"Every year I'm in country. But I've missed a lot of them over the years when I was deployed."

She was quiet a moment, unsure if she should say anything more. But she couldn't help herself. "What's it like?" she asked softly, inwardly cringing a little at the sense of exposure the question brought.

"Like?" He thought about it for a second. "Loud. Chaotic. But nice." A fond smile softened his face. He was twice as good looking when he smiled. It was damn hard to look away from him. "After dinner we sit around and play board games while we eat dessert."

She could almost picture it in her mind. She liked the sound of his voice, too. "What do you have for dinner? Turkey?"

He cocked his head at her, as if curious why she wanted to know. But he probably didn't know that she'd never had a Christmas dinner. Or even celebrated Christmas since she'd been taken into the program when she was small.

There were snippets of memories, though, faded and tattered. A tree glowing with festive lights in front of a window that overlooked a darkened street. A feeling of excitement that Santa would come, and a rush to get into her pink flannel nightie then climb into bed and get to sleep so he wouldn't pass their house by.

There were faces too, but indistinct. Adults. Another child, maybe around Megan's age. A little girl in a matching purple flannel nightie. She had brown hair.

Megan shook the thoughts away, unsure if they were real or imagined. She remembered practically nothing about her life before the program.

"Yes," Tyler answered. "And all the trimmings to go with it. My mom makes apple pie instead of pumpkin, though. And she makes a homemade vanilla custard ice cream to go with it. It's legendary."

It sounded idyllic. It also made her ache in that secret place she tried so hard to hide from the world. "So. Back to work?"

"Wait. What's your favorite thing to eat?"

She withheld a sigh and humored him. "Noodles." Though she rarely indulged because carbs were Satan to someone who needed to keep slim to maintain optimal flexibility and speed when slipping in and out of a target.

"Favorite color."

She couldn't imagine why he cared, but okay. "Cobalt blue."

"Music?"

"Rock."

He smiled. "I like all those too."

Wonderful. And that smile was dangerous, especially when directed at her at close range. "Now can we get back to work?" They were landing in just over an hour. She wanted everything to go perfectly.

He raised an eyebrow. "Worried I won't remember

the plan? This isn't my first time," he added wryly.

"Just want to be prepared. This is my first time on a non-solo op." Let alone posing as lovers. That made it ten times as hard. With someone else it would have been easier. But she noticed Tyler. Too much, and in a way she had trouble ignoring.

"One last thing."

She shot him an impatient look. "What?"

"How do you feel about public displays of affection?"

She blinked at him. Posing as a couple meant there might be an occasion here and there where it would be necessary. Her cheeks turned hot but she gave him a bland look. He'd better not try anything that wasn't expressly called for. "I'm kinda unfamiliar with them." Obviously. She'd had a few hook ups and zero relationships. Came with the territory.

"That's what I figured. But I'm going to be touching you. A lot."

It almost sounded like he was looking forward to it. Which was nuts. "That's not necessary." She was willing to be a professional and play along in public, but let's not get carried away here.

"For me it is. What can I say, I'm an affectionate guy." He leaned in a little closer, dropped his voice. "And attentive. Any woman I'm with won't have any illusions about how much I want her."

She stared, taken off guard by his words and the sensual edge to his voice. By the warmth curling deep inside her.

It was on the tip of her tongue to tell him no way in hell, but if she did that then it proved she was uncomfortable. Valkyries didn't *get* uncomfortable. She could handle this—and him. Besides, it was only for a few days. She'd get through it like a pro and then go back to Marcus's place in Stow and…figure out what the hell to do with the rest of her life.

"I hope you like the whole concept of wooing, then. Because I like to make a man work for it."

A slow smile curved his lips at her challenge, triggering that same little swirling sensation in her belly. His gaze slipped down to her mouth before coming back to her eyes. "I do when she's worth it." His tone suggested he thought she was.

Megan had no idea what the hell to make of any of that, and she wasn't going to waste effort trying. She cleared her throat. This was a job, nothing more. If he thought he had a shot at actually making her succumb to whatever advances he planned to make, he was going to be one disappointed puppy. "Good for you. Now. Back to the plan."

He gave a low laugh that sent a ripple of heat down her spine. "So serious. All right. You're going in the basement to disarm any security systems while I stand watch. Once you're in the condo you'll search for anything that might be of use to us, grab it and get out. I make sure the coast is clear and watch your back."

She tamped down the urge to snort or laugh at that last bit. She might never have relied on anyone before during an op, but she wasn't so much of a bitch that she would throw it back in his face. He'd earned the coveted green beret. He knew what he was doing, knew how to handle himself. And he had worked with others for his entire career. Maybe she would learn something from him before this was over.

He was also calm and self-sufficient. She'd seen those things firsthand twelve years ago. If she was honest with herself, that made him even hotter.

She shoved that unwanted thought right out of her mind. "Right. Now let's go over our contingency plans."

She spent the next forty minutes detailing their escape routes, though she could tell he was merely playing along for her benefit.

"Ladies and gentleman, this is your pilot speaking," a voice announced over the speakers. "We'll be beginning our descent into Prague momentarily. Should have you on the ground a few minutes ahead of schedule."

Tyler reached over and took the tablet from her. "That's our cue," he murmured, and his tone struck her as strangely intimate. Then he upped the ante, sliding a muscled arm around her shoulders.

She stiffened at the weight of it resting on her, the strength and warmth of his hand as his fingers curled around the side of her shoulder. It took everything she had to sit there instead of shoving his arm off her and walking away. Worse, she kind of *liked* how it felt.

Hell. She had days of this ahead and maybe worse to look forward to? Wonderful.

His slight grin told her how much he enjoyed pushing her boundaries, and that he planned on doing it more. "You ready, sweetheart?"

Ugh. She had to unlock her jaw to respond. "I'm ready. But fair warning—get too touchy feely and I'll snap your arm in half, fake boyfriend or not."

Chapter Six

"**O**kay, they're on the move," Megan's voice murmured in his earpiece.

Seated at a picnic table in the courtyard between the target building and the one next to it, Ty didn't respond. To the untrained eye he was just another tourist out enjoying a morning coffee in the summer sunshine, a hat and sunglasses shading his eyes from the glare.

In reality, the shades contained special lenses that allowed him better peripheral vision to watch his surroundings. This whole thing was a strange predicament to be in. His role on this op had been made clear: provide backup for Megan.

He didn't love it. He'd spent his entire career as a member of a team at the tip of the military spear. He was used to taking action, running ops with his A-team. Not being relegated to the background and sitting on his hands while someone else ran the show.

He'd do it for Megan, though. He'd do damn near anything for her.

At first he'd wanted to do this out of obligation and a lot of guilt. Now that was changing. The little things he'd learned about her so far, the pieces she'd allowed him a glimpse of, only increased his attraction to her. And to keep her safe during this mission, it meant keeping his head clear.

He took a sip of his coffee and subtly turned his head. At this point they didn't know for sure who the suspect might be, or even if they were looking for a man or a woman. Everyone was impatient to get a solid lead.

With Valkyries dying, time was of the essence. Inside the condo Megan would search for anything that might give them a clue about their suspect—if he or she was actually staying there—and if they were lucky, they'd find a laptop they could clone or some other kind of electronic equipment for them to analyze.

The front door of the apartment building opened and the young family that was staying next door to the target suite exited, a mom and dad and two young kids, speaking Spanish.

Ty reached up to scratch his jaw, his hand angled to disguise the motion of his lips. "You're clear," he murmured.

There were only a few other people strolling along the pathway between the buildings, and all of the surrounding balconies were empty. He'd done a thorough check of the perimeter before settling at the table. Trinity was posted in a condo located in a building on the opposite side to watch their blind spot and would only communicate if something was critical.

"Copy. Going in," Megan responded.

He maintained silence as he sipped his coffee and kept watch, but inside he was itching to get up and follow her. Intellectually he understood that Megan was well trained and could handle herself—he'd seen that himself firsthand.

Emotionally, he didn't give a shit. He felt protective of her. He wanted to be in that suite with her right now, helping her search. Watching her back up close and personal.

Instead he maintained his role, limiting his movements to switching locations after a few minutes, to a seat in the shade with a better view of the front of the building. Up on the fifth floor the unit Megan was in had the curtains and blinds drawn to keep out the sun. There was zero visibility into the room, giving her total concealment while she searched the place.

After seeing only hints of what she was able to do, he wished he could watch her work. He only knew bits and pieces of what she'd been through, of what the Valkyries were capable of. So far, she'd been a total pro even though it was hard for her to accept working with someone—especially him, given their history.

Had she truly accepted his apology? He still wasn't sure. He wanted to prove himself to her, somehow make up for what had happened. When he'd heard what she'd gone through after he sent her back that night…

Ty was more motivated than ever to earn her trust. And the best way to do that—really, the only way to do that—had been to volunteer for this mission. He not only got to help do something for the greater good, he got to be close to Megan the majority of the time. A definite perk, but also a double-edged sword.

The spark between them was still there, brighter and hotter than it had been before. Maybe because this time they were both single and he was no longer her instructor. Whether the attraction was one-sided, he wasn't sure, but he intended to find out. If she was interested, he was making a move the moment the mission was over. Until then, he had the excuse of their cover as a couple to touch her and make her aware of him as a man rather than just a teammate.

Quiet footfalls sounded to his left. He subtly turned his head to see who it was, did a double take when instead of finding a stranger, Megan strode up the walkway in her cargo pants and tank top, a ball cap covering her hair and sunglasses hiding her eyes.

"Hey. Ready to go?" she asked casually, as if she hadn't just broken into someone's apartment in broad daylight to search it.

Where the hell had she come from? From his vantage point he was able to see both the main and side exits. The back exit was currently blocked off for repairs, so that meant she must have come another way.

Masking his surprise, he stood and nodded. "Yeah, I'm starving," he replied, and when she was close enough, reached for her hand.

She stiffened ever so slightly, as if she wanted to pull away, then remembered their cover and awkwardly laced her fingers with his to walk with him away from the building.

Her hand was cool in his, her fingers slender. In her running shoes the top of her head came up to the tip of his nose. She was the perfect height for him to pull her close and kiss the top of her head, nuzzle her temple and cheek, the edge of her mouth. He hoped he got the chance to do all of those soon.

"How'd it go?" he asked quietly, cataloguing the people they passed. A few families, other couples, mostly older. No one was paying attention to them and Trinity was still silent even though she could hear everything they said, so their six was clear.

Megan shrugged. "Waste of time," she muttered. "I checked the target unit and the ones on either side of it too, just to be safe. Only thing I found was the dollar store safes in the closets. A toddler could open those things, and yet one family left their passports and jewelry in one." She sounded disgusted.

He hid a smile, masking his disappointment. Ops like this often ended with no solid leads or fresh intel, but it meant they'd missed their mark by a matter of hours at most. "I bet you're pretty good at cracking safes, huh?"

"I'm not bad."

Now she was just being modest. *Expert level thief* the redacted file he'd been sent on her said, and that covered a lot of possible territory.

They walked through the main tourist area of the old town to get to their hotel, where they would inform Trinity that Megan hadn't found anything in the suite. If anyone was out there keeping tabs on them, it helped solidify their cover to be seen together as a couple in public. "You hungry?" he asked her.

She glanced up at him with a frown. "We just ate like, two hours ago. You can't seriously be hungry already."

"Hey, it takes a lot of calories to fuel this body." Mostly he wanted to stop and see if they had a tail of any kind.

It did things for his ego when she raked a sidelong gaze over him through the gap at the edge of her sunglasses. "I'm not hungry, but we can stop if you are."

She said it like the idea was the most annoying thing in the world, and he grinned. "Maybe a pastry?"

She huffed. "I don't eat that stuff."

"Why not?"

"Slows me down." She slanted him a look that said she was done talking.

She was adorable when she got annoyed. And he'd sure as hell never had this much fun on a mission. "Ever had a *kolache*?"

"No."

"There was a bakery we used to get them from just off base when I was stationed in Texas, owned by a Czech family. Best *kolaches* ever." He was almost certain no one was following or watching them as they walked along the cobbled streets past pastel-toned, red-roofed buildings. At the next block he spotted a pastry shop. "Perfect. Let's see what they've got."

He swore he heard her groan as he tugged her to the right and headed for the shop. "Smells like Christmas," he said, drawing a deep breath. Cinnamon and other spices.

A lineup snaked along the counter when they entered. The display case had strudel, other pastries he wasn't familiar with, and a few trays of different flavored *kolaches*.

"*Yes*. You sure you don't want one?" he asked her.

"I'm sure." Her tone was completely disinterested but she was covertly watching all around them, maintaining her vigilance even with him beside her.

He squeezed her hand in reassurance. Her heightened vigilance made complete sense given that she'd always been on her own on a mission.

When it was his turn to place his order he kept hold of Megan's hand. The woman behind the counter handed him his order in a paper bag. "*Děkuji*," he said, and led Megan back out onto the cobbled street.

A pair of street violinists were starting a performance in the middle of the square. He stopped at the edge of the crowd and drew Megan close to him, reaching into the bag to hand her a pastry. She shook her head, her gaze fixed on the surrounding crowd. "You don't want to even try it?" he asked, and lifted a blueberry-filled *kolache* to her mouth.

She turned her head toward him. They engaged in a silent battle of wills for a few seconds. He could feel the heat of her glare burning him through the lenses of her sunglasses, but finally she gave in and took a bite.

He couldn't help but stare at the way her lips closed around the pastry, the tip of her tongue peeking out to sweep up a flaky crumb. "Good?" he asked.

"It's okay," she muttered, her annoyance clear.

Fine. More *kolaches* for him.

Deciding not to push his luck with hand feeding any farther, he switched tactics and curled an arm around her shoulders instead, pulling her tight into his side.

She went rigid. So rigid he was sure he'd moved too fast, but she stayed still and, while not exactly leaning into him, didn't pull away either. He'd consider it a small victory in his campaign to win her over.

Something told him it wasn't as much him as it was the close physical contact that bothered her. She'd been orphaned as a kid. She had no other family, no close friends. She'd been put into foster care at five, then recruited into the Valkyrie Program. After the solitary life she'd led and the training she'd undergone, all of this would be foreign for her.

It brought up another thousand questions. Had she ever had a boyfriend? Been in love? Surely she would have at least had lovers over the years.

But what if she hasn't?

The idea stirred something deep inside him. A deep possessiveness that made him want to make up for everything she'd gone without her whole life. Show her every single pleasure that could happen between a man and a woman.

He hated the thought of her going through her entire life alone, with no one to turn to. No one who cared about her beyond whether she got a mission done or not.

He cared, whether it made sense or not. She tugged at him in ways he didn't fully understand.

Her hair smelled good. The urge to nuzzle the top of her head was strong, but he held off. He rubbed her shoulder gently instead then curled his fingers around it as he finished off his pastry, noting the firmness of her muscles. A small reminder that she was stronger than she looked, and deadly when she needed to be.

Across the square, his gaze swept across the crowd…and stopped. A man stood almost opposite them in a brown leather jacket and jeans, eyes concealed by shades. The instant Ty saw him the man looked away.

A low-grade warning tingle started in Ty's gut. He swallowed his mouthful of pastry and casually bent his head to murmur close to Megan's ear, making it look like he was whispering sweet nothings. "Eleven-thirty. Leather jacket and shades." The guy turned and started walking away at a casual pace.

"Yeah, I saw him," Megan murmured. "Recognize him?"

"Nope." But the guy had definitely been watching them. Curious onlooker? Or someone tasked with following them? "One of ours, maybe?"

"Negative," Trinity responded through the earpiece. "Verify if he's a tail."

"Roger."

Megan shrugged his arm off her. "Shall we?" Her tone was all business.

"Sure." He snagged her hand again before she could take off, wound his fingers through hers and started back to their hotel. Neither of them looked over their shoulder on the way.

They both waited until they'd reached the next sidewalk before turning left and taking a cautious glance across the street. Ty's gaze immediately zeroed in on the man in the shades. He'd stopped on the opposite sidewalk, standing there casually as he glanced around. The second he realized Ty had spotted him, he glanced away and started walking faster.

They definitely had a tail.

Megan tugged sharply on his hand. "Keep moving."

"I've got you on GPS," Trinity said through his earpiece. "Can you give me a detailed description?"

Ty murmured the physical details of their shadow to her.

"Got it. I'm having the team search for him with satellite and CCTVs in the area."

They took a zigzag route back, checking for signs of

being followed. "We're clear," he murmured, and Megan nodded as if she'd already determined that. But they circled the hotel twice more just to be sure.

As soon as they were inside the lobby she pulled her hand free of his and put some distance between them. He didn't try to stop her. Even though everything in him wanted to erase every inch between them.

Down, boy.

At their door he waited while Megan checked the anti-trespassing measures she'd left there earlier. It was hard-wired in him to push her aside and check the place himself to make sure she was safe, but that would only piss her off.

So he curbed his initial impulse and waited while she did the sweep herself, then refrained from doing his own to follow up. If he wanted her to trust him, he had to do whatever he could to earn it from her.

Once she determined the room was secure she called Trinity to get an update about the guy who had followed them. "The team got a couple images of him from CCTV footage. They're working on it now," Megan said to him after she hung up.

Trinity had said the guy wasn't one of theirs, but Ty always took the word of government people with a grain of salt. If their shadow hadn't been sent by their own to keep watch, then it was another cause of concern for them to monitor going forward. "She have any more intel?" he asked when Megan got off the call.

"Nope. They're working on something, but she couldn't give me specifics. So for now, we just wait." She flopped down on the other queen-size bed and rolled to grab something from her backpack. An e-reader. She settled back against the headboard and began reading, seeming determined to ignore him.

He couldn't make it *that* easy for her.

"How did you come up behind me like that?" he

asked. It bugged him that he couldn't figure it out.

She glanced over at him. "What?"

"When you left the building earlier. How did you get behind me without me noticing?"

She gave him a pitying look. "Don't feel bad. Getting in and out of unexpected places is what I do. At least you heard me. I can sneak up on most people, even ones with training."

If that was meant to salve his pride, it wasn't much consolation. "So you're not gonna tell me?"

A satisfied smile curved her mouth, showing her dimples. And he couldn't help but wonder if she'd have that exact same look on her face after she'd had an orgasm or two. If things went the way he hoped, once this was over he intended to find out. "Maybe one day."

But not today. Damn, she might not be the same sort of Valkyrie as Trinity, but she sure knew how to get into a man's head. "What else are you trained in?"

She shrugged. "The usual stuff. Self-defense, counterintel, infiltration, ingress and egress. Basic weapons, combat medicine. Augmented memory. Plus my super stealth skills, and other tricks I use to steal things and get into and out of places."

"Like safes and bamboo cages."

Her expression sobered at the last bit. "Yeah."

He stretched out on his own bed, putting his hands behind his head. He wanted to know everything about her. To know what had shaped her into the woman she was now. "Did you really bust out of a bamboo cage that night, while the guards were there?"

She looked down at the e-reader in her lap, her expression bored. "It was dark in the room and they weren't paying close enough attention."

No. But they sure had once she'd been brought back. Because of him.

He internally winced at the thought. "How'd you do

it?"

She was quiet a moment, so quiet he was sure she was either going to ignore the question or tell him to go to hell, but then she answered. "One of them dropped a piece of wire while he was repairing a fence a couple days earlier. I scooped it up while he wasn't looking in case I could put it to good use. I hated the cage. The first chance I got when the guards weren't paying attention, I picked the lock, got out, and snuck past the perimeter."

She was freaking amazing. "Where'd you hide the wire?"

"My mouth."

She'd hidden it there for days. Until she'd seen the chance to use it and free herself. Then, hours later, he'd turned around and sent her right back for more punishment.

God, he wished he could undo that. It had bothered him ever since he'd found out—years after the fact. "I'm sorry I screwed you over." Her words, not his. But they were accurate.

"They would have captured me eventually. I wasn't thinking clearly by that point, I just wanted to get away from…everything. But I knew they'd never let me go."

She said it bravely, as if she'd known what the end result would be. Shit, he wanted to go over there and haul her into his lap, wrap his arms around her tight. "I'm sorry it happened," he said again, not knowing what the hell else to say.

She exhaled almost with impatience, then looked over at him. "What did you think of SERE school when you went through it? You did level C, right?"

She was trying to deflect the attention from her, and he didn't mind answering. "Hated it. All except for the survival part, and even most of that I didn't love because it was in the middle of January and I almost froze to death. Some sick part of me was relieved when I got 'captured'.

At least I was warmer in the prison camp."

"Bet that didn't last long."

He smiled ruefully. "Nope. Pretty quick I decided I'd rather be outside freezing my nuts off in the woods rather than being beaten and water boarded."

Her eyes held a gleam of amusement that he would have found disturbing from anyone else. "Did they put you in solitary too?"

A hard ball of guilt settled in his stomach. "Yeah." Compared to her, he'd had it fucking easy. "A casket. Nailed it shut and blasted death metal overlaid with the sound of a baby wailing." He shuddered. "To this day I can't stand the sound of a baby crying."

She rolled her eyes in commiseration. "The *worst*."

He forced a smile, thinking about what Trinity had told him. That after he'd turned Megan over to the "enemy" at the camp, she'd not only been roughed up more and interrogated, but put into solitary confinement for the rest of SERE school.

Except in her case, instead of a coffin or another bamboo cage, she'd served the duration in a pit they'd dug in one of the outbuildings. She'd spent five nights and four days in utter darkness and without being allowed to sleep, unable to lie down or stretch out. They'd pulled her out only to interrogate her more, then dumped her back into the pit.

That shit turned his stomach. She'd been a freaking twenty-one-year-old girl forced into a brutal program. Yeah she'd had tier-one-level training all the way through, but what she'd endured in the SERE portion alone was worse than anything him or his buddies had undergone, and they were all SOF.

"Was there anything you loved about your training?" he asked to change the subject, hoping there was something good there.

"Oh, yeah, a lot of it was so cool." She thought about

it a moment. "Field craft and theft skills especially. Loved those classes. My instructors for those were the best. Actually, one of them reminds me a bit of—" She broke off and cleared her throat, almost embarrassed that she'd revealed something so personal.

"Of?" Ty prompted, wishing she'd continue. He wanted to know her. Really know her.

"Marcus," she said after another pause. "Anyway, that instructor was…nice to me. A few of them were, but him especially. He even tried to run interference for me a few times, to make things easier on me. When the cadre suspected he was playing favorites, they kicked him out of the program. I never saw him again."

"That's shitty." Sounded to Ty like having an ally of any sort in the program was rare. "How did you and Marcus meet?"

She held his gaze for several heartbeats, and it seemed like she was trying to decide whether or not he was playing her. "Trinity or Rycroft didn't tell you?"

"No. Was Marcus a trainer too?"

She shook her head. "We met in Syria a few years ago. On an op. We…helped each other escape a bad situation. And when the whole Valkyrie scandal blew up in the media I needed to go to ground and had nowhere safe to go. I contacted him and he took me in immediately, no questions asked."

Points for Marcus. But was he a rival for Ty? "You guys seem like you've got a really special bond."

A soft smile lifted her lips, so warm and real it hit him deep in the chest. "Yeah. He's kind of like my overprotective older brother, I guess."

Ty wasn't proud of the leap of relief those words brought. But he was damn glad to know there was nothing romantic or sexual between the two of them. "Cool."

Now that she'd exposed some of her past, it didn't surprise him that she instantly went back to the device in her lap.

"Whatcha reading? Military history?" He figured it was a pretty safe guess after the cover story she'd come up with.

She shot him a long-suffering look that almost made him laugh. "Do you *ever* stop asking questions?"

He grinned. "I'm a curious guy." He sure as hell was curious about her.

Megan picked up her e-reader and started to read, tuning him out completely. "Oh, and to answer your earlier question, I got out by climbing down the balconies."

He stared at her. Down the balconies? In broad daylight? Hell.

Megan had gone back to reading. But she'd talked to him, about personal things. That had to mean something.

By the time this mission was over, he wanted her to let him in completely.

Chapter Seven

Megan woke in a rush the next morning when her phone rang. She grabbed it from the nightstand between the two queen-size beds, her brain once again registering that she was in a hotel room in Prague with Tyler. They'd gotten in late last night, after checking out another possible target here in the city center.

That had been a bust too. It frustrated her that they were always a step behind their suspect.

In the dimness the bright screen display showed Trinity's number. It wasn't even five in the morning yet. "Hello."

"Morning. We got a hit on the guy tailing you."

She sat up. If the guy they'd spotted yesterday had shown up in their databases, then he was a threat. "Hang on, I'm putting you on speaker." Tyler was watching her. She hit the button so he could hear. "Who is he?"

"Contract hitter for the CIA."

Wow. "Who sent him?"

"We don't know. And it looks like this guy hasn't been on the company payroll for well over a year. So, it's likely he's been hired privately."

"By someone involved with the Program."

"Probably."

Tyler was sitting up now too, and switched on the lamp between their beds. His dark hair was all mussed and sticking up on one side, the T-shirt he'd worn to bed molded across his chest and shoulders. Sexy even when rumpled. And he was totally alert now, shaking off the cobwebs of sleep the way only someone with their backgrounds could.

It had taken her a while to fall asleep last night because she wasn't used to sharing a room, but he barely snored and it hadn't been as bad as she'd been dreading. "Is he here for us?" she asked.

"We don't think so. He must have noticed you around the target building yesterday morning."

She glanced at Tyler, who shook his head. It was possible the guy had seen them. "Even if he found out who we are, there's no way he could know why we're here. So then why was he following us?"

"We don't know that either. I just wanted to give you both a heads up so you could take extra precautions. And it looks like our suspect might be on the move. Our analysts think they've pinged some online activity in Vienna. Meet me at the rendezvous point in forty minutes. I'm chartering a private flight for us from a small local airport."

"Got it. Anything else?"

"No. See you soon."

Megan put the phone down and got up, then paused on her way to her backpack over in the corner. She had a roommate to consider. "Do you want first shower?"

He ran a hand through his hair and stretched out on top of the covers. "You go ahead. I'll catch another few minutes' sleep."

She grabbed her things and quickly showered, dressed in a black T-shirt and cargo pants, then pulled her hair into a ponytail and brushed her teeth. When she came out of the bathroom Tyler had all his stuff packed and ready. "Bathroom's all yours."

"Thanks." He reached up to scrub at his hair, making the muscles in his arms flex.

She wrenched her attention away from him and got busy packing her own gear. She didn't *want* to be noticing his muscles. "I'll wipe everything down."

"I'll help you once I'm done."

By the time he'd showered and dressed, she had done most of the sanitization. Didn't hurt to have another set of hands, though. They used bleach wipes on everything they might have touched to get rid of fingerprints, then collected them in a bag to be thrown out elsewhere.

"Ready?" she asked him as she shrugged into her backpack. She tucked her favorite blade away in a sheath strapped to her right calf, and her pistol was safely secured in the holster at the small of her back. Her other tools were stashed in various pockets in her cargo pants.

"Yep."

Rather than finding his presence suffocating or annoying, it was sort of nice to have him there to keep watch as they made their way out of the hotel. That didn't mean she was up for more public hand-holding, however. "Meet you at the RV point," she told him, and headed right.

"Wait." He grabbed hold of her upper arm. "I'm going with you."

Yeah, no. She pulled her arm out of his grasp. "I'll meet you there. If he's still watching, going together will make us easier to spot. This way he'll have to pick one of us. It'll be our best shot at drawing him out."

For a moment Tyler looked like he wanted to argue, but he had to know she was right, and relented. "Alert me if anything happens."

"I can take care of myself."

"Alert me," he insisted.

It was easier to just agree and get moving. "Fine."

She turned around and walked away, paying close attention to what was happening around her. His quiet footfalls retreated in the opposite direction.

Alone, her senses remained on high alert as she wound her way through the historic city center of Old Town. Prague was a gorgeous city. One day, when it was safe, she'd like to come back and explore it more.

She scanned around her covertly as she passed the pretty, pastel-colored stone buildings, using all the trade secrets she'd learned from her trainers and handlers over the years. The weight of the pistol against the base of her spine was reassuring, as was the knowledge that Trinity was tracking her movements. Having backup was weird, but nice.

The city was quiet at this time of the morning and the traffic was light. A lot of the streets were made of cobblestone. Tires made a cool sound as they drove over them.

She stopped at a coffee shop, using it as an excuse to look around her as she waited in line. Except the stupid *kolaches* made her think of Tyler.

Steaming hot coffee in hand, she walked to the street and hailed a taxi. It took her west and then south along the river toward the National Theater, a grand, imposing sand-colored stone building where she would meet the others.

She kept her eye on the passenger side mirror, watching for any signs that they were being followed. Several vehicles were behind them. A delivery truck, two cars and a van.

Climbing out of the cab near the theater, she took a quick look around. Hand on the door, she froze when the black compact she'd seen a minute earlier appeared around the corner. It stopped.

She casually turned away from the cab and started for the steps of the theater, watching the car out of the corner of her eye. It disappeared behind another building.

The theater was deserted. She hurried up onto the steps and slipped behind a column to keep watch.

Her pulse jolted in recognition when she spotted the man from yesterday appear around the corner on the sidewalk. He wore a light jacket, unzipped, and he was heading toward the theater.

She tapped her earpiece to activate it. There was no way he could see her, but if he'd followed her here then he would be looking for her. Moving from her position was risky. And with Tyler and Trinity both showing up soon, she didn't want them walking into a bullet. "I'm here, but we've got company. A block away, heading west toward the theater."

Tyler answered immediately. "Guy from yesterday?"

"Affirmative."

"Can he see you?"

"Not anymore." But he would if she didn't move soon.

"I'm on my way to you," Trinity said. "Tyler's closer."

"I'm two blocks away," he said. "I'll—"

The man veered sharply right and crossed the street, heading straight toward her. "Gotta go," she murmured, feeling weird having to report her decisions to anyone.

She slipped back deeper into the shadows that hugged the base of the building, watching the man. She didn't think he'd seen her, but...

A car parked out front turned on its lights, the beams throwing her shadow against the wall. The man's head jerked toward her and he started running.

With a mental curse Megan turned and ran, the solid weight of her backpack bumping against her spine. She didn't bother updating the others. They'd see her location with the private tracking app on their burner phones.

She raced along the side of the theater, heading for

the next street. When she cut a glance over her shoulder, the man was still in pursuit. His right hand reached into his jacket to withdraw something.

She put on a burst of speed and made a sharp left turn around the corner, darting through traffic and turning sharply left again.

"I'm almost there," Tyler's voice said, serious but calm. "Take your next right and go half a block, then take the alley to the right."

She didn't respond, saving her breath for the run. She did as he said, turning right up a quiet, deserted back street and then right up a narrow alley. Early sunlight streamed through the far end. She squinted against it and kept running, attuned to anything coming behind her.

Running footsteps.

Time's up. She had no choice but to turn and fight.

Without breaking stride she reached back and withdrew her pistol. Whirling, she took aim at the shadowy shape at the end of the alley. They both fired two shots almost simultaneously.

Bullets struck the stone façade of the building to her left, and the figure ducked out of sight behind some garbage cans.

This alley was a deathtrap. There was nothing here for her to hide behind, and the sun lit her entire body up, forming a perfect silhouette. Engaging in a shootout with this guy was beyond stupid. She had to get the hell out of here before she took a bullet in the spine.

She whipped around and raced away, avoiding a straight line because it would make her an easier target. Two more shots rang out. Puffs of dust exploded on her left where the rounds hit the other building, barely missing her.

At the end of the alley she wheeled left and darted up another side street.

"Don't shoot me," Tyler warned.

Huh? Running flat out, she barely avoided plowing into him when he suddenly stepped out of a doorway ten feet in front of her.

She swallowed a gasp and managed to avoid him, her feet sliding. He shot a hand out, grabbed her by the arm and wrenched her back into the doorway with him. With the back of his right arm he pinned her to the cold brick of the building, then ducked his head around the corner of it to check and fired three shots.

"Go," he commanded, shoving her toward the eastern end of the street. "I'll cover you."

What was this bullshit? Just because she was a woman? "I'll cover *you*."

"*Go*," he growled without looking at her, focused on their target.

They could stay here and argue about who would cover who, but that was cataclysmically stupid. Booting her pride aside, she followed his order and ran in the direction he'd pushed her. She veered right at the next street, paused to check behind her, then whirled at the sound of squealing tires and a racing engine.

A delivery van roared up and squealed to a sudden stop in front of them. Megan and Tyler both aimed their weapons at it, ready to fire. The side door slid open to reveal Trinity. "Get in," she ordered.

Perfect timing.

They raced for it together, jumped in, and Tyler yanked the door shut with a slam as the van took off with a squeal of tires.

Ping, ping.

Bullets pierced the rear quarter panel.

Weapon in hand, Megan slid across the bench seat, whipped off her backpack and immediately swiveled to look out the rear window. Tyler settled next to her and dumped his own pack, his hip pressing into hers, pistol in hand as he did the same.

"You wish me lose that guy, yes?" the driver said in panicked, heavily accented English.

"*Yes*," they all responded.

"Hold on." He hit the gas, wrenching the wheel sharply to the right onto Legion Bridge.

"Either of you see a tail?" Trinity asked from up front a moment later, checking out her window and using the passenger side mirror as they sped across the bridge.

"White BMW," Tyler said, having a better vantage point. "Just nearing the foot of the bridge now."

Megan spotted it weaving aggressively in and out of traffic. Gaining on them slowly.

Trinity gave the driver a string of rapid orders. As soon as they reached the far side of the bridge, at the last possible moment he took a sudden left.

Megan shot a hand out to brace herself against the door. Tyler caught her in an iron grip around the waist and hauled her back as the van skidded around the corner.

Per Trinity's instructions the driver made a myriad of turns, winding them back and forth through the warren of streets as he drove them northwest away from the city center.

She didn't see the BMW.

"I think we're clear," Megan said as they reached the motorway. The driver accelerated, merging with the other traffic and then immediately moved into the fast lane to pass it.

She and Tyler kept watch out the back for another few minutes. But at the speed they were traveling, and with no sign of the vehicle, chances were slim he'd be able to find or follow them now.

Tyler exhaled and turned to face front, sliding his pistol into the holster on his hip. She tucked hers away as well. Everyone was silent for a long moment.

"My van has bullets in it," the pale-faced driver muttered, his motions agitated as he drove. "You guys spies or something?" the driver asked as he shot past slower moving traffic on the right.

It broke the tension. Megan grinned but didn't reply, and didn't look at Tyler. She didn't know him very well but she could feel the rigidity in him, as if some inner strain gripped him.

Trinity made a call to relay what had happened to someone, probably Rycroft. Ten minutes later they arrived at the airfield. Megan grabbed her pack and exited the van. Two bullets had punched clean holes through the rear passenger-side quarter panel.

Shouldering her pack, she started for the small terminal building. A small, sleek jet was waiting on the tarmac beyond it, ready to take them to Vienna.

The building was empty except for a man pushing a mop around. He barely spared her a glance and went back to cleaning the floor. Trinity walked past her, still on her phone. Megan followed, tensing slightly at the hard, rapid strides behind her.

She bit back a gasp as two hard hands wrapped around her upper arms and whirled her around. "Hey—" Her words cut off as Tyler yanked her off her feet and dragged her into the men's room, then crowded her up against the door.

She shoved the heels of her hands against his solid chest and opened her mouth to tell him to back the fuck off, but the look on his face made her voice dry up. He was livid, his slate blue gaze drilling into hers, jaw so tight the muscles stood out on either side.

He caged her in against the door with a hand on either side of her head, his huge frame barring her way.

She could have gotten away. A knee to the balls or a shot to the throat and she could easily have escaped. But that look on his face froze her.

"Don't *ever* do something that fucking stupid again," he snarled, right in her face.

"Do what?" she shot back, strangely torn between kneeing him and soothing his ruffled feathers. Or maybe kissing him senseless.

"Argue when I tell you to run. Stand there and fucking argue about who's covering who when there's an armed assassin after us. If I give you an order, it's not because I'm on some male power trip. It's for your safety. So if I give you an order, you follow it. Got me?" His gaze was so hot it was a wonder she hadn't melted under the force of it.

Or maybe...maybe she *was* melting.

It wasn't male pride she heard in his words. Beneath the anger and frustration, she heard his concern for her. His worry about her safety.

No one had worried about her before. No one except a handler, and only because they had been concerned she might fail to complete her mission. But for some reason, Tyler seemed to care about *her*.

She didn't like what that did to her head. Or the flipping sensation it caused deep in her abdomen.

She lifted her chin, refusing to be cowed. She was his equal, dammit, not some helpless female who needed to be coddled and protected, and he needed to recognize that. "Or what?" she demanded.

"Or nothing." His eyes roved over her face. They dipped to her mouth, and he gave a tight, frustrated shake of his head. "God*damn* it," he muttered, then plunged a hand into her hair and brought his mouth down on hers.

Chapter Eight

What in the hell was he *doing*?

The astounded thought blared in his head but Ty ignored it and slanted his mouth across Megan's before he could stop himself. He wanted her and wasn't going to bother hiding it. Not when she could have been shot down in front of him less than ten minutes ago.

He'd told himself to let it go. He'd told himself not to touch her. But when he thought of what could have happened back there, of how close he'd come to losing her...

Fuck it. He was staking a claim right here and now.

The pressure of her palms increased on his chest. He stilled and braced himself, prepared for her to shove him away, her body slightly angled as if she might drive her knee up between his legs.

But she did neither of those things. No, she stood there with her back to the door, unresisting as their lips clung together. Almost as if she was absorbing the feel of the kiss.

He swallowed a groan, wanting to devour her. Christ, he'd imagined doing this to her—and a whole lot more— for years in his fantasies, never believing he'd ever get the chance. Now that he finally had her mouth under his, he wanted more. Anything and everything she was willing to give him.

Needing to get closer, he slid his other hand into her hair, cradling the back of her head as he touched his tongue to her lower lip. A tender stroke meant to coax, meant to make her open for him.

He wanted inside her. To forge that intimate contact. Ached to sink his tongue into her mouth to possess her in even that small way.

As if it snapped her out of a trance, Megan shoved him away, breaking the kiss. They stared at each other for a loaded few seconds, both breathing harder, the wild, latent energy of the kiss swirling between them. Her hazel eyes glittered with silent challenge and something more, a blaze of color riding high on her cheekbones.

Before he had any idea what she was going to do, she grabbed his head and leaned in to seal her lips to his again, plastering the length of her lithe body against him. He released a low groan of need and slung an arm around her waist, locking her to him.

She had a solid hold on his hair with her fists, the tiny burn along his scalp adding to the fire erupting inside him. Her lips parted under his. He licked along her lower one and retreated. Megan mewled in protest and followed his mouth, wanting more.

His entire body responded.

I'll give you more, dimples. Any damn thing you want.

He stepped forward to pin her to the door with his hips and delved his tongue inside the warmth of her mouth. Slowly. Tasting her. Savoring her while his body screamed at him to take more.

She met the sensual caress, touching his tongue with hers. Velvet soft. Slow. So damn erotic he was rock hard in his pants, his dick straining against his fly where it pressed into her abdomen.

She broke the kiss, angling her face away. Bowed her head as her hands came to press at the front of his shoulders. Her breathing was unsteady, her cheeks flushed, eyes closed.

Ty leaned his forehead against her temple and eased up on his possessive grip, breathing in her tempting scent. He was keyed up, his whole body rigid with need.

"That was really stupid," she murmured.

Yeah. Yeah, it was. But he'd be damned if he'd apologize, because he'd loved every damn moment of that kiss and didn't regret a single thing about it.

Megan ducked under his arm to grab her pack from the floor where he'd dumped it, then straightened as she shrugged the strap over one shoulder and met his gaze. "Is this how you usually are with all your female partners on an op?"

"No. Never." He hadn't worked with female partners all that often, and he'd never touched them intimately. Megan was different. She made him lose his head, and that was dangerous for them both.

"Then why did you do that?"

He didn't see the point in lying. It was too late to hide his feelings for her, though she wouldn't know how deep they went. "Because I care about you."

Shock flared in her eyes. "You don't even know me."

"I know enough." He reached for his own pack, sidestepped her and reached for the door handle. He was still hard, his body suffering whiplash from the dual shots of the adrenaline crash and the feel of her warm and willing in his arms mere moments ago.

He walked out of the bathroom without a backward glance, giving Megan some privacy and time to compose herself. Just thinking about the way she'd responded to him made him bite back a growl of longing.

With one kiss she'd singed him, inside and out. He'd gotten a taste of the need and passion hidden beneath the layer of armor she'd been taught to encase herself in.

Now he wanted all the way beneath it. To strip it all away until they were skin to skin and he was buried as deep inside her as he could get, him staring down into her face so he could watch her expression as he made her come apart around him.

He jerked his wayward thoughts back into line when Trinity came into view at a door near the far end of the small terminal building. Behind him he heard the bathroom door open, then Megan's quiet footfalls on the linoleum floor.

"Everything okay?" Trinity asked him as he approached.

"Yep." There was no way she didn't know what had just happened. None. He wasn't going to embarrass Megan further by drawing attention to them right now, however. It was none of Trinity's business regardless. "We good to go?"

She nodded, her gaze shifting past him to Megan. "Wheels up in five minutes." She pushed the exit door open and walked out onto the tarmac to where the jet waited for them.

Ty took a seat in the middle of the plane. He stowed his gear and buckled in for the flight, watching as Megan boarded the aircraft. She'd fixed her hair before leaving the bathroom.

She studiously ignored him as she moved down the aisle into another seat a few rows ahead of him, giving him all kinds of time to admire the shape of her body, the sinuous, confident way she moved. And she was so unpretentious he was willing to bet she had no clue how sexy that was.

Looking out the window he took a deep breath and let it out slowly, willing his body to relax. She'd want to avoid him now, was trying to put distance between them and shore up the barrier the kiss had shaken, but that wasn't possible. There was no going back. No erasing what they'd done, or the pull between them.

In just over an hour they'd be touching down in Vienna to await word on the next target location. Whenever word came in, they'd be heading out together again. There were already too many unknowns going on with this operation for his liking, possibly more hitters coming after them, and having more players involved made this even more dangerous.

If he'd been determined to see this thing through before, after that kiss he was even more invested in keeping Megan safe now.

Ty didn't care whether she liked it or not; unless some unforeseen circumstance made it impossible, he wasn't letting her out of his sight again until this was over.

****

The net was starting to close in around her. She could feel it.

Amber ran up the stairwell to the rental unit on the third floor, pausing only momentarily to ensure that her anti-tampering devices were still intact on the door, and rushed inside. Twice now she'd felt someone watching while she was out in the street, and she'd only been here in Vienna for a day.

Time to move again. This was the second place she'd stayed at in Vienna since arriving yesterday morning, and still she wasn't safe. The constant travel was a grind, but a necessary one if she wanted to remain alive and eliminate every last one of her targets and her training had prepared her for this. She was ready to endure the hardships that came with seeing her mission through if it meant getting retribution on those who had set her up and left her to die.

The good news was, her latest target was missing.

Hannah Miller hadn't shown up to an emergency meeting with her former handler this morning. Amber had intercepted the "secure" email from the handler a little after dawn, checking in with the missing operative, who hadn't responded. Now it was only a matter of time before Hannah's fate was revealed.

"So, you're the hacker."

Amber glanced up from her computer, in the midst of setting up another offshore account for them to funnel away the funds they were about to take from their target. The blond woman stood watching her, dual shoulder holsters revealed as she took her jacket off and draped it across the corner of Amber's desk. "Yeah. You're Hannah?"

She smiled, but it didn't reach her pale blue eyes. "That's me." She flicked a glance down at the screen. "We all set up?"

"Almost." It was so strange to be working with a team. Valkyries were solo creatures for a reason, but they'd banded together to take out a dirty CIA contact and his network of arms dealer thugs. To the victors belonged the spoils, and by night's end, Amber expected to have a little over ten million hidden in various offshore accounts for them to split at the end of the job.

"Good." She patted Amber's shoulder, and the patronizing feel to it rubbed Amber the wrong way. "We'll take care of securing the funds. You just make sure you hide it where no one else can find it." She'd walked away, all attitude, as if she was the badass and Amber a mere computer geek they'd brought along on this op because they'd been forced to.

It had bugged her then, but it infuriated her now that she knew the true depth of their duplicity. All of them, but especially Hannah and Zoya, the ringleaders of the plot.

Unfortunately Amber wouldn't be able to stay here and await confirmation that Hannah had been captured or killed. She had to get out of the city immediately, slip across the border into Switzerland to buy herself some more time. Change her identity once again. Bury her banking information, and see if the shadows she'd sensed at the edge of her consciousness for the past two days would follow here there as well.

She moved around the apartment quickly, packing up her electronics and the rest of the sparse gear she'd brought. Only as much as she could easily carry with her in a backpack.

Get out. Get out now.

The voice inside her was urgent, and she'd learned long ago to trust it.

Shoving the laptop into her backpack, she took one last cursory look around, wiped down the light switches and taps, and left. Her heart beat faster as she took a different stairwell to the bottom floor, hyper aware of her surroundings and on guard for any threats.

Hand on the butt of the pistol in her jacket pocket, she paused, waiting and listening. Once she was satisfied the coast was likely clear, she cracked the door open with a slight metallic creak that made her mentally curse, and glanced around.

The sky was already turning purple. A swarm of bats flitted through the air and across the half moon, heading out to hunt for the night. The trickle of water came from a nearby fountain, along with the faint murmur of distant conversation.

She moved fast, on full alert as she headed for the narrow, cobbled alleyway two blocks east, where she'd left her bike. No one followed her. And no silenced shots fired bullets at her.

She zipped up the leather pocket concealing her weapon, secured the backpack's belt across her waist and straddled the motorbike's seat. It wasn't until she was a few blocks away, heading west that she realized her mistake.

Her treasures. She'd forgotten them in the hiding spot inside the apartment.

Shit. How could she have been so careless? She'd never made this kind of sloppy mistake before.

She pulled over to the side of the road at the next intersection, conflicting urges warring inside her. Stay or go? Flee to safety and the chance to fight another day, or risk going back to get her most treasured possessions?

A cold, hard weight formed in her chest. So cold it burned.

The Valkyrie trainers and powers-that-be had done everything at their command to erase her past. Her memories. Her personality.

To erase whoever she'd been before and leave a reprogrammed assassin in its place.

For the most part, they'd succeeded. She had only a handful of memories from her childhood, little more than confusing snapshots that made no sense. But no one involved with the program had realized that she'd always maintained a part of her own identity. A part they couldn't force things upon or take away from her, no matter what they'd done to make it otherwise.

The things she'd left behind in the apartment were merely a handful of things, meaningless to anyone else. But they were all she had left from a life she didn't remember, taken from a top-secret file she'd found in her last handler's house the night he'd killed himself.

That night she'd lost her only link to the only human being who had ever truly given a shit about her, and inadvertently gained a link to something vastly more precious. Pieces that linked her to fragmented memories long forgotten. Pieces of a puzzle she was working every day to put together.

Who was she, really? Who had she been? What had

happened to her family?

Stay or go?

She'd had a family once. She'd belonged to someone. To people who had loved her, before they'd been taken away. Before she'd been taken away and forced to forget them. Forced to turn into the woman she was now. A weapon those same people had used and then tried to discard.

Except everything that had happened was still there, lurking deep inside her memory in a shadowy place she was only beginning to access. A puzzle waiting to be solved. Crying out for resolution. One she was desperate to find.

Amber pursed her lips and pulled into traffic, decision made. She took the next right and doubled back the way she'd come using side streets, ready to accept the risks and consequences that came with recovering her treasures at all cost.

The Valkyrie Program had already taken everything that had mattered to her. She'd be damned if it took this last piece from her too.

Chapter Nine

Show time.

"You ready to go?" Megan asked impatiently, sliding her pistol into the custom holster at the small of her back.

They'd just gotten word from Trinity about a possible target location to search here in Vienna, and after being cooped up in this condo all day with Tyler going over intel, she was anxious to get moving. Their suspect had proven difficult to find so far. Megan wanted to capture him or her so they could start getting some badly needed answers.

Tyler looked up at her in the midst of taking a spare magazine from his duffel, and the impact of his slate blue gaze hit her square in the chest. Calm. Alert. "Yep."

"So let's move." She needed to get going, expend some of the pent up energy humming inside her and focus on something other than him.

That kiss this afternoon had been a terrible lapse in judgment on her part. Yeah, she'd enjoyed it, but how stupid could she have been? It gave Tyler the wrong idea completely, and worse, now she couldn't seem to shut off her attraction to him.

Worse, it was like the kiss had intensified everything

she'd been trying to keep locked down. Her body was edgy and frustrated around him, the sensation magnified a hundred times when he was nearby.

And since she was going to be close to him for the foreseeable future, that didn't bode well.

She couldn't let it dampen her focus. Couldn't afford to let him distract her, even when they weren't in op mode. Problem was, he seemed determined to deny her the space she needed to make that happen.

She leaned against the wall in the entryway and waited for him to kit up, folding her arms to keep from picking at her cuticles any more. Most of her fingers were picked raw and bleeding in spots. Not unusual when she got keyed up, but he made it worse.

"Trinity's monitoring us on the same frequency as before," she said, sliding in her earpiece.

Tyler eyed her for a second, his gaze stirring heat in its wake as it roamed over the snug black pants and form-fitting, long-sleeve T-shirt she wore. "How many mags have you got on you?"

"Three." One in her weapon and two extras, along with her blade, taser and tools. Her standard loadout.

A wry smile tugged at one side of his mouth. "Okay, then. If we're gonna break local weapons laws, go big or go home, right?" He grabbed two more mags from his duffel and slid them into various pockets in his cargo pants, drawing her attention to the well-defined muscula-ture of his arms and torso.

He confused her. Tempted her in ways that surprised her, and she couldn't figure him out. No other man had shaken her resolve the way he did.

What was his end game? Why had he agreed to work with her on this in the first place? If it was because of guilt due to what had happened in SERE school, then he could just get over himself because she was a lot stronger and more capable than he seemed to think. She hoped she got the chance to prove it to him on this op.

Because I care about you.

That was insane. And it pissed her off that her heart had leaped when he'd said it. She was naturally suspicious at the best of times. Had he said it to make her lower her guard? To get into her head for some reason?

He's in your head right now, because you're still thinking about him.

Bah. She scowled in annoyance and shifted position against the wall, anxious to get out of here and get to work.

Tyler slipped in his own earpiece and came toward her, more than six feet of sexy, masculine power made all the more intense by his quiet air of confidence. He reached past her for the doorknob, gave her a little smile as he opened it. "After you."

Finally. She marched out into the hallway.

The anxious energy humming inside her began to transform into excitement as they drove to the small house on the edge of the historic district.

After circling the building once Tyler parked a block down the street. He would wait in a hidden spot that allowed him to see anyone coming and going from the front, while she installed a camera at the rear entrance to give them eyes there. Trinity was watching the east side of the building from another location.

"Comm check," Megan murmured as she stepped onto the sidewalk. It was dark and quiet out. This was her favorite time to operate. Between two and three in the morning was the best time to perform ops. Most people were dead asleep or at least had their guards down, making her job a whole lot easier.

"Check," Trinity and Tyler both answered.

He was only a few feet from her on the sidewalk, watching her expectantly. It seemed rude to just turn around and walk away without saying anything. "See you," she blurted, feeling dumb for saying anything at all.

He nodded once, his eyes searching hers, making her think of the kiss again. "Be careful."

She pivoted and strode away from him down the sidewalk past the stately, painted buildings, those words playing in her mind. No one had ever said that to her before. Not even her handlers. What if he was for real? What if he actually *did* care?

With a mental smack, she shouldered all that aside and went on alert as she made her way around the back of the house, staying out of the line of sight of the security cameras and motion-activated lights they'd found on the surrounding buildings in a scan earlier.

The two-story target house was supposedly empty but she was approaching it as if it wasn't. If any surprises awaited her inside—human or otherwise—she was prepared to deal with them.

She tugged on her thin, skintight gloves. Then her small, specialized NVGs and switched them on and climbed up the old drain spout to secure the micro camera under the eaves trough.

After activating it, giving the others a sightline of the back alley and the buildings behind it, she climbed back down and slipped her tool pouch from her right hip pocket. Every tool was custom made, and each of them was as intimately familiar to her as her own body so that she could identify and use them while blindfolded. She didn't need to look at them as she chose the first tool and got to work.

The locking mechanism on the back door didn't appear to have any additional security measures on it. She picked it within thirty seconds and gingerly turned the deadbolt so that it made no sound. When nothing happened she eased the door open a fraction of an inch, her NVGs catching sight of the thin bit of wire strung from the knob to the other side of the doorframe.

She stopped and surveyed the entryway, checking for other things she would have to take care of before entering. There were no lasers, nothing high tech that she could see. As long as she could slip in without alerting anyone to her presence—or being injured in a booby-trap—she could be in and out in a matter of minutes.

Megan cut the wire and slipped inside. She found and disabled a motion device set into a light switch on the wall, and two cameras monitoring the hallway from different angles. A far different and more advanced setup than the previous locations. Maybe they were finally onto something solid.

She swept the lower floor and then moved to the second where the bedrooms were. No more devices, and better still, no one at home. Although that could mean they'd missed their chance to apprehend their suspect, because other than the extra security measures, it looked like the place was completely vacant.

No clothes, toiletries or personal items in any of the rooms. Both beds were perfectly made. No dishes in the sink or dishwasher. Fridge empty.

Next order of business was looking for a hiding spot or safe. She checked the second floor first. Finding nothing, she hurried downstairs to look on the main level. In the old boiler room at the back she moved aside a wooden panel on the far wall and grinned, her heart skipping a beat.

"Bingo," she whispered.

"Sitrep," Trinity murmured through the earpiece.

"Found a safe," she whispered back, her voice barely audible in case there were cameras or recorders around that she hadn't found. Doubtful, but not impossible.

"Can you open it?"

She withheld a snort. "Yeah." About the size of a large microwave, the safe was big enough to hold important documents, cash or jewelry while still being the right size to hide easily.

It was old. At least a hundred years old if she guessed right, with three different combination locks, and made of cast iron if she wasn't mistaken.

Ultra low tech, but that was the beauty of it. No one had these anymore. It would take her some time to crack it.

A wave of anticipation swept through her. Oh, *God*, she loved a challenge. And it had been way too long since she'd had one.

"Stand by." Crouching in front of it, she pushed her NVGs up onto her head and slipped her penlight from a pocket in her pants. Holding it in her teeth, she studied her opponent. Three combination dials and nothing else. No scanners, no biometrics.

Sweet. Kicking it old school.

She pulled out more tools and got to work, closing her eyes to hear the clicks better. One of her best skills was identifying exactly when the tumblers clicked into position, and doing it with her eyes open was a distraction.

First seven-digit combo didn't take long at all. She repeated the sequence in her head, memorizing it for later. The second combo had nine digits and took a few minutes longer.

The third dial was different. Tiny. With multiple turns required to find each number. The sound was different too, unlike anything she'd come across before. Higher-pitched, almost tinny, and nearly impossible to detect.

"Eleven minutes and counting," Trinity said.

Megan ignored her, focused on her task. The dial was fiddly, requiring a steady, skilled hand and a keen ear.

"Fourteen minutes. Pick up the pace, Megan."

She didn't respond, busy keeping track of the numbers in her head. Nine so far on the third dial. Ten. Eleven.

Come on, old girl. Talk to me...

She carefully turned the dial three times to the right, searching for the sound that told her she'd found another number.

A tiny click. A shift of the mechanism.

Her eyes popped open. *That's it. I've got the whole combo.*

She wiped the back of her gloved hand across her upper lip, reached for the first dial and entered the initial sequence.

Click. The dial popped out slightly, signaling she'd cracked the first lock.

Now the second. More numbers. The mechanism more precise.

Click. The second dial popped out a bit.

Her heart started beating faster. She grasped the third knob, her lips moving as she repeated the long sequence. *Forty-one. Nineteen. Seventy-three...*

It was time consuming, the mechanism finicky. If she didn't stop at exactly the right place, if she moved a fraction of a millimeter too far with the dial, she'd have to start all over.

Almost there.

Sixty-four. Eleven. Ninety-one...

Click.

She held her breath, paused for a heartbeat and reached for the lever handle. It caught partway down as she pushed it.

Her heart sank. But then the handle gave to her consistent pressure, sliding down.

A quiet thunk filled the silent room as the main bolts slid free in the door.

Megan smiled. "I'm in," she murmured, and eased the door open.

"What do you see?" Trinity asked.

Her heart sunk. "Nothing."

"Nothing?"

A black hole stared back at her. "Not a damn thing." Shit.

She swept her hand over the inside of it, just to make sure there wasn't a false bottom or sides that she'd missed. "It's a bust. I'll keep looking." She closed the safe and spun the dials, annoyed that she'd wasted so much time cracking an empty safe. Had their suspect even known about it?

Moving fast, she went through the place again. Checking behind appliances. Under rugs and furniture. Behind pictures. Any place where someone might hide something.

"I don't see anything else," she whispered, her gut beginning to tighten, that handy internal clock ticking down. She'd spent too long in here already. Time to get out.

"Roger that. Time's up. Exfil and get back to the condo."

She took a step toward the back door in compliance, then paused and looked up at the ceiling as a thought struck her. The bathroom. She'd looked in the most obvious places but maybe...

It was a long shot, but she'd better check one more time.

The soles of her boots were soundless on the carpet runner that lined the middle of the staircase up to the second floor. At the end of the hall, light from the streetlamp outside filtered in through the window above the old, cast iron clawfoot tub.

She walked over to the bathmat beside it, crouched and pulled it back again to sweep a gloved hand over it. No loose boards or a panel beneath it, but when she aimed the beam of her penlight at the floor she saw a few faint scratch marks in the wood. Not unusual for an old home, but the curving pattern was a giveaway.

Maybe the suspect hadn't used the safe because the

safe was too obvious if anyone came looking. Maybe he or she had gone for something more unexpected.

With the penlight secure in her teeth she grasped the edge of the tub and pulled, using her leg muscles to swing the heavy cast iron tub toward her.

As soon as she had room to move behind it, she squeezed into the space she'd made next to the exterior wall and checked the floor. A jolt shot through her.

Son of a bitch!

One of the floorboards was sticking up slightly at the end. She pried it free with ease and quickly reached for the next.

A hole opened up beneath it.

"I got something," she whispered, her excitement growing.

Three more boards, and she had room to peer inside. And there, in the beam of her penlight lay a hidden, thin box. She removed the lid, revealing a small cache of items.

A thin, metallic bracelet. A small, tattered blanket, carefully folded. And inside it, a small, framed picture of—

She sucked in a breath, her hand shooting out to grab the photo. Her heart thudded in her ears, struck by a deep and unexpected sense of recognition.

A couple smiling at the camera. The man stood behind the seated woman, a hand on her shoulder. Young. Maybe in their mid-to-late twenties.

I know them.

Megan stared at it, holding her breath, unable to shake the feeling. She'd seen them before, yet she couldn't place them. Dammit. Where had she seen them? And were the items left behind by a random stranger, or their suspect?

"Megan, time to move," Tyler said. "Two people in the back lane, headed your way."

Was it their suspect returning? "On my way out," she murmured, tucking the items into the box for further analysis later. She slid it inside her jacket, zipped it up and quickly put the floorboards back, then the tub.

"I'm heading to the alley to meet you," Tyler said.

She didn't need the backup if anything went sideways but she didn't bother arguing as she hurried downstairs and started for the door. Then she hesitated. Leaving the cut wires and the disabled devices was a dead giveaway that someone skilled had broken in but she couldn't stop to reconnect them now.

She paused just inside the back door, one hand on the knob, the other curled around the grip of her pistol holstered at the small of her back. "Am I clear?"

"Affirmative," Tyler answered. "The couple's heading to a different building. I'm coming to you from the west side."

Cracking the door open to check the alley, she spotted two people entering a building up the alley. She slipped outside, immediately spotting Tyler's shadow as he appeared around the side of the house to the west.

She shut the door behind her, locked it using her tools, then met him as he reached the side of the house. He curved a hand around her upper arm and drew her into his body as they walked, giving the appearance that they were a couple to anyone watching.

"What did you find?" he whispered, scanning the street before leading her back toward their waiting vehicle.

"Show you later." The image in that photo was turning around and around in her brain. How could someone look so familiar, and yet she couldn't place them? It was going to drive her crazy.

Tyler reached into his jacket pocket for the keys, shooting her a surprised look when he realized she'd already snagged them without him noticing.

"I'm driving," she announced and pulled free of his hand, heading for the driver's side.

Just as she reached for the handle, Trinity's voice came through her earpiece. "You've got company approaching. Single female on foot a half-block to the south."

Megan's scalp prickled as she swung her head around to check behind her and reached for the grip of her weapon. She scanned the opposite side of the street for the woman, ready to end this here and now.

****

The rubber soles of Amber's riding boots were quiet on the sidewalk as she walked the two blocks from where she'd left her bike, using the shadows to help conceal her. As she reached the next street, a warning tingle flared up at the base of her spine.

She was being watched. She just wasn't sure by whom, or from where. But the warning quiver in the pit of her stomach told her there were eyes on her right now and there had been for at least the last minute, maybe more.

She wouldn't go to the house until she was certain she was clear. The picture she had a digital backup of, but the bracelet and blanket were irreplaceable. So she would stay on this side of the street and walk past the rental house before doubling back later, waiting to see if anyone followed. If they did, she'd take them out.

Hands in the pockets of her leather riding jacket, she curled her fingers around the grip of her pistol, pausing when she spotted two people approaching a car parked at the curb across the street, a few hundred yards south of the house. A man and a woman.

The woman had a sleek build and she wore dark, formfitting clothing. She rounded the front of the vehicle and reached for the door handle, then stopped. A second later she straightened and turned her head, her gaze unerringly finding Amber.

Even though the woman wouldn't be able to see her clearly, a shot of alarm punched through her.

They stared at each other, both of them frozen as the second stretched out. And Amber knew.

The woman was here for her.

She spun on her heel and took off, racing back to where she'd parked her bike. No running footsteps came from behind her. Then the sound of a car engine reached her. Coming up fast. Too fast.

She leapt over the hood of a parked car in her way, sliding across the surface before landing back on her feet and continued running. Fifty yards up she darted left down an alleyway and cut over to where she'd parked her bike, watching and listening for signs of her pursuers. They would be coming around the block, either from the left or right.

Amber hopped on her bike, yanked her helmet on and started the engine. She shot out into the street just as a squeal of tires sounded around the corner behind her. Closer than the vehicle that had been chasing her should have been.

She risked a glance over her shoulder as she sped down the darkened street. A different car veered out behind her, its lights off.

Two pursuers.

Shots rang out. She instinctively ducked and turned the bike, sucking in a breath as fire streaked across the bottom of her left ribcage.

Gritting her teeth, she drew her weapon and looked over her shoulder to fire. Both bullets penetrated the windshield.

The driver swerved, the squeal of scraping metal filling the night, but didn't slow. Didn't stop. Coming closer with every heartbeat.

Amber swung back around to face forward and opened up the throttle. She tore down the quiet street, tearing past parked vehicles and darkened homes as blood trickled hot and sticky down her side.

She wasn't sure how bad she was hit. The wound burned but she wasn't going into shock yet and her vision was still clear.

I can make it.

She had to make it.

She made a sharp right turn around the next corner, dragging her inside foot across the ground as the back tire skidded, then gunned it again. She kept her eyes pinned to the road ahead of her, mapping out an escape route in her mind.

The chase was on, and this was a race she would win. She wasn't fucking dying tonight.

Chapter Ten

Their hitter from yesterday was back. Or someone connected to him.

"Buckle up," Megan said to Tyler, then hit the gas.

"Shit," he blurted from the passenger seat, frantically grabbing for his seatbelt as she wrenched the wheel to the left and peeled after the Audi.

Megan kept her eyes pinned to the back of the hitter's car as a metallic click signaled the fastening of Tyler's seatbelt and Trinity's calm voice came through her earpiece announced that she would track them via GPS. With the other vehicle's lights off Megan had to stay close enough to maintain visual contact.

On either side of the street the still houses and cars whipped past as she sped after the Audi, the woman on the bike a half block ahead of it. A hand appeared out of the Audi's driver-side window. Two muzzle flashes and pops came as the driver fired at the woman.

"Look out," Tyler warned as the woman swiveled to return fire.

Megan swerved to dodge the bullets. So did the Audi, catching its bumper on a parked car. Sparks lit up the darkened street.

She pumped the brakes and steered to the right to

avoid a collision as the Audi slid left on the narrow street. The driver managed to recover and race after the motorcycle.

A second later the woman made a hard, tight turn to the right and disappeared up a side street.

The Audi slammed on its brakes, coming to an abrupt halt. Megan did the same, narrowly avoiding plowing into the back of it. Before she or Tyler could lower their windows to fire at it, the Audi tore away, the back end fishtailing on the damp cobbles.

In a split second, Megan made the decision to let him go and chase down the woman on the bike. They needed to get to her before the hitter did, because they had to take her alive.

"Hold on," she said to Tyler, who grabbed his door handle to steady himself, then shoved the transmission into reverse and gunned it, using the side mirrors to steer.

The little car shot backward down the main street. At the side street that the motorcycle had turned up she took her foot off the gas and cranked the wheel hard to turn them ninety degrees in a tight J-turn.

Tyler's chuckle was almost lost beneath the sound of the engine as she yanked the wheel back to straight, threw the transmission into drive and stomped down on the gas to continue the pursuit like a goddamn boss.

"Holy shit, I think I love you," Tyler said, still laughing.

Megan's lips quirked but didn't she respond, busy searching for the woman on the motorcycle. The bike was smaller and way more maneuverable than their car. If they were going to have a shot at stopping her, Megan had to find her damn quick.

"Do you see her?" She had to focus on driving and not killing them in an accident.

"Not yet. She's gotta be close, though."

Well, she'd better be *real* close, or this takedown

wasn't happening. With the shots just fired people would have called the cops by now. Megan wanted to avoid tangling with them at all cost.

"There, ten o'clock," he said, pointing to the left.

Megan glanced over and spotted the bike as it whipped up the street a block over. She took her foot off the gas and made a sharp left, heading toward it.

"Look out!" Tyler said.

The Audi careened out of a side alley into the street in front of them.

Megan hammered the brake and swerved to miss it, narrowly avoiding being sideswiped. "Son of a bitch," she muttered, and gave chase. This asshole was between her and her target. He might still pose a threat to them, and needed to be taken out or he'd just continue to get in the way.

"We have to take him out."

"Roger that," Tyler responded.

Tires squealed as the Audi skidded to the right around the next corner. She followed, the little car's engine racing, the sound growing higher in pitch as she pinned the accelerator to the floor.

This asshole was going *down*. She'd ram him, take the Audi out of commission and finish this.

He veered to the left all of a sudden, barely making the turn.

She cursed and hit the brakes as she sped past the street, forced to throw it into reverse to back up half a block so she could follow. Thankfully there was still no other traffic. "You see the bike?"

Tyler was looking out the passenger window. "She's still heading east toward the river."

If she crossed the Danube, it was pretty much over. "I can't get to her without going through this jackass." Her lips thinned as she sped after the Audi. God, this guy was a pain in the ass.

The driver's window lowered.

"He's gonna fire," Tyler warned. "I don't have an angle."

"I do." She was already lowering her own window to take a shot. She reached her weapon through with her left hand and fired before he could. One shot hit the driver's side mirror. The hand jerked back inside, then the Audi lurched right.

She fired again, hitting the back window on the driver's side. This time the Audi skidded slightly. Had she hit him? He wasn't slowing down yet. She moved left to give Tyler room.

"I'll get the tires." Tyler was already taking aim out his open window. Wind whistled through the interior as he leaned out of it, aimed at the back right tire and fired twice.

The tire exploded. The car veered around the next corner, back end fishtailing wildly. But the driver didn't stop. He was still heading for the river, in pursuit of the female.

His hand appeared out the window again. She ducked when he fired back at them. Two bullets punched through the center of the windshield, inches from her face, cracking the glass.

She and Tyler both ducked but she didn't let up on the gas. "Asshole," she growled.

"I've got him." Tyler leaned out of his window and fired again.

The vehicle skidded a bit, slowed, and Megan seized her moment.

"Brace," she warned, then rammed into the Audi's back bumper. They both grunted at the impact, the seatbelts snapping taut across their chests and shoulders. The Audi jerked forward and kept going, the steering erratic.

Megan steered at the right back bumper this time. A metallic crunch sounded as she rammed it. She hit the brakes and turned the wheel to avoid the Audi as it spun.

This time the driver lost control, the vehicle spinning around in a tight circle across the quiet street. It slammed into a parked minivan along the curb of the empty sidewalk with a bone-jarring bang.

Weapon in hand, Megan threw the transmission into park and jumped out of the car to go after the driver, ducking when a hand flashed out of the driver's side door to fire at them.

Cursing under her breath she ducked back behind her open door while the bullets pinged off the hood inches from her.

Tyler returned fire from behind his own open door. "He's already through the other side," he told her.

Sure enough, the driver had managed to scramble out of the window and use the vehicles parked along the curb for cover. Every second he cost them was another second the suspect had to get away.

"Don't lose him." Megan caught a glimpse of his silhouette as he darted around the corner on foot.

She raced after him, Tyler right behind her. She could take this asshole out herself but she wouldn't complain about having someone to watch her six as she chased the guy.

The hitter was a couple hundred feet away now. Too far to get off an accurate shot. But his gait was rough. Either the crash or Tyler had injured him.

Megan put on a burst of speed, quickly gaining on the guy, tracking him as he darted left and disappeared into another alley.

Shit, she was so tired of this asshole fucking up her op.

Breathing fast, she slowed, her back to the brick exterior of the house on the corner, eyes trained on the edge of it. Tyler did the same, stopping next to her.

Running footsteps echoed up the alley, moving away

from them.

"Go," Tyler whispered.

She whipped around the corner and dropped to one knee, searching for a target. Her heart seized for a second at the sight of the man's silhouette standing so close. His weapon was aimed directly at her.

She braced for the thud of a bullet as she adjusted her aim, sucking in a breath as three rapid shots rang out simultaneously.

The hitter's shot went wild, pinging off the brick building next to her. He staggered, then fell to the ground with a groan. Tyler stalked past her, pistol aimed right at the bastard.

She sucked in a gulp of air as her heart began beating again. Megan raced after him, her own weapon aimed at the man on the ground. He was crumpled on his side, his legs moving restlessly.

His eyes were still open when they got to him, and he was still breathing. Definitely the same guy from Prague.

But he wouldn't be breathing for long given the wheezing, gurgling sounds coming from him and the amount of blood spilling onto the cobbles, glistening in the faint glow of the streetlights at the end of the alley. Tyler had hit him center mass with both shots.

She kicked the fallen weapon away from the man's limp hand, then Tyler hauled the guy's arms behind him. "Who sent you?" Megan growled as she knelt and began to frisk him.

She found a spare full mag in his pocket, a blade in his inner jacket pocket, and no ID. "Who *sent* you?" Voices were coming from the end of the alley. Concerned citizens checking out the situation. She and Tyler had to disappear.

The dying hitter stared up at her with a blank expression, a wet, gurgling sound rattling in his chest.

No time. She seized his hair and yanked his head back. "Answer me. Who *sent* you?" she snarled.

His eyes rolled. His face went slack. He sagged, a rattling sigh filling the quiet alley.

Shit. She let him go and quickly stood, relaying to Trinity that he was dead while Tyler used a device to take the guy's fingerprints. "Let's go," she told him.

Together they ran up the alley and turned right at the next main street, their car a liability to them now. The cops would be on the way, and when they arrived, she and Tyler had better be as far away as possible.

There was no time to check for CCTVs or exterior security cameras that might catch them as they ran. No point worrying about it.

They veered their way through the next few blocks, turning left then right, heading for the river. Then, as they reached the next main street, the faint whine of a motor-cycle engine floated on the warm night air.

Megan jerked her head around to the left in time to see the woman on the bike ride over a pedestrian bridge in the distance.

Dammit. They could easily steal a car to go after her but there was enough heat on them already with the chase and the dead hitter's body lying back in that alley.

Trying to follow the woman was pointless now. They'd never catch up to her even in a vehicle, and since she appeared to be a pro, the woman would no doubt ditch the bike as soon as she was out of sight and take a different vehicle anyway.

Megan stopped running and leaned over to rest her hands on her thighs to catch her breath. The female suspect was gone but at least the threat from that hitter was over. Still, *damn.*

"We've got what she was after," Tyler said beside her, also breathing hard after the extended sprint.

He was good in the field, she'd give him that. She

appreciated a man who could keep up with her. He'd been solid right through this whole thing and hadn't pulled any alpha male bullshit or bitched about her driving. He'd actually seemed to get a kick out of it.

"Yeah, but she doesn't know that," she said.

Would their suspect come back for it a second time? Megan looked up at Tyler, struck all over again by how good-looking he was. And...how indebted to him she was. Not a comfortable realization, but there it was. This was why she preferred to work alone.

Yeah, and if you'd been alone, you might have been dead right now.

"By the way, thanks for back there," she murmured, ignoring the squirming sense of vulnerability the verbal acknowledgment of her gratitude brought. He'd saved her from taking a bullet.

He met her gaze for a moment, then nodded once. "You're welcome." He reached for her hand and she didn't pull away, part of her savoring the warmth and strength of his fingers as they curled around hers. Protective rather than controlling. Caring rather than authoritative. "Let's get out of here, huh?"

"Yeah." The thin box she'd hidden inside her jacket rubbed against her shirt as she walked. If their suspect had come out of hiding for it once, and she didn't realize it was missing yet, then it stood to reason she might come back for it a second time.

If they were lucky.

Megan would bait the trap, cross her fingers and sit back to see what happened.

Chapter Eleven

Another muffled sneeze from the other side of the room had Ty's tired eyes popping open.

Bathed in late afternoon light coming through the slats in the blinds, Megan sat in a chair in the corner, her e-reader beside her and the tablet in her lap. On screen, a live feed from five different camera angles captured the comings and goings around the target house.

They'd been in stakeout mode for the past three days. The night after the car chase he'd provided overwatch while Megan had gone back in to hide the items she'd found inside. Since the analysts working with them on the case hadn't been able to turn up anything useful about their suspect yet, their best chance of catching her was if she came back to retrieve the items. If that happened, it was important the items were in their original place to avoid tipping her off that she was being watched.

Megan sniffed and suppressed another sneeze, turning her face into her shoulder. Her gaze snapped over to him when he shifted. "Sorry," she murmured.

"It's okay." He eyed the clock on the nightstand between their two double beds. He'd only been asleep for maybe forty minutes.

He pushed up and sat with his back against the head-board and covered a jaw-cracking yawn. "You sound worse."

"Nah, I'm fine." She waved a hand at him. "Go back to sleep. I've got some earplugs you can have if you want."

"Thanks, I'm okay." He was up now and wouldn't be able to get back to sleep for a while anyway. And no matter what she said, she was definitely feeling worse. She had shadows under her eyes and she looked pale. They'd both been going on little sleep the past few days between the stakeout, phone meetings with Trinity and Rycroft and surveilling the area.

He glanced at the tablet in her lap. "Still nothing, huh?"

"Nope." She swallowed, seemed to hide a grimace.

He covered a wince. She was tough, so if her throat was that sore, she had his sympathy. "Maybe you should go take a hot bath or something."

Those pretty hazel eyes swung to him. "Is that your way of saying I smell?"

He grinned. "No." She smelled good all the time. Especially her hair. "I just thought it might make you feel a bit better."

"I'm good, really."

He ran a hand through his hair and threw the blankets back, swinging his legs over the side of the bed. She'd turned the air conditioning down and it was close to stifling in the room. "Any updates from Trinity?" She'd flown back to London a few days ago to meet with Rycroft and others from the team he'd assembled. They were analyzing all the data compiled so far.

Since then he and Megan had been taking alternating 4-hour surveillance shifts, watching the cameras for any sign of the female suspect. Whoever she was, she was a pro and able to turn into a ghost. There might also be more hitters out there so they were being extra careful to limit their movements. At this point they were still uncertain whether they remained a target.

"No." She sniffed again. "She's flying back here tonight with another former Valkyrie. A sniper."

"Do you know her?"

"No, but she's friends with Trinity and another Valkyrie named Briar who's apparently helping us stateside. They were all trained together initially, before they were separated into their specialties."

The Valkyrie Program sounded both impressive and dark as hell. Every time he learned something about it, his feelings became more mixed. "Who decides what specialty you're put into?"

"The trainers. They measure us all for different aptitudes from the time we enter the program. They use the scores to divide us into our specialty categories."

Kind of like a military MOS, but involuntary. "Did you have any say?"

"Sometimes. Depends on the girl. Sometimes you might get a choice of one or two areas. Or they might cross-train you in both. I mean, we're all cross-trained in various things, so there's some overlap. But we're usually given missions relating directly to our specialty."

It was damn fascinating, if dark and a little scary. "And they decided you'd make a good thief."

She raised an eyebrow in feigned insult. "A badass thief, thank you very much." She shrugged. "What can I say, I'm sneaky. And bendy."

"I knew about the sneaky part. But bendy, huh? That sounds interesting."

At his loaded tone she grinned, giving him a glimpse of those adorable dimples of hers. "I can't believe your mind went there when I look like this." She gestured to herself with a circling motion of her finger and made a face.

Believe it, dimples. He wanted her more than ever. "How'd you learn to drive like that, anyway?"

The look she gave him said she thought that should be obvious. "I'm a thief. That means I need be able to make a quick getaway."

Ty was pretty sure he could spend years with her and she would never stop surprising him. "Yeah, I guess it does. And you're also a crack shot with your non-dominant hand." Even while driving. Damn.

"I'm ambidextrous."

Of course you are. He paused a moment. "Were you close to any of them? The girls you trained with."

She frowned, deep in thought. "Not really close. I guess the one I was closest to of anyone was Chloe. We were teenagers by then. She was a demolitions expert."

"That sounds terrifying."

Megan chuckled. "You mean awesome." Her smile faded. "I've thought about her over the years. Always wondered what happened to her."

"When's the last time you saw each other?"

"When we got our marks." She patted her left hip. "The day we graduated. We got bandaged up, went out to dinner together to celebrate, and that was that. She was sent on her first mission the next morning. Just...gone."

Damn, she'd been through a lot. "Maybe we'll find her still."

Her smile was a little sad and it twisted his heart. "Maybe."

He got up, brushed his teeth and splashed some water on his face to help push the cobwebs from his brain. Megan was watching the screen when he came out. "Anything more about the picture?" he asked. Before returning the items they'd sent a scan of the photo off to Rycroft's team back in the States.

"Nothing yet. It was probably taken thirty-plus years ago, judging by the hairstyles and clothes." Her eyebrows drew together slightly.

He knew it bothered her that she felt like she recognized the couple but couldn't place them. The bracelet and blanket were a different matter. Those were highly personal items that their female suspect had wanted to recover enough that she'd risked going back to the target house that night. He hoped they meant enough for her to return a second time, though he was starting to think otherwise.

"You hungry?" he asked Megan.

She looked up from the tablet. "I could eat."

He pulled out his phone. "What do you feel like?"

"Soup. The good stuff, made from scratch if you can find a place that does that. Or maybe noodles."

"How about soup *with* noodles?" He'd get her some meds later as well.

Her grateful smile squeezed his heart. "Perfect."

He'd been careful not to crowd her since the run-in with their suspect and the dead hitter, but he still wanted her as much as ever. In all his time doing various contracting jobs for the government, he'd never roomed with a female on a mission.

Megan tested his control. Being in close quarters together day after day made it tough to suppress his feelings, especially after the other night.

She impressed the hell out of him, period, and he was more attracted to her than ever. He'd respected her need for space since they'd kissed and hadn't brought it up again.

Much as he wanted another repeat—and a whole lot more—they were on a job, and now she wasn't feeling well. But man, he couldn't wait for this to be done so he could change their relationship from a working one to something far more intimate if she was willing.

"You trust me to pick something for you?" he asked.

"Sure." She went back to watching the screen.

He pulled up a delivery app on his phone and found an Asian place nearby with scratch-made food and great ratings that took cash on delivery. They were using cash only even though they were using aliases.

He ordered them both a large ramen bowl. "Food'll be here in about thirty-five minutes. I'm just gonna go grab a shower."

She nodded and mumbled an "okay" without looking up. The cameras watching the target house would alert them with a specific alarm on the tablet if anything triggered them.

There were so many things he still didn't know about her, and wanted to. At least he seemed to have gained her trust for the most part. He'd learned enough about her to know she didn't give it lightly, so that was pretty major. Hopefully it would help him convince her to lower her guard around him once this mission was done.

He took a shower, changed, and when he came back out into the bedroom she hadn't moved. "Did you finish your book, by the way?"

"Almost." She didn't look up, completely focused on the task at hand.

With nothing else to do and her attention otherwise occupied, he stretched out on the bed and turned on the TV, finding an action movie playing in English. His phone chimed with a message half an hour later. "Food's almost here."

She grunted.

The urge to take the tablet away was almost over-powering. He shook his head at himself. Man, he had it bad if he was thinking about getting her to pay attention to him.

He tracked the courier via the GPS on the app. When the knock came at the door he jumped up, surprised when Megan put down the tablet and followed. "My treat," he told her.

"Okay." She followed him to the door anyway, brushing his hip slightly as she passed by, filling his nose with her clean, soapy scent.

He checked the peephole and reached an arm out to herd Megan behind him. She snorted but stayed where he put her as he opened the door. He greeted the delivery guy and reached for his wallet to pay the guy.

It was gone.

What the... He stopped, checked his other pocket, then patted his hips and thighs to check the others.

A hand reached past his shoulder, holding some Euros. "No, I'll get it," he argued, turning his head to look at her.

"I know." Megan smirked at him and held up his wallet in her other hand.

He had to grin. "How did you—" He shut his mouth, impressed and intrigued all over again. First the keys to the car the other night, and now this.

Man, she was slick. He kept his wallet in the front hip pocket of his cargo pants. She must have taken it when she'd brushed up against him, but it had been so fast and he hadn't felt a thing.

She paid the delivery guy, gave him a generous tip, then took the bag and shut the door. She raised her eyebrows at Ty while she locked the door. "You were saying?"

He shook his head. "One day I want you to show me how you do stuff like that."

"Maybe one day," she agreed, and sat back in her chair to dig into the bag. "Here," she said, absently handing him his bowl.

They ate together while he watched the movie and she watched the tablet. She might only be two hours into her shift, but she needed rest.

"Oh, that hit the spot," she groaned, setting her bowl on the table beside her.

"I'm glad. Can I have my wallet back now?"

"Oh. Sure." She handed it over.

"Do I need to check the contents?" he asked.

Her chuckle brushed over his skin like a caress. "You can if you want."

"No, I trust you. Mostly. Now go have a hot bath." He nodded at the tablet. "I'll take over for a bit."

She opened her mouth to argue, no doubt that she had to stay at her post. That she couldn't take a break.

He grunted and held up a hand. "Don't argue. I won't listen."

Still she hesitated, and he could almost feel the guilt piling up inside her. "Are you sure?" she hedged.

"I'm sure." He considered it a small victory when she disappeared into the bathroom and ran the water.

She came out fifteen minutes later in a cloud of scented steam, fully dressed and her hair pulled up into a messy bun. She looked sexy and adorable at the same time. And exhausted. "I needed that, thank you."

"Sure." He jerked his chin at her bed. "Get some sleep."

"What? No, I—"

"This isn't a discussion. Go to sleep."

She put a hand on her hip and huffed at him. "It's my turn to be on watch, and I already woke you up from your nap."

He was tired, but not as tired as she was. "Get some sleep, Megan. We need you better in case our suspect shows up again."

Again, she hesitated, staring at him for a few moments in indecision.

"Come on, dimples. Don't fight me on this."

At the nickname something ignited in her eyes. She visibly bristled, maybe because the mention took her back to when he'd first called her that in SERE school.

Something funny, dimples? This is life and death

we're talking about. God, he'd been clueless, thinking how helpless she was out there exposed to the raw elements of nature.

But then she relaxed, her expression softening. Her gaze darted to the bed and back to him. "Well, if you're sure…"

"Sleep," he told her.

She grumbled something under her breath about not needing to be babied, but did as she was told, sliding between the covers. Lucky sheets didn't know how good they had it, being wrapped around her.

Ty picked up the tablet and set it in his lap, dividing his attention between the tablet and the woman curled up in the other bed that was winding around his heart harder every day. There was a softness to her in sleep that wasn't there when she was awake. Awake she seemed to be in constant motion, a ball of suppressed energy, except when she was reading or focused on another task.

When he was sure she was fast asleep, he put the tablet down and stood, ready to run out and find a store nearby to get her some medicine. On impulse he reached over and snuck her e-reader from the nightstand. He switched it on, looked at the book she was reading and stared at it in disbelief.

A romance?

He flipped through the next twenty pages to be sure, skimming the text. An action-based romance, and a steamy one at that, when he'd expected maybe a thriller or military history book.

He set it back to the page she'd stopped reading at and placed the device on the nightstand, then looked over at Megan's sleeping form with a sense of amazement. She never stopped surprising him. She had layers he hadn't even begun to discover yet.

A badass assassin/thief with a romantic heart hidden under all that attitude and armor.

Yeah, he was in serious trouble where she was concerned.

****

Oh, God, it felt like someone had beaten her all over with a hammer.

Megan ached everywhere, even the roots of her hair. Still, she'd die before complaining aloud. She was a freaking Valkyrie. Valkyries didn't bitch or make a big deal out of having the flu. Or whatever hellish germ this thing attacking her was.

Tyler had been incredibly wonderful for the past two days, taking longer shifts and going without sleep much longer than he should have to in order to let her rest and try and fight off this bug. Even with the meds she'd swallowed, it refused to die. Evil bastard.

"Hey, you're awake," he murmured.

She blinked, squinted as his fuzzy image appeared above her next to the bed. "Yeah," she whispered, her throat and face on fire. She'd been dreaming about Chloe. Chloe had been on her mind a lot since she'd told Tyler about her yesterday.

In the dream she and Chloe had been lying in their bunks in their room at the training facility, laughing at something. It made her think about the time Chloe had brought her soup and a can of ginger ale when Megan had come down with food poisoning one night. Her friend had even placed a bucket beside her bed.

God, Megan hoped she was still alive and that they'd be able to see each other again.

Her thoughts scattered when Tyler reached out to lay his palm to her forehead, then cupped her cheek. His touch was so cool and comforting, she couldn't help but lean into it with a groan. "Yeah, you're still burning up. Time for more meds."

"Don't want them," she grumbled.

"Too bad." He shook two out of the bottle on the nightstand, the one he'd run down to the nearest store to buy for her along with a dozen other things to make her feel better. The nightstand looked like a little pharmacy. "Here." He handed her two pills, then held out a to-go cup. "Careful, it's hot."

She pushed upright to accept it. "What is it?"

"Green tea with honey and lemon. My mom used to give it to us when we got sick. The honey'll help your throat and cough."

Tea with honey...

"I put honey in it," a woman's voice said in the background. "It'll make your throat feel better."

Megan was young, sitting on a brown floral couch in front of a TV playing cartoons. It was the middle of the day but she was in her robe. Sick with something. And she was holding a mug of tea in her hands with a picture of Big Bird on it.

She blinked and the memory evaporated. Who had that voice belonged to? Her mother?

Dammit, why couldn't she even remember what her own mother had looked like? It was like that damn picture she'd found. No matter how much she thought about the image, nothing sparked in her memory, and she was sure it had some kind of clue that connected her and their suspect.

It was beyond frustrating. How much of her memory loss was normal because she'd been so young when her parents died, and how much of it was due to the Valkyrie Program and her training?

"You okay?"

Startled, she looked up into Tyler's face, unprepared for the way her heart squeezed. He was damn good-looking. And the way he'd been taking care of her melted her stupid romantic heart. "Yeah, fine. Thanks for all this."

She hadn't been this sick in years and having him with her was comforting. That was a strange and scary realization.

She hadn't had anyone take care of her like this since she was a kid. Maybe it wasn't necessary and it made her feel silly, but she couldn't deny that she liked it. A lot.

She liked him a whole lot, and considering how she'd felt about him for the past twelve years, that was saying something.

"Welcome," he murmured. "I got you some more throat lozenges too. The orange ones you like that don't taste like death."

She cracked a grin. "Thanks. I hate the taste of death."

"Me too." His warm half-smile made her sore, tight chest compress.

He represented part of her past that she wanted to forget and leave behind, but he also drew her in and that invisible pull was getting stronger every day she spent with him. They'd formed a bond whether she wanted one or not.

She also trusted him. Not completely, because she didn't trust anyone completely except for maybe Marcus. But she trusted Tyler more than most. And that was dangerous for someone like her.

The sooner this op was done and behind them, the better for her because he was taking down her protective walls brick by brick and she wasn't sure how much longer she could keep him out. Or worse, whether she even *wanted* to.

"I'll take a shift after I drink this," she told him, the warmth of the tea coming through the paper cup soothing all on its own. Her face was burning hot but the rest of her was freezing, especially her hands and feet.

"Yeah, no."

"Yes. I'm feeling way better than I was."

"Liar." He drew a fingertip down the side of her face,

his eyes delving into hers.

Suddenly she wasn't cold anymore. An internal wave of heat rushed through her.

Then he drew that fingertip down her cheek, paused to curl his hand beneath her chin and swept his thumb across her burning cheek in a tender caress that stole her breath. It was the first time he'd touched her intimately since they'd kissed.

Heart thudding, she stared up at him helplessly, unable to look away much less breathe.

"I don't like seeing you sick." He dropped his hand and shook his head. "Move over."

"What?"

"Just move over."

Moving over was not a good idea if he planned to do what she thought he did, but she felt so damn miserable there was no risk in things getting out of hand. She slid over, warning, "You'll get sick."

"If I do, you can take care of me."

"Oh, God, spare me from the dreaded Man Cold." She withheld a grumbled response. She wasn't the Florence Nightingale type. But for him she was willing to maybe make an exception.

He settled behind her on the bed, staying on top of the covers. A strong arm curved around her waist and drew her into his body.

A shudder rolled through her, as much from the chills racing through her as from the intimate contact. She'd imagined being in bed with him a thousand times, but never like this.

Tyler shifted so that he was plastered as tight to her as possible. His face was buried in her hair, his breath cool on her hot neck. "Sleep if you can."

"The tablet…"

"It's right beside me. I'll keep watch, don't worry." He squeezed her gently. "Sleep, dimples," he whispered.

Her eyelids were so heavy. And he was so damn solid and warm behind her. The nickname he called her was kind of sweet too. Why did that put a huge lump in her throat?

They lay like that in silence for a minute, exhaustion tugging at her but her mind racing. "What if she's not coming back?" she whispered, meaning the female suspect.

"She'll come back."

What if she didn't come back in *time*? They only had another two days here. If the woman hadn't shown up by then, Trinity was pulling them out and sending them back to Marcus's place. Megan didn't want to go back until they'd captured the woman.

"We'll get her, one way or the other," he said.

The conviction in his voice eased the anxiety gnawing at her and reminded her that he was committed to this mission. That he would stand by her and see it through, no matter what.

It meant more to her than he would ever know. And oh, man, it was gonna hurt like a bitch when he left and went back to his own life at the end of all this. That was the only way this could end. "Yeah."

They would capture the female suspect, and start getting some damn answers. Then she would brace for the pain of Tyler leaving her life forever.

Chapter Twelve

The few hours before dawn were the best time to operate.

Amber smoothed a hand over her chin-length, blond wig before exiting the car she'd rented at the train station an hour ago using one of her aliases. She'd waited long enough for the heat to die down before returning here. Now she would grab what she needed and leave Vienna behind for good.

A hot ball of nerves squirmed in the pit of her stomach. Part anxiety. Part guilt.

She might have fucked up. Might have fucked up big time, and she hadn't been able to find out for sure yet. But if she had...

If she had, then there was a chance Hannah Miller might be innocent.

The odds were slim, but based on intel she'd scooped up last night, there was still a chance. Someone had been feeding her lies. And it was too late to stop this now because Amber had already sold Hannah's information to one of the most ruthless criminal groups in Syria.

She couldn't think about that now. She had to keep a clear head and not let any of this cloud her senses or judgment.

Maintaining a straight and upright posture pulled at the healing bullet wound on her side. She was lucky it had been shallow. The round had passed through her external oblique muscle without hitting any bone. She'd hastily stitched it up that night in the cheap motel room a few hours after leaving Vienna, once she'd crossed the border into Slovakia.

The sewing job wasn't the neatest. The wound still seeped and was sore as hell, swollen and puffy and red. That, added with the fever she was running, told her it was infected. After she retrieved her things from the safehouse she would get some antibiotics from a local pharmacy and head for the Hungarian border. There she would hole up for another few days and monitor her security situation before planning her next move.

She still didn't know exactly who was after her. Her efforts to identify the man and woman chasing her had turned up nothing. Though the man who had shot her was now dead, the last Valkyrie she'd sold information on wasn't. Wherever Hannah was, she was most definitely still alive.

For now, at least. And the threat against her and Amber's lives increased steadily with every hour that passed.

Taking a deep breath of the warm night air, Amber walked toward the safehouse. She'd passed it twice earlier today to make sure it was still unoccupied. Once on the bus, once in an Uber, then just before parking her rental on a side street a block over.

Coming here again was a huge risk, especially so soon and in her weakened condition, but it was a risk she was willing to take. Once she retrieved the items, she could dig more into the intel she'd found on Hannah, and act accordingly. All the other dirty Valkyries were dead.

After the situation with Hannah was taken care of, she could start targeting the people responsible for dreaming up and implementing the Valkyrie Program.

The people responsible for destroying her life.

Her handler's final message to her before killing himself still haunted her.

I'm sorry for my part in all of this. I'm sorry for the things I covered up and the suffering I caused you. These belong to you and now I've returned them. I hope you can use them to find answers, and then a measure of peace after all that was taken from you.

She'd admired and looked up to him. A long time Air Force intelligence officer, Barry had been her mentor for the nine years she'd been assigned to him. They'd developed a close relationship. He'd always had her back.

But he'd lied to her too, by omission, and that cut deep. Now the photo, blanket and bracelet were the only clues he'd been able to leave her.

They were the keys to unlocking the mystery of her past.

Now they would either be her salvation…or her undoing.

****

The past couple days had been rough, but today was much better. No more sore throat or fever, just a slight headache and fatigue. Megan was ready to rock, and more motivated than ever to find and protect the missing Valkyries. Right after she took this hacker bitch down.

Tyler's quiet breathing and the air conditioning were the only sounds in the condo as Megan sat in the chair by the window watching the tablet and wishing she was immersed in her most current read. A romantic thriller with a kickass heroine that reminded her of Chloe.

Not as kickass as a Valkyrie like her or Chloe, but still, pretty damn awesome. Currently the heroine was waiting to spring a trap on the villain—a skin trade kingpin far too close to some of the human pieces of shit Megan had targeted over the years—and all his underling, wastes-of-skin minions. The heroine had the entire hideout rigged with Symtex.

Megan couldn't wait for her to blow them all to hell.

A soft beep came from the tablet in her lap. She grabbed it, a surge of excitement hitting her when she saw the alert from one of the cameras posted on the building down the alley from the target house.

Staring at it, she held her breath as a woman came into view. Alone. She had chin-length blond hair but her height and build were right for their female suspect.

The woman walked at a casual pace, her posture relaxed, gaze straight ahead. No sign of nervousness, no glancing around. Her hands were hidden in the pockets of her leather jacket.

Time seemed to slow as Megan watched her, praying this was their long-lost suspect.

The woman walked up the cobbled alley and turned left toward the target house. She stepped right up to the back door and reached for the doorknob, keys in hand.

Gotcha.

"Tyler."

He jerked awake instantly and pushed up into a sitting position, on alert. "What?"

"It's her. We gotta go."

As he jumped out of bed she was already reaching for her weapons. After inserting her earpiece she alerted Trinity, who responded that she and another former Valkyrie she'd brought to Vienna yesterday would move in from the north and east while Megan and Tyler came from the south and west.

Megan smiled, more than ready to take this woman down.

Time to kick some ass.

****

For the moment luck seemed to be on her side. Amber hoped it held. All she needed was six or seven minutes to get in and out of the house, then she would be free and clear once again.

The wire she'd put in place from the back doorknob to the edge of the doorframe was still there and intact. A measure of relief trickled through her. She disabled it and stepped inside with her weapon drawn, locking the door behind her as she looked around.

Everything appeared exactly as she'd left it.

She swept the lower floor anyway, then moved up the stairwell, her heart beating faster. She checked each room to be sure no one had been inside while she was gone, more relief hitting her when she finally reached the bathroom without incident. She slid the pistol back into the concealed holster in the waistband of her jeans.

Pulling the end of the clawfoot tub across the wooden floor, she held her breath and shone her penlight at her hiding place. One of the boards appeared to be higher on one end than she remembered.

She paused, taking a closer look to be sure it hadn't been tampered with. The chances of anyone finding this were almost zero. Still...

A soft sigh escaped her when her gaze landed on the thin box inside the hiding spot, the tension in her chest dissipating. The bracelet was on top of the folded blanket, with the framed photo inside it. Exactly as she'd left it.

Moving fast now, she gathered the items up and tucked them inside her jacket where they would be safe, then put everything back the way it had been. On her way out she reset the cameras and wires, checked to make sure the coast was clear, then locked the door and headed around the back of the house toward the alley.

"Drop it and put your hands up," a female voice said

from the shadows.

Shit. Amber whirled and drew her weapon—

Just as four armed people emerged from the shadows to encircle her.

****

Megan kept her pistol aimed at the woman's chest as she stepped forward out of the shadows. "Drop it," she growled, her finger on the trigger. If this woman so much as twitched wrong, Megan was taking her down.

Tyler was to her right, guarding the approach from the alley. Trinity was to her left. The former Valkyrie sniper Georgia was behind her, fanning out toward Megan. The female suspect had nowhere to go. It was four against one.

The woman stared right at her. Her expression was hard, her weapon gripped at hip level. Never looking away, she slowly bent her knees and crouched, lowering her gun hand. Megan kept her gaze locked on it until the weapon rested on the pavement and the woman straightened once more.

Still she watched the hands. No telling what other kinds of weapons the woman had, or what she would do now. A cornered suspect was the most dangerous of all. "Hands up."

The command earned her a cold stare. The woman stood there in defiance for a few moments, then slowly raised her hands.

"Take her," Trinity said.

As one, they began moving forward. Tightening the noose.

The woman's gaze darted around the circle. She took a step back, her hand going behind her.

Nope. Megan fired.

The dart hit her in the side of the neck. The woman

grabbed it, whirled to flee and managed to wrench it out of her skin. It fell to the cobbles just as her knees buckled.

She sprawled out on her stomach. Tried to struggle to her knees. Managed to prop herself up on her elbows just as Megan reached her.

Megan grabbed the woman's arms, wrenched them behind her and secured them with plastic flex-cuffs. "Who are you?"

No answer. Not surprising. Narrowed green eyes squinted at Megan. Unfocused.

Trinity knelt next to them to take the woman's fingerprints digitally and send them off for analysis. Megan found another pistol in the woman's pocket, a military-style knife strapped to her thigh and a switchblade hidden in the sleeve of her jacket. No ID.

"She's wounded."

Megan stopped and looked down at where Trinity had pulled the woman's shirt up to expose a bandage taped across her lower left ribs. It was stained with fresh blood but not saturated, not an immediate concern. They'd wait to get a better look at it later.

She unzipped the woman's jacket and found a small bundle resting against her chest. The bracelet and photo were folded up inside the tattered blanket.

Megan tucked them into her own zipped-up jacket, staring down at the woman's slack face. Why the hell were these items important enough for her to risk her life to come back for them not once, but twice? It made no sense.

Just one of the many mysteries they would hopefully unravel once the tranquilizer wore off and they could start getting some answers. Who she was, the Valkyries she had targeted, and why.

Megan checked their suspect thoroughly for more weapons, then reached under her shirt to check for anything hidden in her bra. She came up with a tiny flash drive.

Bingo. She tucked it into her pocket. "Okay, let's go," she said, hoping this little device held the intel they were desperate for. If they could find out where Hannah was, then maybe they could still save her.

Tyler hurried forward. He holstered his weapon, bent and scooped the woman up, effortlessly hoisting her over one broad shoulder. The woman's hair slipped.

A wig.

Megan pulled it off. Long brown hair about the same shade as hers was carefully pinned into place beneath it.

She handed the wig to Trinity and started walking down the alley at a fast clip, anxious to get out of the city and back to safer turf.

Together they swiftly made their way to the waiting van parked up the alley. Megan and Georgia stayed in the back with the unconscious woman lying between them while Tyler drove and Trinity rode shotgun.

"Here." Megan handed Trinity the flash drive to plug into her tablet. Not that she expected them to find much. If this woman was a good enough hacker to be responsible for selling out the other Valkyries, then she would have encrypted the files and covered her tracks.

"They're all corrupted," Trinity announced ten seconds later.

Surprise, surprise.

"Shallow bullet wound," Georgia said, tucking a lock of long blond hair behind her ear to take a closer look at the damage beneath the woman's bandage. "Looks like she stitched it up herself. It's infected and she's got a fever. I'll—"

She went silent so fast that Megan immediately glanced down. The blood rushed out of her face and her gasp sliced through the silent interior.

Trinity whipped around in her seat, frowning in concern. "What?"

Megan swallowed, staring at the mark on the woman's left hip. "She's one of us," she said hoarsely, her throat tightening under a sudden rush of rage.

She'd wondered. They'd all wondered. And they'd all hoped otherwise. But now they had irrefutable proof.

One of their own had tried to destroy them.

Thick, silent tension throbbed inside the vehicle. "We'll get her patched up on the flight to Germany," Trinity said, and faced forward once more.

A fellow Valkyrie had sold out their sisters and set them up to die. Maybe even Chloe.

For what? For money? It made her sick. Made her want to give the bitch the antidote and revive her just so Megan could give her the beating she so richly deserved. How could one of their own betray them that way?

Loyal Unto Death.

The world had been harsh enough to them. Making them all orphans and then forcing them into the program. Enduring whatever the trainers dished out. Then, after graduation, the ops they'd performed.

Only the best made it through. The most skilled. The most dedicated.

She was proud of it. Proud that she'd come through it all, and proud of her service to her country. The things she'd done and the kills she'd made had all made the world a better place. Her conscience was clear. She was part of something that even after all she'd been through and all she'd seen, she had stupidly believed was incorruptible.

Megan looked away from the woman and stared blindly out the window, struggling to shove her reaction deep into her internal vault with all the other things she refused to acknowledge, and drew a breath to calm herself. The bitch would pay. They would all see to that.

She caught Tyler's gaze briefly in the rearview mirror and looked away. She couldn't face him right now.

He headed straight for the private airstrip where the jet was waiting. Megan pulled out the items she'd tucked inside her jacket. The baby blanket was made of a flannel material, worn soft with use and age, tattered around the edges.

She opened the folded layers and stared at the photo in the flickering bars of light coming in through the van's tinted windows as they drove. She'd memorized the image, yet staring at it now, something tugged at her. The woman's face specifically, tormenting her with its familiarity.

Dammit.

She folded everything up and put them back inside her jacket. Once they were airborne they could get the woman patched up, then revive her and begin the interrogation.

Chapter Thirteen

They were twenty minutes into the flight and their captive still hadn't regained consciousness. When Ty walked into the small cabin in the aft of the aircraft, she was lying across the twin bed there, her wrists still cuffed behind her.

"How much sedative was in that dart?" he asked Megan. Her vitals were strong at least, but damn.

"Enough to keep her under until we're at cruising altitude," Megan answered as she removed the woman's bandage with gloved hands to inspect the wound. "They having any luck with Rycroft's team?"

Georgia and Trinity were up front on the phone with someone named Briar back in the States to see if she could help identify their mystery Valkyrie. "Not yet. Her fingerprints didn't show up in the system."

"No surprise there."

"They're also trying to crack the encryption on the flash drive files right now."

She snorted. "I won't hold my breath on that one." She set the bloodstained bandage aside. "Can you pass me that med kit?"

He handed it to her and knelt next to her to take a closer look. "That's a pretty sloppy sewing job." The stitches were uneven and clumsy. Obviously she'd done them in a hurry, probably in a few minutes when she'd made a quick stop either to fuel up or because she'd been forced to do something more to stop the bleeding during her getaway.

"She just wanted to stem the blood loss so she could keep going. Making a pretty scar wasn't a priority."

He stopped her in the act of reaching for the pack of steri-strips, curling his fingers around her slender wrist. Her pretty hazel eyes flashed up to his face. "You okay?" he asked softly, stroking his thumb across her pulse point. Finding out one of their own might be responsible for helping kill them off must have been tough for her.

She lowered her lashes, jaw tight. "I'm angry."

He would be too. "You have every right to be."

She met his gaze again. "She broke the oath."

"What oath is that?"

She shot the unconscious woman a look so full of resentment it made the hair on the back of his neck tingle. "Loyal Unto Death. We all pledge it when we graduate. When we...get our marks." She touched her left hip.

"What does the mark signify?"

She shifted to undo the button on her pants then pulled one side of the waistband down, giving him a tempting glimpse of purple lace before she bared her upper hip. The mark was a little larger than a silver dollar. A crow with spread wings, clutching a sword in its talons, a scroll with the word *Valkyrja* inside it.

And it wasn't a tattoo, as he'd assumed. It was a fucking brand.

She met his eyes at his sudden intake of breath. "The crow is an old symbol for the Valkyrie. In Norse legend they were the choosers of the slain, and of who went to Valhalla. It's our symbol because we choose who lives or dies. Only graduates get it."

"What happens to non-graduates?"

"They're put into other programs. Intelligence, things like that."

"A brand," he murmured. That had serious ownership overtones. Like whoever had implemented it regarded the women as property rather than human beings.

"It used to be a tattoo, but someone along the way decided this was more badass. It's a mark of honor that represents who we are. And we bear the pain in silence during the branding ceremony as a matter of pride." She pulled the material back up and fastened her pants. "Chloe and I got ours together. Hurt as much as I thought it would, but in all honesty, the healing phase was way worse than the actual brand itself."

Jesus Christ. It must have hurt like fucking hell. And it would have taken months and months to heal. "They used a hot iron on you?" he asked, horrified.

"No, cold one, submerged in liquid nitrogen." She shrugged like it was no big deal. "It's an initiation ceremony of sorts."

Yeah, an archaic and brutal one. The training these women had been put through was harsh enough, then they were fucking branded like livestock? He didn't understand why she wasn't horrified by it too.

He wanted to touch it. Stroke his fingertips across her scar, wished his touch could make up for the pain it must have caused her.

Megan released her hold on her waistband and swiveled back to tend to the woman once again. Ty studied her profile as she worked with calm efficiency, the urge to slide his hand around her nape and turn her face to his so he could kiss her overwhelming.

He'd reined in his desire for her every day since they'd kissed but it and his feelings just kept building, expanding inside his ribcage until it was hard to breathe sometimes. He'd seen the softness she concealed beneath the steel. The vulnerability she didn't want anyone to know about.

He was falling for a female assassin who was probably going to crush his heart into dust beneath her heel when this was all over. His life was back in the States and she was in hiding. But it was a risk he was willing to take for the chance to have her even once.

Megan worked quickly to close the seeping wound with the steri-strips, then loaded a syringe with antibiotics. The moment Megan jabbed the needle into her hip, the woman let out a soft groan and her lashes fluttered.

Megan stiffened like someone had zapped her with a cattle prod and stood, slipping the syringe into a sharps container as she stripped off her gloves. "Get the others," she said to him softly.

Before he could move, the woman's eyes snapped open. Green. Unfocused for a moment, then they sharpened and locked on Megan, who stood facing the prisoner with her arms folded across her chest and a cold expression on her face.

Their prisoner lifted her head, glanced at him and her surroundings, then slowly pushed up into a sitting position with her elbow, watching them warily. "Where am I?" she said hoarsely.

"I ask the questions, not you," Megan snapped.

The two women stared each other down in a silent battle of eyeball chicken, both of them refusing to be the one to blink first.

And there was something…eerie about it. About the similarity in their expressions. The tilt of their heads. Their coloring.

Glancing from the woman to Megan, a terrible possibility hit.

No freaking way... Oh, shit. Shit, shit, shit.

"Get the others," Megan repeated, never looking away from their prisoner.

Ty exited the rear cabin and rushed up the aisle to get

Trinity and Georgia, wishing he were wrong.

A MUSCLE TICKED in Megan's jaw as she stared the woman down, the rage building, burning hotter. She had to curl her fingers into her palms to keep from smashing her fist into that traitorous face. This staring contest was pissing her off more.

Keep on pushing me, sweetheart, and you'll regret it.

The cabin door opened. Trinity and Georgia came in behind her. "Ah, you're finally awake," Trinity said, her tone cool, almost lazy.

"What did you do to me?" the woman shot back.

"Dragged your sorry ass onto this plane and fixed you up," Megan said in a clipped voice, tamping down the rage boiling inside her. Tyler came to stand next to her. She absorbed the comfort of his steady, protective presence. "And I'm already regretting it."

Trinity gently pushed her aside to confront the woman. "We're transporting you to a detention center in London for interrogation. No reason why we can't start right now, though."

The woman stared back at Trinity, unblinking, expression completely devoid of emotion. Megan clenched her back teeth together to keep from growling. Tyler set a steadying hand on her shoulder and squeezed lightly.

I'm here, the touch said. *No matter what happens, I'm here.*

The rage slipped a notch, blending with something like helplessness. And a grief so sharp it cut her.

Her heart was trying to pound its way out of her chest. Time was running out for Hannah and any others in harm's way. If this woman didn't want to talk, they'd never get anything out of her. They were all trained to take their secrets to their graves.

She fought the helplessness threatening to take over. The remaining Valkyries the team was scrambling to identify were either dead or missing. It might be too late to save any of them now. Because of this woman.

A deep, aching sadness spread through her chest, squeezing at her heart, her lungs. She tried to pull in a deep breath. It caught in her throat, almost came rushing back out as a cry of rage.

Her whole life had been taken away from her. All her choices made for her. The one thing she'd always held sacred was her Valkyrie oath. And now it turned out even that was a lie.

As if he sensed her internal struggle, Tyler's hand curled around the side of her shoulder and exerted gentle pressure. She didn't resist the pull, leaning into his side slightly while she forced the lump of emotion back down her tight throat.

"Why did you do it?" she blurted, unable to help herself. "How could you do it?"

The woman turned her head and met Megan's eyes with that cold stare. And said nothing.

Something inside her snapped. Megan lunged forward, would have attacked if Trinity hadn't blocked her and Tyler held her back with an arm across her upper chest.

He pulled her tight to his body, his arm banded protectively over her sternum. "Don't," he whispered. "It won't help."

Seething, Megan drew a steadying breath and contented herself with filleting their prisoner with her gaze. Attacking the woman wouldn't get them any answers. And she was handcuffed. Not a fair fight, and that's what Megan was itching for right now.

Her chest heaved as she fought to get her emotions back under control. "Where's Hannah?" The Valkyrie this traitor had betrayed. The one they'd been trying to locate and save. "Or Chloe?"

Trinity cut her a sharp look and turned her attention

back to the woman, a slight frown creasing her forehead. "You gonna tell us your name, at least?"

So even Briar hadn't recognized her. Megan had hoped she would, to make this easier.

When the woman said nothing, Trinity continued. "We've got a team of NSA-sanctioned cryptologists working on the files we found on the flash drive you were carrying."

The captive Valkyrie's mouth curled up on one side. "You didn't find anything. And you won't. So you can keep me locked up for as long as you want, do whatever you want to me, but it won't do you any good." She glanced around at them. "Any of you."

Fuck. You. "What about the picture?" Megan shot back.

That hard green gaze sliced to her. And held.

A weakness? "The bracelet, blanket and picture meant enough for you that you risked your life twice to get them. Who's in the picture?" That was the part of the puzzle that wouldn't stop nagging at her. The answer was there in the back of her mind, just out of reach.

No answer. Just that hard, frigid stare.

Trinity was watching her. Megan could feel the weight of it. Trinity looked back and forth between her and their prisoner, then seemed to come to some sort of conclusion.

"You and I are having a little chat in private," Trinity announced to the woman. "Everybody else out," she ordered, opening the door and waiting for the rest of them to leave.

Megan pushed out a ragged breath and reluctantly walked out with Tyler. Georgia came out next, then shut the door and stood guard outside it.

Tyler looped an arm around Megan's shoulders and led her up the aisle. She allowed him to urge her into one of the seats. "She's not gonna talk." She almost choked on the words.

He sat beside her and cupped her cheek in his big hand. He searched her eyes for a moment, then pulled her to his chest in a hug that made her heart tremble. "We'll find out what we need to know," he murmured, his mouth right at her temple. "One way or the other."

She shook her head in frustration. "Waiting for her to talk is a lost cause. She'll never break unless she *wants* to tell us. The only shot we've got at finding Hannah or Chloe is if the cryptologists manage to find something in those digital files."

He let her go, but the weight of his gaze made her glance up at him. There was something in his eyes that gave her pause. Something that looked a hell of a lot like sympathy. "What?" she demanded.

He shook his head once and paused as if searching for the right words. "Did you notice anything when you looked at her?"

"Yeah, a lying, traitorous piece of shit capable of selling the rest of us out and getting us tortured and killed for money." Scorn dripped from every word.

"Besides all that."

His tone made her go still. "What are you getting at?"

"There's a resemblance between you," he said carefully. "Your expressions. Mannerisms."

Megan stared at him as her lungs constricted. Everything froze inside her as little fragments suddenly started coming together, like pieces of a jigsaw puzzle.

The people in the picture. Her certainty that she knew them. That constant niggling at the back of her brain.

And their prisoner had similar hair color, texture and complexion as her. They were close in age. Had the same build and height.

Cold spread through her, forming an icy ball in her gut.

"No," she whispered, blanching.

Tyler lifted a hand as if he was going to cup her face but she stood and rushed past him, heading for the cabin at the end of the aisle. "Out of my way," she growled at Georgia.

She lifted a blond eyebrow. "Care to tell me what's going on?"

"Out. Of my *way*. I need to see something." She was almost shaking.

Georgia stared at her for a long moment, then relented and stepped aside. "Be my guest. But it's locked from the inside."

Megan's hands were unsteady as she took her toolkit from her pocket and made short work of the locking mechanism on the door. It clicked open within seconds.

Cold tendrils of dread coiled around her spine. Was it true? If it was, was she ready to face this?

Heart thudding in her ears, she threw the door open.

Trinity and the woman both looked over at her in surprise, but Megan was totally focused on their prisoner. "Who *are* you?" she whispered, her voice shaking. It couldn't be true. It couldn't.

But this time even she couldn't deny the resemblance between them.

The woman stared back at her, unmoving.

"Wake up! Santa came!"

She gasped and leapt out of bed, the skirt of her pink flannel nightgown flowing behind her as she raced after her sister. Christmas carols were already playing in the living room as they hit the staircase. Halfway down, the glow from the Christmas tree lights filled her heart to bursting with excitement.

The tree sparkled before the window at the front of the house. Dozens of wrapped presents surrounded it. And at the fireplace, all four stockings were fat and bursting with things Santa had filled them with.

She looked over at her sister, who was dressed in a

matching purple nightgown. "Can we open the stockings?"

Her older sister shook her head. "The rule is we have to wait for Mom and Dad."

Her shoulders sagged. "But they're still sleeping."

"No, we're not."

Both of them gasped and whirled around, smiling as their parents came into view at the bottom of the stairs.

A wave of dizziness hit Megan as she stood there, waiting. She was vaguely aware of Tyler standing behind her, had the passing thought that his presence was wasted, because he couldn't protect her from this.

No one could.

"Those people in the picture," she managed through the sudden restriction in her throat. "They're my parents. And that means you're my…"

The woman paled, staring at her in shock.

My sister.

A HIGH-PITCHED ringing filled Amber's ears. Her stare remained locked with the woman in front of her.

Her younger sister?

It wasn't possible. They'd told her Carly was dead, soon after they'd been taken away from each other. It was in the official records Amber had hacked. Complete with death certificate and autopsy report. Blunt trauma to the head had been the cause of her sister's death, supposedly from when the car had hit her.

But they'd lied about everything else. Why not this too? And the proof was hard to refute given the resemblance between them and the picture of their mother…

This woman looked like Carly would have, had she lived into adulthood. Same hair and eyes, facial features like their mother's.

Jesus.

First the potential screw up with Hannah, now this.

The Carly look-alike stared at her through narrowed eyes. "Is it true?" she rasped out.

Amber didn't know what the fuck to say, she was still trying to process this. Her pulse was racing, her lungs suddenly too tight to draw breath. Could it be true? Was she losing it?

"Megan, I need you to step outside," the raven-haired, blue-eyed woman said.

Megan.

Carly look-alike shot the woman a cold glare. "I'm not leaving until I get an answer."

"We'll figure all this out soon. Just…" The black-haired one looked at the man. "Ty, will you take her?"

Ty reached for Megan's arm. Megan wrenched it away and nailed Amber with a look so full of anguish it pierced through the armor plating around her hardened heart. "This isn't over," she hissed before spinning and stalking out.

No, it wasn't. And Amber didn't think it ever would be.

Chapter Fourteen

Her *sister.*

Standing at the window of the modern skyscraper gazing out over the London skyline hours later, Megan bit the inside of her lip and fought the burn of tears. It angered and embarrassed her that she was nearing the edge of her emotional control. But nothing in all her extensive training had ever prepared her for something like this.

The shock had barely begun to fade. She might as well have dropped a bomb into their midst when she'd said it on the plane. The others had been just as stunned as her, the prisoner included.

Amber. The hacker suspect was apparently her biological sister, and her name was Amber. Trinity had told her.

That fragmented Christmas memory of Megan's lost family remained the only one she'd managed to hold onto from her childhood. All the others were missing so far.

How was that possible? How had she forgotten everything else, and how had the people behind the Valkyrie Program been able to get away with such a thing?

The burner phone in her pocket vibrated. Marcus,

calling after she'd texted him earlier. "Hey," she answered quietly. There were ears and eyes everywhere in a place like this.

"Y'alright, love?" His tone was urgent, his Yorkshire accent more clipped than normal.

The mere sound of his voice almost pushed her to tears. "Yeah, I'm okay. There's just been... A lot's happened since I saw you last."

"Do you need me t' come down there?"

She loved that he'd offered. Could picture him halfway to his Land Rover, keys in hand, cane in the other. "No. But thanks."

He grunted. "You don't sound alright."

She rubbed at her tired eyes. "I found out some things this morning. Things I'm not sure what to do with."

"Like what?"

"Like I have an older sister."

His stunned silence filled the line. "How is that possible?"

"It's a long story I'll tell you all about over a brew when I get back." *If I get back.* "To top it off, she was the primary target we captured this morning. We think she's the hacker."

"Fuckin' 'ell, Meg." She could clearly visualize the deep frown on his face as he spoke. "You sure you don't want me to come down? I could be there in just over two hours."

"I appreciate it, but no. I've got Tyler here."

Another beat of silence. "Tyler, the bloke you hated?"

The insane urge to laugh struck her. "That's the one. Turns out I don't hate him." *Just the opposite.* "I like having him around."

A pause. "Are you under duress? I need an ID check. Which is your favorite horse in my stable?"

She smiled. "Rollo."

He grunted. "Alright. I'm looking forward to that proper brew when you get here."

"Me too. Not sure when I'll be back, though."

"Let me know if you need anything, won't you?"

God, she wanted to hug him so bad. "I will." She swallowed, hanging onto her rapidly dwindling control. "It's so good to hear your voice."

"Good to hear yours. Remember, I'm here if you need me."

She loved him dearly for that. "Thanks. I'd better go."

"All right. Tarra, love."

"Bye." She ended the call and slipped her phone back into her pocket, staring down at the busy city below. All those people, all with their own stories. They had families. Friends. Pasts, and the memories that came with them. They knew who they were.

Her past had been erased. She only knew who she was now. And who she hoped to become one day.

Amber—or whatever her real name used to be—had been the only family member Megan had left after their parents died. And yet the powers that be within the program had taken them away from each other.

Had she blocked it out because it had been so horribly painful? Now her big sister was her enemy, locked up in an interrogation room at this secure holding facility where enemies of the British government were held. Megan had no clue what would happen now.

Tyler walked into the room, took one look at her and closed the door behind him. She straightened and composed her expression into a calm mask, but too late. He'd already seen the heartbreak in her face.

Without a word he walked straight over to her and drew her into his arms. She went into them willingly, winding her own around his back and rested her cheek on his chest. She needed the comfort. Needed to know that at least this was real. That he truly cared about her.

"You hanging in there?" he asked quietly, his deep voice as soothing as his embrace.

She nodded, even though she wasn't sure. "It's been...hard to digest."

"I know." He kissed her temple, ran a soothing hand over her back.

"The pieces were there. I just didn't put them together before." God, how surreal.

"You can't blame yourself for not knowing."

She exhaled a ragged breath, fighting to control the torrent of emotions raging inside her. "How could they do it?" Split them up and erase them from each other's memories. She didn't remember any of it, obviously, but she must have asked about her sister. And they'd lied to her. "She was all I had left."

"I don't know. But if the public ever found out about some of the things we've uncovered so far, the people responsible would be crucified."

Megan was in the mood to personally pound a few nails into the people responsible. Whoever had dreamed up and implemented the Valkyrie Program had covered their tracks well. The public knew only minor details about the program, due to the fallout from the Balducci case. Hell, Megan and the others were only scratching the surface of what had really gone on.

"I barely remember her," she said. "Little flashes, that's all. The clearest is that Christmas morning. I can see our parents standing in the living room doorway, smiling at us. But that's it. I don't have anything else about them."

Tyler gathered her closer and just hugged her. "I bet more will come with time."

She closed her eyes and leaned into him, grateful for his comfort. "I don't know if I can face her again."

"It doesn't have to be today. Give yourself some time to adjust." He stroked a hand over her hair, pushing her closer to tears.

She'd always put on a brave front no matter what. With Tyler she was tempted to let everything go. Though it went against what she'd been taught, she trusted him that much.

"It's been a long week," he continued. "Why don't we go to the townhouse and you can sleep on it? It's not like she's going anywhere."

Maybe she was, though. Maybe Rycroft was pulling some legal strings to have Amber extradited back to the States as they stood there. "We need answers. It can't wait. If Hannah and Chloe are still alive, we need to find them." It didn't matter that she didn't know Hannah Miller. She wanted to find all the surviving Valkyries and bring them in before it was too late.

Except forcing Amber to give them the intel was impossible if she didn't want to cooperate. Megan hoped Rycroft's hacker analysts were one-tenth as skilled as Amber, otherwise the rest of this whole operation was pretty much screwed.

A tap came at the door. Megan pulled away from Tyler just as Trinity pushed the door open. Trinity studied her for a moment, as if assessing her emotional state. "The medical team is done treating her and she's being fed. You want to see her?"

Megan lifted her chin. "Yes."

Trinity nodded. "Right this way."

Tyler caught her arm, making her look up at him. His handsome face was full of concern. "You sure about this? Say the word and I'll get you out of here to the townhouse. I'll get you the biggest bowl of ramen London has to offer and you can just relax for the night. Decompress, get some sleep and I'll make sure no one disturbs you."

Because he would personally stand guard and watch over her.

A sharp pain pierced her heart. "Can I get a rain

check for that? I need to do this now."

He nodded once, not looking too happy about it. "All right."

Leaving him behind, she followed Trinity down two floors to a brightly-lit corridor filled with locked doors. Her heart rate picked up when Trinity stopped at one halfway down. "This is it."

Megan nodded, bracing for the coming confrontation. "Did you get anything else out of her earlier?"

"Not really. She's denying that she had anything to do with the others disappearing or winding up dead."

Well, of course. She wasn't going to admit anything, and was skilled enough to cover her tracks. They all knew Amber had done it. They'd found the encrypted files on her, and if she wasn't talking, she had to be guilty. The burden was proving it so that they had enough evidence to hold her.

Trinity reached for the knob. "Ready?"

"Yes." Disguising her anxiety as best she could, she put on a calm mask and entered the sterile room.

Her sister sat at a rectangular table with her hands cuffed in front of her, dressed in an orange prisoner's jumpsuit. Her cool green gaze never wavered from Megan as she walked over to sit in the chair on the opposite side of the table.

For several long heartbeats they stared at each other. "I didn't remember you until this morning," Megan finally said, unable to stop studying Amber's face. They did look alike in some ways. The bone structure and hair. Like their mother. "Do you remember me?"

To her surprise, Amber nodded. "Not until a few months ago, though."

"What do you mean?"

Amber held her gaze.

"Tell me, dammit. If you know something more about our past, about us and our parents, then I want to know." She deserved to know.

Her sister raised an eyebrow. "You sure about that?"

"Yes," she responded through gritted teeth.

"All right." Amber consented with a nod. "The night my handler killed himself, he sent me a message just beforehand. He'd saved some things for me that I never knew existed. So I went to get them before anyone else found out and tried to beat me to it."

Megan was too surprised to answer for a moment. How much of this could she believe? Was any of it true? Or was Amber just spewing lies to fuck with her head?

"And that's when I learned the truth."

The way she said the last two words sent a warning prickle down Megan's spine. "Which is?"

"That I'd had a little sister. That it wasn't just my mind playing tricks on me all these years."

Something sharp like grief sliced through her. "So what..." She swallowed, fought for control. "What happened?"

Amber peered at her more intently, frowning. "You really don't remember anything?"

"Just a bit from one Christmas morning. I was wearing a pink flannel nightgown, and you had on a matching purple one."

Her sister looked almost disappointed. "I guess that's to be expected. You were even younger than me when our parents died."

The curiosity was killing her. "Do you remember what happened?" she couldn't help asking. She was desperate for answers, and prepared to listen even if Amber fed her lies. She could dig on her own later with help from maybe Rycroft's people and sort fact from fiction.

"Not really. But I remember when our aunt came for us."

She blinked. "Our aunt?"

"Our mom's sister, a few years older than her. She

was our guardian."

It triggered nothing but a blank screen in her mind. "Then what happened? Why didn't she keep us?"

"She was too busy with her job, traveling all the time. We went into foster care."

Foster care. God, she didn't remember any of this. Was it true? "For how long?"

"Little over a year." She gave Megan a funny look. "You don't even remember when they came to take us to that special boarding school?"

"No."

"I was almost seven. You would have been five. But it wasn't really a boarding school, was it," she finished bitterly.

Her heart beat faster. Her life had changed so much. Maybe with all the trauma she'd blocked it all out to save her sanity. "What was it?"

She gave Megan a pitying look. "It was a cover for the program. They split us up shortly after we got there."

Megan shook her head, struggling to absorb it all. "How do you know all this? Why should I believe anything you say?"

Amber looked her dead in the eye. "Because I hacked all the classified files from their system before they could wipe them out when they shut the program down. Including our sealed backgrounds. It was all in there."

Holy. Shit.

Amber leaned forward to rest her bound wrists on the table, her expression earnest. "They separated us almost immediately, Megan. We were orphans. We were both scared and lonely and they separated us to sever the family bond between us. They put us into different training facilities on the opposite side of the damn country. They lied about it all and made us both forget what really happened." Her eyes burned with hatred. "They made us forget everything to turn us into what we are now."

"A thief, and a hacker willing to sell the others out for money," Megan responded, her voice flat.

Amber's mouth thinned and she sat back in her chair. "Anything I did, I did because I had to."

"Really. You had to betray the rest of us by selling us out to the highest bidder and watch us all get killed one by one by our enemies?"

"That's hearsay. No one can prove anything. And whatever I *did* do, was out of necessity." The steel in her voice was enough to make Megan's skin crawl.

"Wrong. Revenge isn't the same as necessity. Goddammit, you were wrong to do what you did, and you're my *sister*." She shot out of the chair, unable to sit there and look at her sibling one second longer.

She didn't care that the others were standing on the other side of the two-way mirror, watching. Didn't care that Tyler was hearing about her past and witnessing her coming unraveled.

This hurt. Hurt so much she couldn't breathe. If Amber was telling the truth about their past, then most of Megan's life had been a lie. She'd been manipulated to suit someone else's agenda and put her life at risk to do their dirty work. And so had the rest of them.

"They left me to die."

The softly spoken words pierced the building storm of anxiety and grief. She looked back at her sister. "Who did? What are you talking about?"

"My enemies." She wasn't looking at Megan. She was staring straight at the mirror, talking to Trinity. "They sold me out and left me to die so they could get away and keep all the money for themselves. But I got out and kept all the proof of what they'd done. Then my handler left me that message and blew his brains out, and I learned the truth. The whole, ugly, blackened and rotten truth. And I'm not going to be anyone's pawn anymore." Her gaze sliced to Megan. "It had to stop."

Megan gaped at her. It wasn't an admission of guilt. It was a mission statement. A cryptic message for Trinity and the others to decipher if they could. But Megan knew in her gut that no matter how long and how hard they searched, they'd never find any hard evidence linking Amber to the disappearances and deaths of the other Valkyries. They would only get that if Amber chose to give it to them.

Drawing a deep breath, Megan shook her head, trying to absorb it all. Amber had given her a lot to think about. Maybe her sister's kills hadn't been so evil or black-and-white after all.

She drew herself up straighter. Time to get real and put her personal problems aside. They had a mission to complete, and time was running out. "Where's Hannah? Is she still alive? And what about Chloe?"

"I have no idea, and I don't know Chloe." She said it with a straight face, not so much as a flicker of emotion to betray her. Talking to her any longer was a complete waste of goddamn time.

Fuck this. Megan had heard enough.

She turned and strode for the door.

"Megan."

Her feet halted without her permission just as she reached for the door handle, that voice freezing her in place.

"It's…good to see you again. I'm glad you're okay."

Still facing the door, she squeezed her eyes shut. *Don't listen to her. Don't trust her.*

But she wanted to. She'd never wanted anything so badly in her life than to reconnect with her sister, except maybe being free to finally live her own life…and a future that would allow her a chance at happiness.

Maybe even with Tyler.

The missing Valkyries were still in grave danger,

even with Amber behind bars. Megan might not remember what it felt like to have a family, but Chloe had become a kind of "found family" to her.

Don't wish for something you can never have.

Inhaling a painful breath, Megan reached for the handle and walked out of the room. Trinity and Tyler were there, along with Georgia, and Alex Rycroft.

Tyler took a step toward her, his eyes worried but she warned him off with a tight shake of her head. "You heard everything," she said to them all. "I've got nothing else to say."

"Megan," Trinity began.

Megan whirled on her. "No. I'm leaving." She stalked past them down the hallway, blinking back tears, relief swamping her when she heard the rapid footsteps coming behind her. She knew it was Tyler without looking.

He caught up with her a second later and reached for her but she shook her head again and refused to look at him, barely hanging on. If she looked into his face now, if he touched her, she wasn't sure what she'd do. Crumble to pieces right here in the hallway, clinging and crying. Or maybe scream and start throwing punches.

"What do you need?" he asked her quietly, and the concern in his voice almost broke her.

You could ditch him here and disappear for a while. Ditch them all and not come back until you're ready.

As soon as the thought formed she dismissed it. Her instinct was to disappear and hole up by herself so she could think and get a grip on her emotions.

Except she didn't want to be completely alone right now. She wanted to be with Tyler.

"I need to get to the townhouse," she managed, striding for the security doors at the far end.

Tyler caught her hand, squeezed in reassurance as the guards opened the doors for them. "Car's right out front," he said, and led her through the exterior doors into the hot summer sunshine that could never penetrate the chill inside her.

Chapter Fifteen

Seeing that lost, wounded look in Megan's eyes fucking killed him.

Ty kept his mouth shut as their hired driver took them to the townhouse Marcus owned, his mind busy dissecting everything he'd heard in the interrogation room.

It made him think of his own sister. How it had torn him and his parents up when they'd lost her, but at least they'd had all those years with her before that. To know that Megan had been so young when she'd been put into foster care and then ripped away from the only person and source of comfort she had left made him both sick and want to hunt the bastards responsible down.

She was quiet, staring out her window as they wound their way through the late morning traffic. She hadn't said a word in almost twenty minutes since leaving the facility. Now they were in the upscale Chelsea neighborhood on the north side of the river, passing ultra-expensive townhomes made of brick and white plaster lined with glossyleafed magnolia and cherry trees.

Needing to touch her, Ty reached out and wrapped an arm around her shoulders. When she glanced over at him in surprise, then gave in and leaned her head on his shoulder, pain ripped at his heart. He kissed the top of her head, wanting to do so much more than just hug her. Wishing he could somehow make her hurt less.

The driver double-parked in front of a row of white, Georgian-period townhomes that looked like something out of a movie set. They were made of aged brick and white plaster, all meticulously kept.

Ty had no idea how Marcus had the kind of money to afford this and the manor in the Cotswolds. For certain he hadn't paid for them with his SAS salary, even if he'd managed to put away most of his earnings over the years.

He followed Megan up the front steps and inside the five-story townhome. She disarmed the security system, drew her pistol and started to do a sweep.

Okay, then. Either she wasn't as emotionally wrecked as he'd thought, or she was operating on autopilot.

Without a word, he took the right side of the townhouse while she took the left, then they checked the remaining floors together. "Clear," he said after checking what must be the guest room on the top floor.

She holstered her weapon as she came out of the other suite, her hazel eyes dull with fatigue. "I'm pretty bagged. Gonna take a shower and then crash."

"Do you want company?" He wasn't sure if she wanted to be alone.

"No, I... No. I need some time to myself right now."

He hid his disappointment, understanding why she'd want that. She had a lot to process. "Okay. Can I take this one?" He hooked a thumb over his shoulder to point at the guest room.

She hesitated a moment before responding, watching him. "Of course." She backed into the other doorway, gave him a stiff smile. "See you in a while."

"Sleep well." He stared at her closed door for a few seconds before going into the guest suite, fighting the urge to barge into Megan's room and drag her into his arms. If she wanted privacy and space he had to give them to her, no matter how much he hated it.

He glanced around him. Everything in this place was immaculate and elegantly finished. The large, walk-in shower had four different spray nozzles and a rain head in the center.

He stripped and stood under the flow of hot water until the ache in his neck and shoulder muscles began to ease, then got out, dried off and pulled on fresh clothes from his backpack.

Megan's door was still closed when he peeked out into the hall. Too wired to sleep, he wandered downstairs to the kitchen. It was bright and airy, with top-of-the-line appliances.

The whole place was incredible, but it had an impersonal feel to it, almost like a hotel. There were no personal touches, no photos or anything else that suggested Marcus even owned the place. Although, maybe he never came here.

He must have alerted someone that they were coming, though, because when Ty opened the fridge he found it stocked full with all kinds of fresh groceries. So he busied himself making a sandwich and then looked up ramen places on his phone, intending to either pick it up or have it delivered so it was here when Megan woke up.

He froze when she appeared around the corner wearing a white bathrobe that cinched around the waist, her freshly washed hair hanging loose around her shoulders. She didn't have a drop of makeup on and there were dark circles beneath her eyes, but one look at her was still like a punch to the chest. "Hey. Feeling any better?"

Rather than respond she skirted the marble-topped island and walked toward him, her gaze locked on his. Ty's heart kicked into overdrive, his mouth going dry. She looked…intent. Hungry, even, and he prayed it wasn't for food.

She stopped directly in front of him, her pretty hazel eyes on his. In that moment he was afraid to touch her, because if he did, he wasn't sure he could hold back.

"I don't get...involved with guys," she said quietly. "And obviously never when I'm on a job. But you make it so damn hard to stay away." She raised her chin while his heart tried to pound its way out of his chest. Was she really saying what he thought she was? "So even if this is all we can have, I still want you—"

Ty plunged his hands into her hair and crushed his mouth to hers, cutting off whatever else she'd been about to say. She'd said enough—more than he'd dared hope for, and he was done holding back.

She opened for him instantly, making them both groan, and wound her arms around his neck. There was no tentativeness in her, and no teasing from him this time. Only need and hunger and the desire to give her more pleasure than she'd ever had with anyone else.

Ty had to be different than any guy she'd been with. He wanted to stake his claim and imprint himself in her so deeply that she'd never be able to forget him. So that when this mission was over, she wouldn't want to walk away.

Megan pressed her body to his, the feel of her firm curves setting him on fire. There was so much of her he wanted to see and touch and kiss. So many things he wanted to do to her.

He locked an arm across her shoulders and walked her backward until she came up against the wall, then pressed his hips and aching erection into her as he reached for the belt on her robe. Their tongues stroked and caressed while he undid the belt and let the two halves of the robe spread apart.

Lifting his head, he stared into her eyes for a heartbeat before easing back to look down her body. The robe had fallen open all the way to her hips, the folds of fabric trapped between their pelvises and covering all but an alluring line down the center of her body.

Ty took a step back, his gaze drinking up the sight of her as the fabric fell down her legs. He pushed the halves aside, his heart pounding when her naked breasts finally came into view. Small and round with tight, coral-pink nipples that begged for his mouth. Sleek lines defined her abs, her body toned and supple—both a weapon and a tool for the role she'd been trained for.

He dragged his eyes back up to hers and leaned in to nip at her lower lip, then plunging his tongue inside for one last taste before kissing his way down her neck. He paused when he found a sensitive spot that made her gasp and cupped her breasts, gliding his thumbs over the taut peaks.

Megan shivered in his hold. She squirmed, all restless energy and sank both hands into his hair, urging his face lower.

Ty was only too happy to oblige.

He rubbed his face between her breasts gently, scraping his stubble over her soft, creamy skin. She smelled of soap and arousal, making his head spin.

He wouldn't forget her scent, the sounds she made. But he wasn't walking away without a fight. He would do whatever it took to keep her with him.

"Ty."

Yes. His tongue traced the curve of one breast, then the other while his fingers closed around the hard nipples and twisted softly. Her mewl of pleasure sliced through him and he couldn't wait a second longer. Grasping her upper ribcage, he licked his way to one nipple and sucked it into his mouth.

"Ty." Her back arched, her hands moving impatiently over his shoulders, grabbing at the fabric of his shirt.

"Take it off me," he rasped out, and kept sucking, his

dick growing even harder when she peeled the material up and over his head.

The way she moved was such a turn-on. Small, restless squirms and wriggles that were both sinuous and impatient. So consistent with her personality, showing him how eager she was for more.

But Ty refused to be rushed. Not when he'd wanted her for so long. And more than any other woman.

He moved to the other nipple, sliding one hand down to grip the curve of her hip. Christ she felt good, firm yet supple.

He rolled his tongue across the captive flesh and slipped his free hand down to her thighs, brushing his fingertips down the silky soft inside to her knee, then back up. She widened her stance, giving him more room, her breathing unsteady as her hands flexed into his shoulders.

Ty eased his hand higher and cupped her, groaning at the feel of that silky heat against his palm. He pressed gently, rubbed the heel of his hand at the top of her folds while he teased her nipple.

She gasped and pushed at his head. "More," she whispered.

Hell, yes. *Everything*.

He sank to his knees in front of her, rubbing his face down the center of her body until his chin rested against the strip of hair between her thighs. His hands squeezed her hips as he drew in her clean, soapy scent, underlaid with the wild scent of her arousal.

Dying to taste her, he leaned forward and nuzzled her with his lips. Touched the tip of his tongue to the top of her flushed folds.

Megan hissed in a breath and tangled her fingers in his hair, pushing her hips against his mouth. He eased his tongue deeper. Flattened it and gave her a long, slow lick from bottom to top, pausing directly over the swollen bud of her clit.

"Oh, God, don't tease," she whispered, the muscles in her thighs tensing.

He loved the desperate, breathless edge to her voice. He would never get tired of knowing she needed him.

Ty closed his eyes and gave her what she needed. Licking and caressing. Worshipping her with his tongue. Making sure he focused on the exact spot that sent her up on her toes with a strangled whimper, her fingers clenching around his hair until his scalp burned.

The slight sting combined with the taste of her and the husky edge to her voice made him so hard he ached. He stayed on his knees as he drove her closer and closer to the edge, then shifted his grip to sink one finger into her soft, slick heat.

The broken moan she made was the sexiest sound he'd ever heard. She trembled, her fingers clenching in his hair. He stroked her inside and out, letting her pleasure build, savoring the sounds he pulled from her, the impatient rocking of her hips while she rubbed against his tongue.

"Oh, that's so good," she groaned, quivering now.

"Want to hear you," he murmured, licking and caressing, adding a second finger inside her. "Gonna make you come." He needed this. To satisfy her this way before they did anything else.

She let her head fall back and closed her eyes, soft, husky moans spilling from her parted lips. Her body squeezed around his fingers, signaling she was getting close.

He slowed his tongue, finding the sweet spot inside her with his fingers. Megan mewled and bowed against his mouth, a shudder rolling through her as she started to come.

Triumph surged through him. *His.* In that moment she was completely his. Surrendering to him, letting her protective walls down.

When she'd settled and relaxed against the wall he kissed her open folds one last time and eased his hand from between her thighs. Then he kissed his way up the center of her body, chuckled when she grabbed his arms to pull him up to her mouth.

He met it gladly, turned on even more by the way she didn't shy away from her own taste. Her hands roved over his naked chest, down his stomach to the top of his jeans.

He was throbbing, so hard he hurt. He didn't even feel it when she undid his jeans, too busy kissing her and dying for the feel of her hands on his aching flesh. He'd never felt this way about anyone. This level of need had a sharp, raw edge to it. She eclipsed everything.

She shoved the denim and cotton down his hips and he groaned into her mouth when her fingers curled around him at last. He flexed into her hand, hissed in a breath at the pleasure that ripped up his spine. But she pushed him back with a solid hand on his chest and went to her knees in front of him.

Ty caught his breath, barely had time to absorb the sight of her there with her hand wrapped around him before she lowered her head and traced her tongue around the sensitive head.

Air hissed between his clenched teeth. He caught a fistful of her silky brown hair and squeezed, his heart thudding against his ribs and his whole body drawn taut with anticipation.

She tipped her head back a bit, looking up at him through her lashes as she closed her lips around him. Slowly. As if she was enjoying it as much as him.

Pleasure rocketed through him. His entire body went taut. He bit back a raw groan and braced one hand against the wall, struggled to find his voice. "I want inside you," he ground out, reaching for her shoulders.

No, he *needed* it. To connect with her completely, on a level of intimacy neither of them had before.

She shoved his jeans and underwear down his legs but pushed his reaching hands away as he kicked his jeans aside. Giving him one last, slow suck that made his lungs constrict, she stood and fused their mouths together.

With a low growl, Ty grabbed her around the hips and hoisted her off her feet, heading for the stairs. Her low, sexy laugh went straight to his head, then her legs wrapped tight around his waist, rubbing her open folds over the length of his pulsing cock.

Somehow he managed to get them upstairs, but by the time they reached the first bedroom he was convinced he would die if he didn't get inside her in the next heartbeat. She laughed again when he tossed her onto her back on the bed, and her smile remained as he stretched out on top of her.

He shoved up onto his hands to look down at her, breathing hard. *Shit.* "I don't have anything."

"I do." She twisted around and leaned over the edge of the bed, arching backward at an impossible angle.

Reaching for her discarded robe on the floor, she came up with a condom from the pocket. She gave him a sexy, confident smile and pulled herself up in an impressive display of core strength. "See? Told you I was super bendy."

"Yes, you did." And he was damn glad she'd wanted him enough to come downstairs prepared. Grinning, he caught her chin in his fingers and bent to capture that luscious mouth once more.

He got to work revving her back up again, searching out new places that made her gasp and moan, and spending lots of time on the spots he already knew she loved. When she was panting and quivering, slick and ready against his fingers, he allowed her to roll the condom onto him and settled between her open thighs.

Megan curled her lithe thighs around his hips, her eyes heavy-lidded with anticipation as he braced his weight on his forearms and slowly pushed inside her. Wet heat surrounded him. Her eyes closed, her head tipping back into the pillow.

God. Nothing had ever felt this good. He surged forward until he was buried inside her, dropped his face to her throat for a moment to let the sensation shudder through him.

Her arms came around his shoulders, her hands stroking his hair as she cradled him deep within her body. If he died right now, he would die happy.

She smelled so damn good. Felt even better. He couldn't get enough of her. Couldn't get close enough. Her skin was like satin under his mouth as he cruised up her neck to her jaw, her mouth. He twined his tongue with hers, came up on one elbow to ease his other hand between them and find her swollen clit.

She moaned into his mouth and arched her hips. Ty gave into the need ripping through him and started to move. Slow, smooth thrusts, his touch on her clit light and steady. She pulled her mouth from his and whispered his name, her arms and legs tightening around him as they began the climb together.

His breathing turned choppy, his heart thundering in his throat as he thrust faster, a little harder.

"Oh, yeah, like that," she breathed, then pushed his caressing fingers aside and took over with her own.

Ty watched her face as she stroked herself, dying a little each time he thrust forward into her warmth. She clenched around him, her moans turning to whimpers, her face a study in ecstasy. Then she cried out and bucked as the orgasm hit, taking him with her.

He drove forward and stayed locked there, let the pleasure rocket him over the edge. By the time he could open his eyes again he was sagging over her, his arms weak. His heart squeezed when she drew him down into her embrace and just held him, his face buried in her hair spread across the pillow.

He barely had the presence of mind a minute later to shift up and withdraw to deal with the condom, then wrapped her up in his arms and rolled them onto their sides, her cheek resting on his shoulder. A profound sense of contentment spread through him as they held each other.

Exhaustion hit him, dragging him down while he ran his fingers through her long hair. "You feel so damn good," he whispered.

"Mmm, and I love all your muscles," she whispered back sleepily. Her fingers stroked the spot over his heart gently. But she definitely wasn't sliding off to sleep as he was about to. He could practically hear her mind humming.

"What are you thinking about?"

"Different things." A slight pause. Then, "Can I ask you something?"

"Anything."

"What happened to your sister?"

The question threw him so much that he tensed, yanked out of his contented glow.

"You don't have to answer," she said quickly.

She must be thinking about Amber. Of course she was. "No, it's fine. I just haven't talked about her in a long time."

"What was her name?"

"Gloria. She was two years older than me."

"Were you close?"

"We didn't get along that great when we were little, but we got much closer when we both hit our teens." He closed his eyes, focused on the feel of Megan curled into him as he continued. "None of us could wait until she got her driver's license. My parents did shift work and in between they were constantly running us around to various sporting events and other activities. When Gloria got her license right after she turned sixteen, she started driving me to and from games and practices to give my parents a break."

"That was nice of her."

"She loved any excuse to drive my mom's car around, so it wasn't exactly a hardship for her. And she always let me pick the music." He smiled as he said it, the memory not quite so painful anymore. "In the summer my mom would sometimes give us money to get an ice cream. We'd go through the drive through so we didn't have to get out of the car."

Megan made a soft sound, encouraging him to continue.

"That's my last clear memory of her. She was singing along to a song I'd found on the radio. We were at the drive through window. She handed me my ice cream, a big smile on her face as we sang along to the chorus."

Megan tipped her head back to look into his face. "What happened?"

He took a deep breath. "She dropped me off at my teammate's house. I had just shut the front door behind me when I heard the screech of tires and the impact."

He paused, the memory so vivid he could still see the ice cream tumbling from his hand on the front step when he threw the door open and saw what had happened. "An uninsured driver sped down the street without his lights on as she backed out of the driveway. He T-boned her right at the driver's door. Broke her neck on impact. I was the first one there."

He'd torn down the front steps screaming her name, his teammate and the parents right behind him. "Her eyes were open but she was struggling to breathe. She was terrified. She looked right at me, knew I was there. But there was nothing I could do. She died before anyone could even call an ambulance."

"I'm so sorry."

"Thanks." He tucked her back into his chest, buried his nose in her clean hair. "I had a hard time with it. Mainly because she'd died after dropping me off. I felt like it was my fault. But watching her die without being able to do anything was the hardest part."

And that's why I hate not being able to protect you from everything.

He hugged her tight. "Were you thinking about Amber?"

"Yes. I can't remember being separated from her, but they must have done it to make us forget each other."

"They probably did." No telling what the people behind the program were capable of after the things he'd learned.

"She also said some Valkyries betrayed her and left her to die to get a bigger cut of the money they'd earned on a joint op." She shook her head. "I can't stop thinking about it. It could all be lies, but what if it's not?"

"We'll dig until we know the truth."

She looked up into his face, a smile curving her mouth. "We?"

"Yeah, we." He tucked her back into his hold and wrapped his top arm around her back, willing her to relax and sleep. She needed it. "You won't be facing this alone."

This or anything else if he had any say in it.

Chapter Sixteen

Megan woke to utter darkness, surrounded by warmth.

Tyler was holding her. They were in Marcus's townhouse. He'd stayed with her all night, helping to chase away the demons lurking in her subconscious.

But he couldn't shield her from the horrible reality that her sister was being held for questioning by the U.S. government.

It weighed heavy on her mind. Even when she'd finally dozed off, she'd dreamed about Amber. Now awake, the fragmented memories she'd carried around all these years had come to life, full of new meaning.

Yesterday had changed everything. First the bombshell about having a sister, and Amber being implicated in the exposure and deaths of an unknown number of Valkyries.

Then there was Tyler.

Sleeping with him had been the most intimate experience of her life. These past twelve hours with him had blown her emotional shields off. Now she didn't know what the hell to do.

People like her didn't have relationships. Not real ones. They couldn't. Not when she had no clue what a real relationship even looked like, and not with the danger she would bring to Tyler.

It was stupid to even hope that they could be a couple. Her reality was far different from the romance novels she read so voraciously. She was meant to be alone, and Tyler deserved more than she could give.

And yet... The thought of walking away from him was unbearable.

Anxiety roiled inside her, quickly edging toward panic. There was too much going on. She needed space. Needed to clear her head and rebuild her emotional shields before she faced Tyler again.

But first, she needed to see her sister.

Making sure she didn't wake him, she eased out of Tyler's hold by degrees, pausing when he rolled over in his sleep. She made sure he was deep under before leaving the bed to get dressed.

She told herself it didn't make her a coward to leave without a word. She needed to sort out her feelings and figure out what she wanted to have happen going forward, and it wasn't like she was ghosting on him and planning to never see him again.

There was a message on her phone from Trinity. Time stamped two hours earlier.

Need to talk to you. Call me when you wake up.

Megan wasn't calling her at this hour. Besides, she had something to take care of first.

The sun hadn't even touched the eastern horizon yet when she silently set the alarm, slipped out the front door and made her way to the nearest tube station a few blocks over. She felt naked without her pistol but carrying here in the UK was illegal, though she kept her blade strapped to the inside of her right calf.

Not technically legal, but given the situation there was no way in hell she was walking around without some sort of a weapon to defend herself with.

On the journey to the facility she stood with her back to the corner of the train car, watchful of the few people who got on with her, but her mind kept spinning. In spite of everything, she had a sister. In spite of everything, she wanted to believe Amber had told her the truth.

Faint shades of rose and gold touched the eastern sky as she walked the final block to the detention center. The guards checked her ID and took her blade as she entered. No one but the guards were armed inside the building. "Who are you here to see?" one of them asked her.

"Amber Brown."

He frowned and checked his computer. "She's listed as restricted access."

"Alex Rycroft has given me personal access to her. Check her file."

He typed something into his computer, studied first her ID and then her. "So he has." He rose and radioed someone, alerting them that she was coming. "They've moved her to the third floor. If you go up there, someone will escort you to her," he told her, and buzzed her through the first set of secure doors.

Though it was early and no one else was around, the building was fully lit. Another guard let her into the elevator and rode up with her to the third floor, where another waited.

The new guard escorted her down the hall of cells and stopped in front of one. "We've removed her restraints but I can put them back on her. Did you want me to come inside with you?"

"No to both." She wanted to talk to her sister alone, and not while Amber was in chains.

He swiped a keycard into a scanner and entered a code. "The cell's under video surveillance. When you want to come out, signal us." A small light above the door turned from red to green and he opened it for her.

Amber sat up on her bunk fixed to the far wall, blinking at the glare of lights as Megan stepped inside. The door shut soundlessly behind her.

They stared at each other for a long moment. Then Amber pushed her long, chocolate-brown hair over one shoulder and swung her legs over the side of the bunk. "What time is it?" Dark circles lay under her eyes.

"Just after four in the morning." She crossed her arms and leaned against the wall. Seeing her and the resemblance between them was still surreal. "You get any sleep?"

"A little. They were here until two."

Megan frowned. "Who was?"

"Trinity and Rycroft."

Trinity must have texted Megan just after finishing up here. They'd left the lights on, making it hard for Amber to sleep. Why? Trinity had to know that sleep deprivation wasn't going to work. "What did they talk to you about?"

That wary, green stare measured her. "You know what."

The list. The names of the Valkyries Amber had targeted and any other names contained in the encrypted files she had, so they could determine who was at greatest risk and take action.

"We made a deal, so to speak. To show good faith."

Good faith? Megan drew a calming breath. She'd come here to see for herself if what Amber had said was true. Time to see if her sister was willing to share anything. "Did your trainer have any information about us when we were kids?"

"There was a partial file. Most of it was redacted. So I hacked the rest from the main system before they were able to erase it all."

"And that's when you found out about the foster care?"

She nodded. "I remember being taken away from you."

Megan's skin prickled. *Screaming. A little girl screaming, the sound so full of anguish and fear that it made her heart race and clap her hands over her ears.*

"No, I won't go! That's my sister, you leave her alone!"

A little girl struggling as a man picked her up and started to carry her out of the house. Her face was streaked with tears as she twisted around and cast a desperate look behind her. "Carly, no!" She shoved at him, trying to get free, her voice hysterical. "I need to stay with Carly!"

Megan swallowed, shaken as realization slammed into her. *She* was Carly. She'd watched the man carry her sister out of the house. "My name was Carly?"

"Yes. Mine was Ashley."

Her pulse kicked up another notch as that name triggered another piece of her past.

"Ash, wait! I can't keep up." She'd pedaled her bike as fast as her legs would go, trying to catch up with her sister as they rode down the sidewalk. It was summer, the sun beating down on her. She was sweating. Ashley was way up the street now, almost at the next block.

She tried to keep up but her sweaty hands slipped on the handlebar grips. The front wheel wrenched sideways and she fell off the bike, skinning her knee.

She was trying not to cry as she got up and tried to get her bike back up on its wheels. It was brand new, with pink training wheels and matching streamers in the handlebars and now she'd scraped the paint off it.

Ashley rode up and stopped close by, her eyes wide as she jumped off her two-wheeler. "Are you okay?"

Her knee stung as much as her eyes as she wiped at the embarrassing tears. "I ruined my bike."

Ashley reached out a hand to help her up. "Come on,

it's okay. Mom will fix your knee and Dad will fix the bike."

Megan shook herself. The recovered memory was so vivid. How many more were locked up inside her? "Did you by chance find our old address?"

"Why?"

"I want to see something."

Amber gave it to her.

"What city?"

At that Amber gave her a look full of empathy. But she answered. "Pasadena."

They were from California? Yes, that made sense. In the bike memory it had been hot and dry. And she could see palm trees as she replayed the clip in her mind.

Willing her hands not to tremble, Megan pulled out her phone and typed in the address to check a satellite view of the house. Her heart stuttered when it appeared on screen.

A little white-shingled bungalow with a terra cotta tile roof. She recognized it instantly, and that window at the front that looked out onto the street.

Amber had told her the truth. At least about this.

Megan swallowed and turned the phone around for Amber to see. "The Christmas tree used to be in front of the front window. Do you remember that?"

Amber nodded, a sad smile on her lips. "Do you want to know our parents' names?"

"Yes."

"Beth and Randy Amesworth."

To Megan's horror, her throat closed up. She looked away, tried to compose herself but the tears burned the backs of her eyes regardless. Hearing her parents' names, her and Amber's real names, made this all too horribly real.

"There were forms in there about our foster care time, too," Amber continued in a quiet voice. "But when

I checked it, the paper trail went nowhere. Because it was all fake."

Megan nodded, took a breath. "How did our parents die? Was there anything about that?"

"Not in the file my trainer had. But I found information in the files I hacked. It said they died in a car accident in Pasadena."

She had a vague recollection of Amber—Ashley—and her huddling on a bed together one night, crying, and her struggling to understand what it meant that Mommy and Daddy had gone to heaven together. "So, our aunt ditched us, and the foster care system was a front for the program. Then they split us up and put us into different training facilities."

"Yes. I stayed in California and you were taken to Virginia."

Unreal. All that was missing from her memory too. "I thought I'd been born and raised there."

The look in Amber's eyes chilled. "That's what they wanted you to believe. They were experts at manipulating us, and we were way too young to question them. They told me you died soon after they separated us. That you got hit by a car when you were out riding your bike one day."

God, it was so awful. Megan stared at her sister, her mind whirling. What else about her life was a lie? "What about the others? You said they set you up and left you to die."

Amber's expression closed up, but anger burned in her gaze.

"What?"

Her sister stared at her for a long moment, the hard look on Amber's face sending a chill of foreboding through Megan.

"Come on, what?" Megan demanded.

"It wasn't just the others who set me up."

Megan shook her head, frustration building like a pressure cooker inside her. "What's that supposed to mean?"

A bitter smile curled the edges of her sister's lips. "Trinity and Rycroft didn't tell you."

Before? Or was this what Trinity had wanted to talk to her about? "Tell me what? I haven't seen or heard from them since yesterday. They don't know I'm here right now. What did they say?"

"The government. Someone from inside the program, probably. They orchestrated the op I was on that went bad. After the program was shut down."

"How were you even operating at that point?"

"Officially it was shut down, yes, because of the media exposure with the Balducci trial. But a few of us were still operating, this time on a group op to settle an old score one of us supposedly had. But someone else had insider intel on that op. They knew I'd been up and left behind to fend for myself during the extraction. I think they planted some of the files I hacked on the others afterward, and some of the intel in them might have been fabricated."

"Why?"

"Because this person knew I would want revenge. They were betting on me taking action on my own." Amber looked away, her throat moving as she swallowed. "And they were right, because I sure as hell did."

A lead weight settled in the center of Megan's chest. She shook her head. "No." Who would do that? Why?

"Yes, Megan," she insisted, her posture tight. "Don't you see? We're liabilities to them now. All of us. A threat because we know things that would shake the intelligence world if any of this went public." Her gaze drilled into Megan's. "Especially me, after what I hacked from their systems."

Suddenly it all became horribly clear. The pieces pulling together. "The hitter in Vienna. He was a former

CIA contract agent."

Amber lifted an eyebrow. "But he wasn't just after me, was he? He wanted you too. And there are others. They're out there hunting us right now. Any of us who are still alive."

Blood rushed in Megan's ears. This whole scenario was a nightmare. "But they knew we'd all go to ground. That we would all fall off the grid and lie low until the media attention blew over, and then disappear for good. They have no reason to eliminate us if we do that."

Amber scoffed and gave her a get-real look. "They're not going to leave loose ends."

The ribbon of alarm she'd been trying to suppress wound around her stomach and pulled tight. Back when the Balducci case hit the media, she'd dropped everything and disappeared off the grid, just as she'd been trained to.

Eventually, when things had settled down a little, she'd taken the risk of contacting Marcus. Since then she'd stayed at his house, waiting for the pressure to ease so she could disappear and start over in a new place with a new identity.

But that whole time she'd been looking over her shoulder. Because she'd been afraid of exactly what Amber was describing. Of reprisal from someone within the government.

Her sister continued. "The media only leaked the name of the program and hinted at the corruption going on within the intel community. The public has no clue what really went on. A secret government program that took young orphan girls and turned them into black ops assassins? Assassins responsible for hits on some of the most prominent people and organizations in the world? Hits ordered from the highest levels of our government? They'll do anything to keep all that from coming out, and that means eliminating us by any means necessary." She paused. "Including turning us on each other."

Megan's insides twisted at the implication in her sister's last words. Jesus. Is this what Trinity had wanted to tell her? Now Megan wished she'd called her before coming down here. "What are you saying? That the Valkyries killed recently were actually innocent?"

"Most of them, no. But Hannah..." Amber looked down at the ground, exhaled a hard breath.

"Hannah what?" she demanded and took a step forward, afraid of the conclusion she'd just come to. *No. No, no, no...*

Amber stiffened, her expression turning eerily blank. Ready to attack or defend. Megan recognized it because she'd been trained to do exactly the same when facing a possible close-up threat.

"Is Hannah innocent?" Megan pressed, feeling like her heart was being crushed in a vise.

"None of us are innocent. But...the night before you captured me, I found some intel that suggests it's possible she wasn't involved with the plot to set me up. At least directly," Amber admitted, her jaw and shoulders tight. "I was still looking into it when you captured me."

Megan dragged a hand over her mouth and chin. "So, is it too late for her?" she asked, feeling numb inside.

"I'm...not sure. I couldn't find anything on her and I didn't hear she'd been captured. There's a chance she might still be okay."

But she might not be.

It was stupid, but part of Megan had been hoping there might be a chance for her and Amber to reconcile. Somehow salvage their past relationship. Now?

She stared her sister down. "But it's also possible that you led her enemies right to her, and she never betrayed you? That an innocent person—a fellow Valkyrie—is either dead or being horrifically tortured right now because of you?"

Amber closed her eyes. "I don't know," she whispered. "I don't know, and I can't verify anything from inside this damn cell," she added in frustration.

Yeah, well, none of them knew shit about anything right now, did they? "Jesus Christ," Megan whispered, shaking her head.

"I'm going to find her. I told Trinity and Rycroft I would."

Megan looked back at her sister. "It's probably too late. She's been missing for days now."

Amber pulled in a deep breath. "I'm the one who put her in danger, so it's on me to fix this. I'm going to find her. I'm going to make things right. And if she's been captured, I'll get her out."

And what if she's dead? How are you going to make it right, then?

Megan was too sick to her stomach to respond immediately. Hell, at this point she didn't even know what to think. She was reeling. In free fall without a parachute and nothing to break her fall. "If they let you out of here, you'd better find her." A warning.

"I will."

"And what about me? Was I on your list too?"

Amber scoffed. "You were never in any danger from me."

"And why's that?"

"Because you never did anything wrong. And besides, you're my little sister."

So reassuring. "What about Chloe? Was she on your list?"

"No. I remember seeing her name in the files I hacked, but no. She wasn't involved with the op."

God help her, Megan wanted to believe that. And so she needed to leave because her grip on her emotions was slipping.

"I gotta go." She turned and strode for the door. Then

signaled for the guard and waited, the tension in the cell so thick she could barely breathe.

Seconds later, the locking mechanism clicked free. She stood back so the guard could open the door, analyzing everything Amber had told her. She would call Trinity as soon as she left the building and find out what she wanted. But Megan was going back to the townhouse immediately. She needed to see Tyler and tell him what she'd learned.

The door began to swing open. A hand shot through it.

"Down!" Amber shouted.

Megan dropped to one knee, catching a glimpse of Amber launching off her bunk, and automatically reached for the long-barreled pistol in the man's hand. The silenced shot was surprisingly loud in the confined space. It buried in the ceiling as Megan wrenched the weapon up and back, thrusting upward with all the strength in her legs.

Another set of hands shot out to help her from behind, the arms sleeved in bright orange. Megan twisted the weapon hard to the right, snapping the guard's wrist as Amber rammed her weight into the door, slamming it shut on his forearm.

His howl of agony split the air and the pistol clattered to the floor. Megan bent to scoop it up, straightened as he shouldered his way through the opening, a knife in his other hand.

Amber jerked out of the way as the wicked blade sliced downward in a deadly arc meant to cut her throat. She danced back, hands up in fighting position as the man barreled into the cell.

Megan brought the pistol up and fired.

Nothing happened.

As he rounded on her she hit him across the backs of the knees with a roundhouse kick, sweeping his legs from under him. Amber was on him before he'd hit the ground. She locked both hands around the wrist wielding the knife and shoved upward, trying to break his grip. He twisted, snarled as he threw her off him.

Megan lunged. The blade was coming at her. She wrenched back just as it swept past her head, wincing at the burn as it sliced across her upper arm.

Amber let out a feral sound, stepped back and hit him in the jaw with a solid roundhouse. His head snapped to the side as he fell.

Megan lunged forward to grab the knife-wielding wrist. Then she locked her legs around his neck from behind and squeezed, at the same time digging the fingers of her free hand into the brachial plexus at the side of his neck to make his arm go numb. Amber came at him, smashing her fist into his purpling face once, twice.

Bone crunched. Blood spurted.

Finally, he fell limp.

Breathing hard as he keeled over, Megan kept her legs locked around his neck, refusing to let up in case he was playing her.

Amber disarmed him and staggered back.

The knife was in her hand. The cell door was open.

For an instant, she and Megan stared at each other. And for those few endless heartbeats, Megan wondered if her sister would use that knife on her in order to win her freedom.

Amber's posture relaxed, and she tossed the knife onto the bunk behind her. "He's out."

Megan released him and scrambled to her feet, her legs a little weak, and not just from the fight. God, her guard had been down and it shouldn't have been. Not after what Amber had told her.

Amber reached for Megan's upper sleeve. "You're bleeding."

She pulled her arm away, only now feeling the full

extent of the burn along her upper arm where the knife had cut her. "I'm fine."

Amber's mouth thinned and she shook her head in disgust. "I swore to myself that no one would ever hurt you again. And yet, we're not even safe in here."

The vow stunned Megan, unerringly hitting a vulnerable place inside her she hadn't even known existed until yesterday. She ran an assessing gaze over her sister. "Are you all right?"

"Yeah, I'm okay."

They watched each other in strained silence for a few moments, then finally the sound of running feet made Megan whirl and slam the cell door shut to protect them from further attack.

By the time she ascertained that the new guards weren't a threat and got everything straightened out, medics had arrived to look at the attacker. He was unconscious but breathing.

One guard started to cuff Amber. It ripped at Megan's heart. "No." She said it so sharply everyone stopped and looked at her. "She didn't do anything wrong. All she did was defend herself, the same as I did. Don't you dare put those things on her."

The guard gave her a wary look. "I'm just following orders—"

"Then I order you to put the cuffs away."

At that familiar voice Megan whipped around to see Trinity coming toward them down the corridor. Though the woman had only had a couple hours sleep at most, she looked like she'd just left a day spa, hair perfectly styled, makeup flawless, dressed in a sapphire-blue wrap dress and heels.

Her deep blue eyes raked over Megan before shifting to Amber and the unconscious guard on the floor. Then they settled back on Megan. "What happened?"

As she was relaying the sequence of events, the

guards began taking Amber away. Megan stopped and instinctively reached out toward her sister. "No, wait—"

Amber caught her hand, squeezed it and gave her a reassuring smile. "It's okay."

"No way." She stepped between Amber and the guards, staring them down. She didn't give a shit what they thought about it. "They're not taking you anywhere unless I know you'll be safe."

"I'll make sure she's safe," Trinity promised from behind her. "Come on."

Megan and Trinity flanked Amber on the way downstairs to where a car waited. Trinity eyed Amber warily. "My gut says to cuff you, but I'd rather not. You going to make me regret that?"

"If I'd wanted to escape, I could have earlier," Amber said wearily.

Megan nodded. "It's true."

"Then why did you stay?" Trinity asked Amber.

"You know why." She glanced at Megan, the show of loyalty piercing her.

"So, you told her everything?" Trinity asked.

Amber nodded. "Yes."

"Good enough, then. In you get." Trinity opened the back door and Amber slid inside.

Megan caught her sister's gaze and another memory slammed into her brain. Of her standing on the front steps of their foster house maybe as Amber drove away in the back of a car.

Amber was twisted around on the seat, staring through the back window. She'd pressed her open hand against it. As if she'd wanted to reach through it for Megan.

Megan forced herself to breathe past the painful image and gave Amber a little smile. "See you soon?"

Amber smiled back, tentative but relieved. "Yeah."

Trinity shut the back door of the sedan and opened

the passenger door in front of it. "I'll call you once we're settled in a new facility," she said to Megan. "In the meantime, get that looked at." She nodded at the blood soaking Megan's sleeve through the bandage she held there.

Megan nodded and stood on the curb as the car pulled away. As she turned back toward the building, another car came speeding up the street. She tensed, ready to run, but the car stopped a safe distance away.

The back door popped open and her heart skipped a beat when Tyler jumped out. His gaze locked on her, his face a mask of concern as he raced toward her.

Chapter Seventeen

Ty's heart was in his throat as he ran toward Megan. It had been stuck there from the moment he'd gotten the message from Trinity saying there'd been an incident at the facility and Megan was hurt.

She hadn't answered her phone and it had taken him what felt like a fucking eternity to get here. Waking up to find her gone had been bad enough, but this?

From fifty feet away his gaze locked on the blood dripping down her left arm as Megan stood there on the sidewalk, and the smile she gave him hit him like an arrow to the chest.

He ran right up and wrapped her up tight in his arms, careful of her injured arm. "Tell me you're okay," he breathed into her hair.

"I'm okay." She sounded amused.

Fucking *amused*, while she stood there bleeding from a wound. He dragged in a deep breath and eased his hold enough to look down into her face. "How bad are you hurt?"

"It's just a scratch."

Considering the source, he'd take that with a big-ass grain of salt.

He grunted and reached for her injured arm, grasping

her elbow gently so he could get a better look. A blade of some sort had sliced through her upper sleeve and into her skin.

He pulled the edges of the fabric apart and removed the bandage to see the cut, bit back a curse at the curving slice that marked her upper arm. It was pretty deep. A hell of a lot more than a scratch.

"Anywhere else?" He stepped back to scan her with a critical eye. She had a bruise forming on one cheek and probably had others hidden from view.

"No, I'm fine. Tyler," she said when he kept looking her over. He met her gaze. "I'm okay. Promise."

That remained to be seen. "What the hell happened?"

"Tell you as soon as we get back to the townhouse and I get this thing dressed properly. Is that our ride?" She indicated the car idling at the curb with a nod.

"Yeah. Come on." He took the bandage from her and pressed it to the wound himself, holding it there as he walked her to the vehicle.

"Wait, how did you find out?"

"Trinity texted me. She said there'd been an incident, you were injured and she was heading there immediately."

"Oh."

The driver raised her eyebrows when she saw Megan's arm and the blood on her clothes. "Do you need to go to the hospital?"

"No. Just back to where you picked me up," Ty responded, sliding in next to Megan in the back seat.

He kept his arm around her waist all the way back to the townhouse. He couldn't wait to get her alone, make sure she really was okay and not just putting on a brave front. Then he was going to find out what the hell had happened.

He hadn't known how to set the alarm so upon arrival he ordered her to stay put and did a quick sweep of the townhouse to make sure everything was secure. Then he towed her into the guest suite bathroom and sat her on the edge of the soaker tub to take her bloodstained shirt off.

"Really, it's nothing," Megan insisted, humoring him by staying perched on the tub. "It's hardly even bleeding now."

As she said it a fresh rivulet of blood welled up from the wound and dripped down her arm, splattering into the tub. "Pants off too," he ordered.

"Why? You just can't control yourself around me?"

"Because I need to see for myself if you're really okay or not."

She huffed out an irritated sigh and reached for the button on her jeans. Ty knelt to strip them down her legs, relieved when he didn't see any more blood. Just a few bruises forming on her hip and back.

"What happened?" He took the medical kit from beneath the sink and found some sterile gauze pads along with some antiseptic wipes and steri-strips. "I woke up and you were gone. Then I got Trinity's message."

"I went to see Amber. I wanted to talk to her alone."

He didn't like that she'd taken off without a word—especially after last night. Maybe he was an idiot, but he'd hoped last night had shifted things between them for the better. "I would have gone with you."

"I know. But I needed to do this by myself."

Ty listened incredulously as she detailed everything she'd learned, followed up with the guard who had attacked them. It made him insane to know he hadn't been there to protect her. "Was he after her, or you?" he finally asked as he cleaned the knife wound. He hated seeing her hurt.

"Her, I think. Both of us, if he got lucky."

Well, he almost had, the asshole. "This is pretty deep up here," he said, cleaning the upper portion of the wound where the blade had carved into the meaty part on the outside of her shoulder. She didn't so much as flinch.

"I feel like you're always taking care of me," she said in a wry voice.

Ty looked up into her face, completely unprepared for the gentle smile she gave him, or the way his heart rolled over. He cupped the back of her neck with one hand and leaned up for a slow, hard kiss. "I want to take care of you. But you don't need me to."

That was the kicker. The absolute hardest part of this whole thing. She didn't need him. Not really. And wasn't that a kick in the ass. How was he supposed to convince her that she should give a relationship with him a shot if she didn't need or want to be with him?

Megan reached her right hand up to run her fingers through his hair, a fond look on her face. "I want you. I like having you around, which is more than I can say for any other guy I've been with. And I love that you can handle yourself in any situation thrown at you."

Yeah, any one but this. He was at a complete loss as to what to do about her. She'd been trained to be totally autonomous and never rely on anyone else. It was ingrained in her. And yet here he was, hoping she would fall in love with him. "Well, that's something, I guess."

Her smile widened. "For me, it's huge."

Well then, yay for her. Didn't make him feel any better about their situation—even though he respected her ability as an operator. If he'd been with her this morning he would have stood guard outside the room while she talked to Amber. He would have prevented the attack from ever happening.

"Hold still. I'm gonna see if I can close this up with some of these strips and save you some stitches."

She sat there placid as a doll while he applied the strips, pulling the edges of the upper part of the wound together. He applied some antibiotic ointment to the shallower part at the bottom and covered the whole thing with a bandage to keep it clean. "I'm guessing you're up to date on all your shots?"

"Yes."

He grunted as he washed his hands in the sink. "And I'm guessing you won't take pain meds?"

"I will if it'll make you feel better."

"I want *you* to feel better." Some bastard had fucking knifed her. If the blade had hit her jugular or carotid or punctured a major organ, she might have bled out and died on that cell floor before anyone could stop the bleeding.

He pushed out a hard breath, bracing his hands on either side of the sink, then looked up into the mirror when her arms came around him from behind.

Megan pressed her soft, warm weight to his back and just leaned on him, her head resting between his shoulder blades. "I'm sorry I left without telling you. I'm not…used to having anyone else to consider. I didn't mean to worry you."

Worry him? He'd woken up alone and immediately assumed she'd taken off for good. Then he'd calmed down a little because he'd decided there was no way she would leave London while Amber was being held here, so he could still find and see her again. Then that text from Trinity had sent his blood pressure plummeting.

He hadn't been able to get out of the townhouse fast enough. He'd jumped in front of the first cab he'd spotted, nearly got run over in the process but all he'd cared about was getting to Megan as fast as possible.

"Were you coming back?" he asked quietly.

She tensed slightly. "Yes. Even before the guard attacked I wanted to come straight back here and tell you everything."

That small reassurance eased something inside him.

Made him think that last night might have meant something to her too. "Thank you."

She wrapped her good arm around him and hugged him tighter. "Ty..."

"What?"

"I don't know what I'm doing here."

He straightened and turned around to face her, curving his hands around her hips. "Here? Or with me?"

She held his gaze. "Us. I shouldn't have slept with you while we were on a job—"

"The job was done when we landed in London. So you're off the hook there."

"You know what I mean." She shook her head slightly. "I never meant for this to happen. I didn't want to care about you, and now I..." She looked away.

Nuh-uh. He needed to hear this.

He caught her chin between his thumb and fingers and tipped her face up until she met his gaze. "Now you what?" It felt like he was standing at the edge of a precipice. Her next words would either pull him back from the brink or shove him over the edge to the rocks below.

She made an exasperated sound and pulled free of his grip. "Now we're both going to get hurt."

His gut tightened. "You sound pretty sure about that."

"How can we not?" She turned away and retreated to lean her uninjured shoulder against the doorjamb. "Your life is back in the States. Mine—such as it is—is here for now, and who the hell knows where I'll end up in the future, or even if I'll survive? I just discovered I've got a sister, I've got a target on my back, and so does anyone close to me."

"Including Marcus. Yet you're okay living at his house."

She paused, her expression closing, becoming wary. "Marcus and I have an understanding."

"What kind of an understanding? What's the story with you two?"

For a moment he didn't think she would answer. Then, "I was on a job in Aleppo. I heard rumors of British military hostages in the area. I found where they were being held. By the time I was able to infiltrate, Marcus was the only one left alive, but barely. He was in bad shape. I wasn't sure if he'd make it."

Ty absorbed that in silence. He imagined it all in his head, even as his mind rebelled against the idea of Megan being in such a deadly place.

"I...dragged him out. He didn't want to be saved. I didn't listen. And a few days later, we got pinned down in a bad spot as we tried to escape the city. He saved us both. Together we managed to hold off the enemy until his command sent in a team to get us on a helo."

Okay, Ty hadn't expected all that. "So you and Marcus have been through hell together, and that's why you stay with him."

"He knows the risks and accepts them."

He laughed shortly. "And I don't?" What, was his green beret not as worthy as Marcus's beige one in her eyes or something?

She exhaled. "My current options are to live underground or on the run. I can't give you anything more than I already have. Even if I wanted to, I can't be in a relationship."

Bullshit. "And do you want to?"

The question hung in the air between them. This was the heart of the matter.

Her eyes remained steady on his. "It doesn't matter what I want."

"Yes, it fucking *does*, Megan." He ran a hand through his hair, battling the frustration and the sharp edge of his temper she was bumping up against. He had a long fuse but he was reaching his limit with this. "You make the decisions about your life now. No one else. Just like I make them for my own."

"Like I said, I've only got two options right now."

He stopped and faced her, hands on hips. "Do you want to be with me, or not?"

She shook her head, her eyes filled with a disappointment that made his gut clench. "It's not that simple and you know it."

"It is that simple. I'm a big boy, and as you said, I can handle myself. So yes or no?"

Even as he issued the ultimatum he was aware of the warning buzzer going off in his head. He was pushing her to a place she clearly didn't want to go, and he might well not like the answer she gave him.

Well, fuck it. He needed to know where he stood with her and refused to pretend he was okay with this ending with her just walking away. Not after everything they'd been through.

"What do you want from me?"

"Everything."

Shock flared in her eyes as his meaning sunk in. "You can't mean that."

She said it as though she couldn't fathom why any guy would want to be with her. "The hell I can't."

"Tyler, you barely even know me."

"I know everything I need to know. I want you. I care about you. I want to *be* with you. I'm not walking away."

"You think that now because of everything that's happened since the start of this mission. It's new and exciting, but what happens weeks or months from now when I'm still off the grid or on the run? That's not a life."

He stepped toward her. Stopped just shy of touching her. This went way deeper than her current security situation. The woman read romance novels and secretly craved affection, though she tried to hide both. She wanted what he was offering, but she was afraid to risk going after it.

"You don't trust anyone to stay because everyone you've ever loved has disappeared."

She paled and spun around to leave.

He gently caught her good shoulder, stepped up close to slide his other arm around her waist and held her, his lips next to her ear. "I'd stay. Through everything."

Megan bowed her head. "You can't promise that."

"Yes, I can. I'm doing it right now."

"You have a life back home. A family that loves you."

"My family will understand. If you don't want to be with me, then that's your choice. I'm standing right in front of you, telling you I want to be with you, that I want to make this work. If you walk away from us, that's on you. You're not doing it for my own good. You're doing it because you're fucking scared."

She turned toward him, and this time she let him see the torment in her eyes. Anger and confusion and...fear. "I don't..."

She was going to turn him down. He could see it in her face. That she desperately wished things were different and thought they never could be.

To stop her, Ty took her face in his hands and kissed her. Slow and soft at first, rubbing his fingers along her scalp.

He licked at her lower lip, delved inside gently to stroke her tongue. She moaned softly and leaned into him, her hands pressed to his chest. Softening. Melting.

The ring of a cell phone blared from the kitchen.

Megan broke away. "That's Trin."

Ty let her go, exhaling a deep breath. He was so fucking lost over her it wasn't even funny, and yet the tighter he held on, the faster she slipped through his fingers. Like grains of sand through an hourglass, he could feel their time spilling faster and faster and he didn't know how to stop it.

She answered the phone, listened for a moment and looked up at him. "Okay. We'll be there." She lowered the phone. "She's got Amber in a new location. She wants to have a meeting with all of us. We're supposed to be there in forty minutes."

At least he was being included this time. "Okay."

The meeting amounted to a stay of execution for their budding relationship. He'd take it, because it gave Megan the bit of space she clearly needed right now, and it gave him the chance to work on a strategy.

Because if Megan was only saying no to protect him, then he wasn't taking no for an answer. This was a different type of mission for him, one he had no experience with, but he would win at all costs.

Chapter Eighteen

Tyler was quiet on the drive to the meeting and Megan was glad. He was still upset with her because she hadn't told him what he wanted to hear, but telling him they could have a relationship would be a lie because that was impossible. Even if it was exactly what she wanted.

Except the thought of walking away and never seeing him again tore her up inside. And that's exactly what would happen when Rycroft cut him loose, probably anytime now that they had Amber in custody.

It was for the best, she told herself, no matter how much it hurt. To keep him with her would be selfish. In the end, he would see she was right and be glad to be rid of her.

Megan mentally shook herself. She and Tyler had created a hell of a mess for themselves in a short amount of time. It was exactly why she'd avoided getting her heart involved with the handful of guys in her past.

He made that impossible, however. Even if she did the right thing and walked away after this mission was complete, after what they'd shared it was far too late for her to move on unscathed.

She shoved that down into her internal vault as well.

She couldn't deal with the thought of losing him right now. She would face that when the time came. Until then, she would make the most of the time they had left.

The new holding facility was near the MI6 headquarters near Vauxhall Cross on the south side of the river. They walked to the front door together, Ty's hand warm against the small of her back. It was little things like that, his natural protectiveness and the way he touched her that she would miss the most.

Inside the lobby, a tall, well-built man with graying hair and wearing a blue dress shirt and black slacks was talking on his cell phone near the reception desk. When his gaze landed on them, he stilled, then said something to whomever he was speaking with and ended the call.

"It's Rycroft," she murmured, surprised. If he was here, this meeting was a bigger deal than she'd expected.

"Megan," Rycroft said with a smile that warmed the cool silver of his eyes. "You got your arm taken care of?"

"Yes, sir. Nice to meet you."

"Call me Alex." He switched his attention to Tyler. "Bergstrom. Good to meet you in person finally."

Tyler shook his hand. "You too."

Rycroft tipped his head toward the elevators. "Shall we? Everyone else is already upstairs."

They followed him into the elevator and rode in silence several floors down in the basement. As they walked down the narrow hallway past a series of closed doors, he spoke.

"The guard who attacked you is a former British Army sergeant who did security contracting. As far as we can tell this was his first attempted hit. We don't know who hired him yet but we're looking into all possible suspects." He entered a code into a keypad outside a door at the end of the hall that opened into a larger office.

Two guards stood beside the door to an interior room, its windows frosted over to prevent anyone from seeing inside. Rycroft paused at the door to place his palm on the biometric scanner.

Inside, Trinity sat on one side of a large conference table. Georgia was beside her. Amber sat at the far end, and Megan was pleased to see her sister without handcuffs and wearing street clothes rather than an orange prison jumpsuit. And at the other end...

A startled smile broke over Megan's face when she saw Marcus. "Hey." She was so damn glad to see him. What was he doing here?

He inclined his head, gave her the slightest hint of a smile before running a concerned gaze over her. "Meg."

Pulling her attention from him, she focused on the newcomer opposite Trinity and Georgia.

"I believe you've met everyone here except for Briar," Rycroft said, indicating the dusky-skinned, dark-haired woman.

Megan nodded at her. "Nice to put a face to your name."

Briar nodded back, her liquid-espresso eyes watchful. A sniper's eyes. "Likewise."

"Officially she's on maternity leave, so while she won't physically be participating on any ops, we'll be using her in other capacities," Rycroft said. "Now. I've brought all of you here because we've got some important decisions to make going forward. This entire effort is being conducted off the books and with little funding, so we've got limited resources and have to make the most of all of your skill sets."

He walked to the head of the table opposite Amber and sat, leaning back in his chair in a posture that radiated power and command. A man completely at ease in his role as leader, and given his reputation in both his military and government service, it was no wonder why the entire intelligence community respected him so much.

Megan sat beside Amber, Tyler next to her. Megan

shared a tentative smile with her sister.

"So. First things first," Rycroft continued. "Given the attacks in Prague, Vienna and this morning, all of you are considered possible targets. Which means you're going to have to stay vigilant until we can pinpoint where the ongoing threat is stemming from and neutralize it. While we try to find out who's behind all this, our first priority has to be keeping all of you safe as we locate and extract all remaining Valkyries. Starting with Hannah Miller. If she's still alive."

"I can find her."

All eyes swung to Amber.

"How?" Rycroft said, his voice and expression calm.

"Any intel you have on her is too old now. You know about my skills as a hacker. I've already got information I can use to find her, but I need to start fresh and I can't do that from in here. You need to let me out, and either let me operate on my own, or give me a computer and bring me fully on board as a member of the team."

Trinity let out a humorless laugh. "Not a chance in hell."

"In light of recent events, everyone's safer with you in here," Rycroft said in a flat tone. "If we decide to bring you on board at some point in the future, you can work while in protective custody."

"You can't find her without me, and you know it."

He raised an eyebrow. "I've got some of the best cryptologists in the world working on cracking your files."

"They won't crack them," she said, her expression and tone teetering on the razor's edge of arrogant.

Rycroft's silver eyes remained focused on her, his laser-like gaze no doubt intimidating to most people. But Amber wasn't most people. Valkyries didn't do intimidated. Unless it came to matters of the heart.

"They might. And if they find anything incriminating in them, you'll be heading somewhere a lot less cozy than this place." He paused before continuing. "You're in protective custody right now because I'm allowing it. If you won't give us what we need to find Hannah Miller, I can make things a whole lot worse."

Amber's chin came up, and Megan was once again startled by the resemblance between them. She did that same move when challenged. "As I've already told you and Trinity, I'm no longer a threat to any of the remaining Valkyries."

Megan got the feeling Amber said it aloud to fill her in. And Megan also was pretty sure that Amber was no longer a threat because she'd already eliminated all the dirty Valkyries on her list. Except for Hannah. Hopefully not Hannah.

"I'm committed to finding Hannah and the others and getting them out of harm's way. I have leads I can follow—"

"Which you won't give us because you know they'll incriminate you."

Amber sliced him a look and kept going. "And given everything that's come to light so far, I'm sure you can understand why I'd want to regain my freedom and reclaim my life. I now have a sister I'd like to get to know again." She glanced at Megan, the quiet yearning in her eyes hitting Megan like a punch to the chest. "It's my fault Hannah's at risk. Considering that and the ongoing threat from an unknown source, I should be the one to undo this."

"Then prove you're serious," Rycroft answered. "Give us access to all the files, prove your innocence and help us recover Hannah and the others. Then we'll let you go."

Amber's expression closed up. Her eyes hardened like steel. "I've already given you the evidence you need to show what really happened on that op, and who was guilty."

Streamers of anxiety flickered in the pit of Megan's stomach. Amber might be lying to cover her ass, but she was also right. With her hacking ability and insider knowledge of whoever she sold Hannah's information to, she was the best shot they had at finding her.

Unconsciously Megan began picking at her cuticles. Peeling at the healing skin around her nails. This new threat confronting them all added another layer of risk to the mission.

She kept thinking about what Amber had said to her earlier. If it was someone from within the government, someone with insider knowledge and connections to the people within the Valkyrie Program who had cause to want her and the others killed, then the danger was formidable.

Beneath the table Tyler reached over to grasp her hand and pulled it onto his thigh to stop her from picking, squeezing once. She didn't look at him, but she also didn't pull her hand away. Their time together was ticking down and she wanted to spend as much of whatever remained with him.

"What comes after that?" she asked to break the tension.

Everyone looked at her. She hid her growing unease. "If we find Hannah and the others and bring them in safely, what then? We need a plan for what happens to everyone afterward."

"What do you want to happen?" Rycroft asked, looking around the table at her and the others.

"All of us will need to work together as a group to make this happen," she continued, indicating the other Valkyries around the table. "With the ongoing threat against us, it's too complicated to keep us scattered. It makes more sense to bring us into a secure, central location so we can coordinate and work as a team. And we could use Amber's expertise."

"Everyone can come to Laidlaw Hall," Marcus said. "Every Valkyrie you bring in and vet as a non-threat can come and stay there. It's out of the way, and private and fairly secure. There's plenty of room. You can all stay at the manor together, use it as a base of sorts."

Megan gave a startled smile, taken aback by the offer. Marcus was an extremely private person and liked his space, a borderline recluse. Yet he'd offered up his private sanctuary to aid their cause. Because he cared about her that much.

"Thank you," she murmured, tightening her hold on Tyler's hand. He squeezed back.

"That's a generous offer, Marcus, thank you," Rycroft said. "And it could work."

"We need some kind of protection for everyone throughout the remainder of this mission, however long that lasts, and we also need it for afterward," Trinity said.

Rycroft nodded. "Any suggestions?"

"We bring all the missing Valkyries in and set up a WITSEC-style program of our own," Amber said.

Everyone looked at her in surprise. From Amber's quick response, she'd obviously put some thought into the idea previously.

"We don't have the resources for something like that," Rycroft said, his expression inscrutable.

"Then we get the resources. We find and bring the remaining Valkyries to the manor house. Once everyone's accounted for and safe, we create new, fully-fleshed out identities for everyone. I'm talking right down to credentials, fake backgrounds, new bank accounts and passports, the works. Then everyone gets an equal, lump payout and we scatter to new locations that nobody knows about. No one," she emphasized, looking around the table and stopping at Rycroft.

"And we pay for all that with what money?" he asked.

She held his stare. "I'll get us the money."

Megan bit back a smile. Her sister had serious balls. And from what Trinity had hinted at, a shitload of money saved up in an offshore account somewhere.

"That might be tough," Rycroft returned, "from the inside of a prison cell."

"Let's put a pin in that and come back to it later," Trinity said coolly. "Our immediate priority is to locate Hannah."

"Let me go after her," Amber said again. "I can find her."

"No, we need you here, helping us crack the coding on your files and doing other hacks going forward," Trinity said.

So we can keep an eye on you. The unspoken thought was clear to everyone in the room.

Amber shook her head, her expression defiant. "I'm her best chance at this point. I'm her *only* chance."

Trinity stared back at her, frustration burning in her eyes. "We can't trust you. And due to reasons already discussed, none of us works alone anymore. We're in this together, and from now on we operate as a team."

Amber didn't back down. "If you want to save her, you need to give me immunity and let me go. Now."

"That's not happening," Rycroft said as his phone rang. He checked it, pushed his chair back and stood. "This meeting's over." He hit a button to remove the frosting on the windows and waved the guards in as he answered the call.

Megan pushed to her feet as the guards came to get Amber, a pair of handcuffs in one man's hand. Handcuffs wouldn't hold her for long if she wanted to get free, but attacking the guards in this facility if she tried to escape meant the end of any chance of Rycroft trying to help Amber.

"Wait," Megan began.

Amber looked over at her, her expression softening with a tiny smile. "No. It's okay." She put her hands behind her, submitting.

Everything in Megan protested the cuffs going on her sister. Tyler's hand was solid on her unhurt shoulder as Amber was marched past them, presumably down to an ultra secure cell in the bowels of the building somewhere. "I'll go with you," Megan blurted.

"Bergstrom, Megan. Need a word with you both before you go," Rycroft said.

Near the door, Trinity, Georgia and Briar glanced back at her and Tyler. "We'll go with her. She'll be safe, I promise," Trinity said, then followed Amber and the guards out of the room.

Torn, Megan stood there gazing after her sister while Rycroft opened a file on the table and slid it over to them. "I want to thank you personally for your service on this mission," he said to Tyler. "Your signed contract is in here, the terms of which you've now fulfilled."

Megan's stomach plummeted as Tyler stiffened beside her. "Sir, I—" he began.

"With Amber in our custody, your part of the mission's now over. And per your NDA, you can't discuss or disclose anything that happened during the term of your contract with us."

Rycroft nodded at the page he'd opened it to and slid a pen across the table to Tyler. "Sign at the bottom of that document and we'll wire you the rest of your payment. Due to the current security situation we've taken the liberty of booking your flight back to the States. You leave first thing in the morning. The ticket's been sent to your email."

The blood drained from Megan's face. First thing in the morning? *No. Not yet. Not yet.*

She hid her reaction, fought to contain the panic scraping at her insides. Tyler glanced at her, held her gaze for a long moment, waiting. For what, she didn't know. A miracle that would give them more time together?

She wanted him to be safe. To have a good life. He couldn't have either with her.

Rycroft kept watching him, waiting.

Frustration burned in Tyler's gaze as he stared at her.

It was hard to breathe. "Sign it," she told him softly.

Hurt flashed in his eyes a split second before they chilled. After a long, tense moment he looked down at the form, his jaw tensing.

Pain spread through her chest, expanding until she couldn't breathe. *Sign it. I can't let you give up your life for me.*

Then he picked up the pen and signed his name in an abrupt, angry motion.

It felt like her heart was being ripped apart.

He tossed the pen onto the file and started for the door without looking at her. She followed behind him, numb.

"Megan."

She stopped, looked over her shoulder at Rycroft as he picked up the folder. "Yes?" she managed.

His silver gaze was full of empathy. "Are you okay?"

She forced a nod. "Of course."

But no, she wasn't okay. And she was pretty sure she would never be okay again.

Chapter Nineteen

Frustration and disappointment rivaled for position as Ty rode down the elevator beside Megan in silence. He'd been a soldier for most of his adult life. He was used to receiving dismissals. But not from a woman he was falling in love with.

He checked his phone on the way down. Sure enough, there was an email containing his plane ticket.

"Is it there?" she asked.

"Yep. Flight leaves at 08:00 hours from Heathrow." Which meant he'd have to leave the townhouse by 05:30 at the latest.

That left them with just over fifteen hours together. Fifteen hours to win her over and change her mind.

They might have officially dismissed him, but that didn't mean he was done protecting Megan on his own. Or that he was giving up and getting on that plane in the morning.

They stared at each other as the seconds seemed to slip faster through the hourglass. "I didn't expect it to happen so fast," she said.

"Me neither." She'd told him to go. Was that really what she wanted? He didn't buy it. She was trying to protect him. From pain and hardship. He was almost certain of it.

The elevator stopped and the doors opened at the lobby. Trinity was standing near the reception desk with Georgia and Briar. She looked at him. "Alex says you're leaving us."

"Looks that way." He wasn't in the mood for small talk at the moment. All he wanted was to get Megan alone so they could talk about them. He didn't want to get on that plane in the morning. Hell, he didn't want to leave her, period.

Trinity stepped toward him and offered her hand. "Thanks for everything."

He shook it. "My pleasure."

Trinity switched her attention to Megan. "Amber's safe in her cell. She asked for you."

Megan's gaze sharpened. "Did she say why?"

"Nope. But if anyone can get her to talk about what she knows about Hannah, it's you. You up for giving it a shot?"

Megan looked up at him, regret clear in her eyes, then back at Trinity. "Yeah. I'm good."

His heart sank a little. He curled a hand around the upper part of her uninjured arm. "Can I talk to you for a minute? Alone."

He led her to the other side of the lobby to a leather couch set near the exterior wall for some privacy. The other three Valkyries watched them for a moment, then dispersed. Except for Trinity, who leaned against the desk, apparently waiting for Megan. But she wasn't staring at them, giving them at least the illusion of privacy.

"I know the timing sucks, but if I can get anything useful out of her, I have to try. It might save Hannah's life," Megan said to him.

"I get that. But you shouldn't go in there alone. You still don't really know if you can trust her."

"I trust her. And she's the best shot we have at finding Hannah."

"You don't know her anymore. Who's to say she won't try to manipulate you to get what she wants? I'll go in with you. Or at least stand guard outside to prevent another insider attack."

"No. If she's going to give me anything, it'll only happen if it's just her and I." She pulled her arm free of his grasp but took his hand, her hazel eyes earnest. "I have to do this. But I'll make it as fast as I can. Because I want to…"

"You want to what?"

"Have as much time with you as I can before you go."

She was seriously just going to sit back and watch him leave. He pushed out a frustrated breath. "What if I didn't go?"

Sadness filled her expression. "It might give us a few more days together. Weeks, maybe. But with you off the team now, I'll be leaving the moment we get intel on Hannah or one of the others, and you'd have to stay behind."

"I'll figure it out." He hated being sidelined but he'd handle it if it meant being with her when she came back.

"Ty." She bowed her head, her hand gripping his tight. "It doesn't matter what we want, or how much we wish things could be different. It's never gonna happen."

"The hell it won't. You don't know that."

Her gaze came up to his, bright with pain she'd never let him see before. "Yes, I do. And deep down, so do you."

He shook his head. "I'm not giving up."

She let go of his hand, looking tired all of a sudden. Pale. Heartsick. "I can't talk about this right now. I need to see my sister."

He folded his arms to keep from grabbing her. To keep from kissing her senseless, or shaking some sense into her. Maybe both. "Yeah, she's your sister, but that doesn't mean shit at this point. She's lied and manipulated her way this far, and she'll do or say anything to cover her own ass. You can't trust her. *Think.*"

"I *am* thinking," she fired back, those gorgeous hazel eyes blazing. "You weren't there this morning. You didn't see what happened or what she did. She had all the time in the world to use that knife on me. She could easily have attacked me while I was fighting with him. But she didn't. She protected me and then surrendered."

"She protected herself." Ty threw up his hands. "God, I can't believe I even have to say this, but seriously? I know you want to believe her, and I know this has all been a hell of a shock for you, but make sure your head's on straight before you go down there."

"I need to see her. Alone."

A muscle jumped in his jaw as he stood there watching her. After the attack this morning he wanted to be at her side wherever she went. But his toes were already flirting with the line she'd drawn in the sand. His fiercely independent Valkyrie didn't need him and if he didn't respect her abilities and let her handle this, he'd lose her for sure.

It was tearing him in two. "I won't let you put yourself in danger like that again. Not for her."

Her expression closed up, telling him he'd gone too far. "Lucky for me, that's not your call. I don't answer to you just because we slept together." She turned to brush past him and he had to force himself to stay still, suppressing a growl.

He shoved out a ragged exhalation. Fuck, he'd screwed this up so damn bad. If this was the end, he didn't want to spend the remainder of their time together fighting. "Wait."

She stopped, shot him a glare over her shoulder.

"I'll stand outside the room. At least then I'll know there won't be a repeat of this morning."

Some of the anger bled out of her expression. "Thanks, but I'll be fine. She's my sister." She turned and headed for Trinity.

Yeah. That's what worried him.

****

Trinity eyed her on the way to the elevator. "Tyler looks pissed. Everything okay with you two?"

It made Megan squirm inside to have someone ask her something so personal. "Yeah."

"Okay. By the way, what Amber told you about your childhood, the recovered records and your history, it's all true. We think she's right about being set up, too. The files she so graciously recovered for us proved it," she added in a dry tone.

Megan drew in a relieved breath. "That's good to know."

"Yeah. But she's still not giving us anything on Hannah or the other missing Valkyries." Trinity swiped a key card in the elevator's security system and pressed the button for the second floor underground.

Out of habit, Megan paid close attention to all the details, just in case. Location of any security cameras she noticed. Number of guards. The schedule she'd glimpsed at the reception desk showing when the next shift change happened.

"So, Tyler's leaving tomorrow, huh?" Trinity asked.

Megan cut her a sidelong look. "Yeah."

Trinity nodded, her gaze on the electronic panel giving the floor numbers as they descended. "You okay with that?"

"Doesn't matter if I am or not."

She looked over at her. "Why doesn't it?"

You know why. "Because."

But then Megan's gaze dropped to Trinity's left

hand, to the sparkly diamond ring on her third finger. And dammit, she wanted to know how Trinity had done it. How she'd managed to move past everything she'd been taught, everything she had been, and found a man she loved and trusted enough to spend the rest of her life with.

"You're engaged," she said.

"Mmhmm."

Even after this op, even though they shared so much with their training and past experience with the program, they were little more than strangers. Megan didn't know anything personal about her, and she wanted to. "What's your fiancé's name?"

"Brody."

"Where did you meet him?"

"At the end of an op. I was running for my life, actually." She glanced down at the ring, her fingers fiddling with it. "He's a sniper on the FBI's Hostage Rescue Team."

Sounded like a great story. And it made so much sense that Trinity would fall for someone with that background and level of training. "When are you getting married?"

Trinity stilled for an instant, then went back to watching the elevator display in front of her. "We haven't set a date yet."

"Oh." Something in her tone was off. "How come?"

One side of her mouth turned up in a sardonic smile. "Same reason you're afraid to risk a relationship with Tyler, I guess."

Megan's cheeks heated. "I'm not afraid."

Trinity locked her gaze on Megan's. "We're all afraid of falling in love. It's our biggest battle."

Her heart thudded painfully in her chest. "But you did it. You love him, right?"

She faced front again. "More than I imagined I was capable of. And in case you're wondering, no, it never gets any easier. Risking that part of us we were trained never to reveal to anyone. Trusting that we deserve something real. But it's worth it. So you might want to think long and hard about that before you let Tyler go."

"I didn't let him go," she muttered. "He was released from his contract and he's off the team. Rycroft's sending him home and I have to focus on Hannah and the others." It hurt to even say it aloud.

"Ah. Okay, then."

The elevator stopped and the doors slid open, saving Megan from making any response. But Trinity's words echoed in her mind as they passed through a guarded security door and turned left down another hallway.

Megan counted the guards, made note of the cameras and other security measures she could see. Her back was up. Ready for any new threat.

"Here we are," Trinity said, stopping at a cell door on the right. "Not as high tech as the last place was, but it's secure enough for the time being."

Megan memorized the code Trinity typed in. "I'll be out here in the hall if you need me," she said to Megan, and stepped aside as she opened the door.

Amber sat up on her bunk as Megan entered, her face relaxing with what appeared to be a genuine smile. "I wasn't sure you'd come."

Megan spread her arms out. "And yet here I am."

"How's your arm?"

"It's okay." It ached and stung, but it didn't hurt half as much as the pain in her chest. And the scar it would leave was nothing compared to the mark Tyler would leave on her heart.

There was a small table with two chairs in the middle of the room. She bypassed it, choosing to sit on the bunk a few feet from Amber. "I still can't get over how eerie this all is. Every time I see you, I pick out something else in how we resemble each other."

"Same." Amber drew her knees up and looped her arms around them, her chocolate-brown hair draped over one shoulder. "I've been trying to remember everything I can from when we were little. Do you remember the tire swing in the backyard? Dad hung it from the old oak tree."

"No." She imagined it, though. Had they been happy? She wanted to believe that.

"We shared a room together."

She mirrored Amber's posture, looping her arms around her updrawn knees. "We did?"

"I had the top bunk because you were afraid of going up and down the ladder."

Megan scowled. "I'm not afraid of heights."

"Well, you were little," Amber said with a grin.

Something warm and light spread through her chest. Even with the temptation of Tyler waiting upstairs, Megan couldn't have stayed away from her sister.

Amber was her sister by blood, not just by creed or the brands on their hips. And no matter what suspicions Tyler or anyone else had about Amber, her sister had protected her today.

Megan got right to it. "What about the oath we all took?" *Loyal Unto Death.* "It doesn't mean anything to you?"

Amber didn't pretend to misunderstand. "It does. And I followed it until it was used against me."

"And now?"

"Now my loyalty is to me and those I want to protect. Like you, and the remaining Valkyries. I get to choose my own path now. The government doesn't own me anymore."

The fierceness in her tone and the somber expression in her eyes squeezed at Megan's heart. "Maybe we can be part of an extended family one day. With the others we save."

215

Amber inclined her head. "Maybe." She shifted, resting her head against the cinderblock wall. "So, what's the scoop with you and Tyler?"

Megan blinked at the abrupt change in subject, and couldn't help but grin. Until the cautious conversation with Trinity on the way down here, she'd never had a girl talk before. It felt so great to be able to talk to another woman about certain things.

She wanted to be able to open up and share thoughts and hopes and dreams and... Even fears and insecurities she wasn't supposed to have. It would be amazing to do all of that with Amber. To be real sisters and not just in name or by shared genetics.

Though the vulnerability made her heart pound, she womaned-up and took the risk. "He's leaving in the morning."

Amber frowned. "So you two aren't...involved?"

She hated the warmth that rushed into her cheeks, but she couldn't help it. "We kind of are."

Her sister raised her eyebrows. "Kind of? You either are, or you aren't. And you definitely look like you are."

"Okay, yeah, we are." She picked at the edge of her front hip pocket rather than at her fingers. "But I don't know what to do about it."

"Ah."

Megan was insanely curious about her. "Have you ever...gotten involved with someone?"

"Once. A few years ago." Amber's eyes took on a faraway look. "It didn't end well. But that was my fault, not his."

"What happened?"

"I got cold feet and took off. It didn't feel right, and I told myself I was protecting him by leaving."

"Oh." Wow, that sounded familiar. "Did you love him?"

Amber's smile was sad. "I thought I did, but the truth

is, I'm not sure what love even looks like." She paused, searching Megan's eyes for a long moment. "Do you ever wonder if you're... broken?"

Megan swallowed. "Yeah, all the time."

"Me too."

She exhaled, a smile tugging at her lips. "Glad it's not just me." Amber smiled back, and Megan felt the first link in the long lost bond between them join back together.

"God knows I've made a lot of mistakes." Amber's gaze turned intense. "I want to find and recover Hannah and the others."

"What if Hannah's not innocent?"

"Then I turn over my evidence against her and let Rycroft handle the rest."

Good answer.

"I want to be part of getting them to safety and helping set them free to live the lives we've all secretly dreamed of and never believed we'd get the chance to have. And after that..."

Megan leaned forward, hanging on every word. "What?" she whispered.

Her sister's green eyes hardened like shards of jade. "I want to find out who started the Valkyrie Program and bring them and that entire inner circle down."

Megan held her breath, her heart racing. God, she wanted those things too. The need for vengeance pulsed inside her, demanding she bring those responsible for so many others' suffering to justice. And if meting out that justice meant killing...

So be it. *We are the choosers of the slain.*

Amber's gaze was earnest as she continued. "Look what they've taken from us. Look at all the lives they've destroyed. We've served our purpose and been cast aside. And now they want us all dead to cover up their sins."

It was true. "The situation's so much more complicated than I realized."

"I want them to pay for what they did," Amber said in a hard whisper.

A chill crawled across Megan's skin at the venom in her sister's tone. But the desire for vengeance burned the cold away. "I do too."

Amber reached out and gripped Megan's hand, her expression both pleading and sincere. "I can find Hannah, I swear. Do you believe me?"

"Yes." Maybe she was crazy, but hell yeah, she believed her sister.

"But I have to act fast. You have to make them let me go."

Megan sat there unmoving for several moments, weighing her options and the costs. She and Amber wanted the same things. They all wanted this threat hanging over them to be gone. And Amber was right. She was probably their only chance at finding Hannah before it was too late.

If it wasn't already too late.

The plan that came to mind was risky, however. They had no clue who was watching their every move and listening to every word they said.

She squeezed her sister's chilled fingers, decision made and a plan already in mind. Rycroft and Trinity would never let Amber go. So Amber was going to have to get out of here on her own.

"I'll see what I can do," Megan promised.

The way their grasped hands were positioned was close to what Megan needed but not exactly right. There were two cameras in the walls near the ceiling: one at the front of the cell and one near the back.

She maintained her grip on her sister's hand and shifted them up a few inches, blocking any view someone might have of the pocket on her outer thigh closest to the wall.

Amber remained motionless, watching her, as if she sensed something important was about to happen.

"Tell me more about what you remember from when we were kids," Megan said, putting on a soft smile and acting for the cameras while she held her sister's hand.

Amber didn't miss a beat. "We had a cat named Squishy. And he hated everyone except Dad."

While Amber spoke, Megan used all her sleight of hand tricks and skill to reach into the outer thigh pocket for her burner phone, pulling it free. Moving only her eyes, with lightning quick glances down at the keypad and tiny motions that gave nothing away, she typed in a brief message.

Make security cams go down @ 11.

Amber kept her gaze on Megan's as she told more stories—whether they were real or made up, Megan didn't know or care. All the while, Megan slowly eased the phone across the plastic-covered mattress, keeping it between the wall and her thigh, safely out of sight.

Amber's fingers touched hers. Closed around the phone and began sliding it back toward herself as she talked about Squishy the cat and other things from their childhood that had been lost to Megan.

As soon as Amber had the phone, Megan released her sister's hand and eased back to drape her forearms across her upturned knees, her posture and expression utterly relaxed.

They shared a smile as Amber finished her story, then her sister's expression turned serious, her gaze delving into Megan's. "Lima uniform delta," she murmured, using the phonetic alphabet.

A thousand needles pricked the backs of Megan's eyes at the acronym's meaning. "Lima uniform delta."

Loyal Unto Death.

Chapter Twenty

After talking with Amber, Megan stayed for another meeting with Trinity and ate dinner together after. By the time she left the building hours later it was already dark out, and Megan was extremely conscious of the time.

She had until just before twenty-three-hundred-hours to gather what she needed and get back here.

The urge to call Tyler was overwhelming. She checked her phone again for the twelfth time. There was no message or text from him. That made her a little sad, but what did she expect? He'd been dismissed, and then she'd done pretty much the same thing by choosing Amber and the mission over him.

She didn't like the way they'd left things earlier, and wished she could go back to the townhouse to spend the rest of the night with him, but this had to take priority.

As she neared the Underground station at Vauxhall, something made her glance over her shoulder. Something that told her subconscious she was being watched. Maybe even followed.

This area was busy, full of traffic and pedestrians

even after dark. She didn't see anyone that set off her internal radar, so she dismissed it and kept going, aware as always as she loped down the stairs to catch the train. As well stocked as Marcus kept the townhouse, the equipment she needed had to be acquired elsewhere.

That niggling sense of being watched continued to follow her on the train to her first stop. She surreptitiously glanced around, but still couldn't see anything that alarmed her. Was she just being paranoid because of the threat hanging over her and the others? There was no sense of alarm, no grinding anxiety in her gut.

The hand in her pocket curled around her new burner phone. She itched to call or at least text Tyler, but she didn't want him involved in this. Best she could do was get this done as quick as possible, then she could return to him and spend their remaining few hours together. After everything they'd been through and shared together, they at least deserved a proper goodbye.

She hit up the bank first, making a withdrawal from an emergency fund she had under an alias. Next was a fifteen-minute train ride to a market at Covent Garden, then another ten minutes north to a military surplus store that carried the rest of what she needed.

She put everything into the backpack she carried and started back to her point of origin. As she stepped out of the last shop and walked to the nearest Underground station, the mild buzz of awareness at the back of her mind became an insistent vibration.

She paused on the sidewalk, automatically reaching for the pistol that wasn't there. All she had with her was her blade.

Unease threaded through her. What if whoever was behind the ongoing threat had somehow discovered that they'd captured Amber? What if they knew where she was being held, and they'd had someone follow Megan?

If someone was targeting her, she had to deal with

the threat alone. She wasn't going to lead them to Amber.

On full alert, she took the Piccadilly line to Green Park Station, then changed trains to the Victoria line that would take her to Vauxhall. But she got off one stop early, at Victoria Station.

The platform was still fairly busy as she made her way up the stairs, preventing her from spotting her tail. The person was still there. Dammit. Why couldn't she see them? If she hadn't been able to shake them, they were damn good.

Anxiety built with each step she climbed. It was already 10:42. She needed to be at the building soon to get everything ready in time.

There was no way she would allow this person to follow here there. So her only choice was to stand and confront whoever it was.

At street level Megan turned right as she exited the station, then headed down a side street. It was quiet and dimly lit. And when she heard footfalls coming faster behind her, she whipped her blade from its scabbard and whirled to confront the threat.

She sucked in a ragged gasp when she saw his face.

"Jesus, Ty," she breathed, the rush of relief leaving her lightheaded.

TY STOOD HIS ground while she lowered her blade. When she'd gone down to see her sister earlier, he hadn't been able to leave. She hadn't wanted him to stand guard outside the cell, but that didn't mean he was leaving. He wasn't going anywhere until he was sure she was going to be safe.

So he'd waited around the corner from the building's main entrance until Megan had finally come out hours later wearing dark cargo pants, and a fitted, black long-sleeved shirt. She'd been wearing jeans and a different top earlier.

And yeah, he'd also waited partly because he'd been worried that she might not return to the townhouse, and he wanted the chance to talk to her after she'd had some time to process everything.

She sheathed the knife and pulled her pant leg over it, letting out a little laugh. "Why the hell didn't you just show yourself earlier?"

"Because you'd have taken off if I had."

Her smile faded. "I was planning to go back to the townhouse later."

But she didn't want him to know what she was up to. He eyed the backpack. "You've been busy. Doing a little last minute shopping?" She'd stopped at a bank, a food market, and a military surplus store. Whatever she was up to, it was well planned. "Going on a trip, maybe?"

She glanced around to make sure they were still alone before answering. "No. It's not for me."

The tightness around his ribs eased a bit. He'd been worried she'd planned to disappear on him and leave the country without a word. "So who's it for? Everyone's flying out tomorrow except for you. And your sister," he added pointedly, watching her.

She huffed out a breath and shifted her feet. "Look. The less you know, the better off you'll be."

But she didn't deny it. "You sure you know what you're doing?"

She raised her chin. "Yes. And I only have a few minutes left, so—"

"So nothing." Worried, he stepped forward until he could reach out and cup the back of her head in his hand. "Have you already forgotten that you're a target?"

"No. But I have to…take care of this. And as soon as I'm done, I'll meet you back at the townhouse."

She seriously thought he was going to go wait there while she did this? He snorted. "Not a chance."

She reached up to grasp his wrist, her expression earnest. "Tyler. You don't want any part of this. Trust me."

The stubborn woman was going to do this whether he liked it or not. "No, trust *me*. Because I'm not leaving your side. So whatever you've got planned, you need to read me in right now."

Megan shook her head at him in exasperation, then a rueful grin tugged at her mouth, one dimple popping out. "You might regret this."

"Maybe. But I'll regret it more if I don't help you. Now. What are you doing?"

****

The stubborn man stood to get his ass in a sling because of this, but he'd refused to budge or listen to reason, and even though he didn't trust Amber, he was helping her anyway.

Damn, Megan loved that about him.

Poised halfway up the rope trailing down the side of the tall building, she tuned out her awareness of him and studied her watch, counting the seconds down as the top of the hour approached.

Ten.... Seven...

Three. Two. One.

At twenty-three-hundred-hours on the dot, all the lights in the building went out right on cue.

Amber smiled to herself. Damn, Amber was good. If she could pull this off in a few hours with just a phone, imagine what she was capable of with a computer and an internet connection.

NVGs in place, she glanced back to aim a grin at Tyler, standing far below her on the street. Over his protests she'd made him promise to stay and keep watch while she executed the mission. Getting in and out of places she didn't belong was her area of expertise. Besides, he was too big to go where she was headed.

Moving fast, ignoring the ache in her cut shoulder, she climbed the last few feet up the side of the building until she reached the large air intake grate on the wall. Using a customized power screwdriver from her toolkit, she removed the cover and let it drop into the dumpster below that Ty had opened up for her.

The inside of the heating vent was still hot, but not enough to burn as she squeezed through the opening and began crawling her way toward her target. Speed and stealth were key here. They had a limited number of minutes before everything came back online, including locks, cameras and alarm systems. She had to have Amber out of here before that happened, or they were all screwed.

Sweat beaded on her face, back and under her arms as she crawled to the first down shaft at a fast clip. Her sore shoulder pulled as she grasped the edges of the vent to lower herself down the short section to the next horizontal one below it, and descended again.

And again. All the way down to her sister's floor, and then laterally along the ceiling.

Twenty-seven yards.

She counted them out in her head as she crawled, pausing when she neared the spot to feel around for the panel that was supposed to be there. Her gloved fingers found the edges of it, and her tools allowed her to remove the screws.

Sliding the panel aside almost without a sound, she leaned down to look below.

A hand reached up through the darkness.

Megan grasped it, shifted her weight and gritted her teeth against the pain while she pulled her sister up and through the opening. Amber scrambled to one side while Megan put the cover back and secured it. Then she handed Amber another pair of NVGs and signaled for her to follow.

Sweat rolled down the sides of Megan's face as she slid along. She retraced her route, her heart beating faster as they reached the final upward section.

This was gonna be close. Security personnel would be swarming the building. Every second counted.

Then a breath of cool air wafted through the vent, signaling they were close to the exit point.

Hurry. Hurry.

The rappelling rope was still in place, Tyler standing at the bottom to hold it steady. Megan went first, easing out backward through the vent to grasp it and make her way down. If she had time she would replace the vent cover, but it wasn't critical.

Tyler caught her near the bottom and lifted her down, his arms crushing her tight to his chest for a moment. "You okay?" he whispered.

"Yeah. We still clear?"

"For the moment."

She leaned into him a second, then looked up at her sister. Amber was halfway down, about forty feet up. Megan glanced at her watch. Yikes. Any second now, and—

The lights went back on.

Amber froze on the rope, then slipped and lost her balance, maybe blinded by the sudden light.

Megan gasped and bit back a cry of warning as Amber lost her grip and dropped a few feet before catching herself, dangling from the rope.

Before Megan could move Ty had pushed her out of the way, grabbed the rope and started climbing. Within seconds he'd reached Amber. He clamped an arm around her waist while she wrapped around him, then dropped, letting the rope slip between his gloved hands. Seconds later they were on the ground and Megan could breathe again.

"Let's go," she urged in a whisper, then grabbed her backpack and took off up the side street, the others right behind her. She kept to the shadows as she ran, following the route she'd mapped out earlier.

Several blocks away she stopped and turned to face the others, shrugging out of her backpack. "The boat leaves in twenty minutes," she told Amber, pulling out a packed duffel and the disguise.

Amber put on the wig and hat and wrapped the gray woolen shawl around her shoulders. "We've got to write a book about this someday," she said, tucking her hair up under the short wig.

"One day." Megan smiled and handed her the small duffel of cash and other supplies she needed to leave the country. Burner phone. Passport. A thick wad of cash. Food, water. "You're coming back, right?"

"If I can."

Megan scowled and shoved Amber's shoulder playfully. "Well, then, make sure you can."

"I'll try."

It would have to be enough. Megan nodded once, then, overcome by a surge of emotion, she reached out to wrap her arms around Amber and squeezed tight. "Try hard."

Amber stiffened slightly in surprise, then laughed quietly and returned the embrace. "Okay. I will." Stepping back, she faced Ty. "Thanks for not leaving me hanging back there."

His lips quirked at her dry humor. "Find Hannah and call your sister, and we'll call it even."

"Deal." Amber's gaze swung back to Megan, and her expression turned wistful. "Be careful."

"You too." She watched her sister walk away and disappear into the shadows with a heavy heart.

Ty wrapped a solid arm around her waist and pulled her in close. "Let's get going."

She nodded and they headed back to the townhouse to make the most of the few hours they had left together.

Chapter Twenty-One

Tyler let out a relieved breath when he shut the townhouse door behind them.

She took a step toward the fridge. "I'm starved. Have you eaten?"

He stopped directly in front of her and gently captured her chin in his hand. They hadn't talked on the way back and he had so many questions. "Did she tell you where she's going?"

"No. But I know she's going to find Hannah."

Ty didn't argue, because what was done was done. Now she needed to hold onto the hope that she'd done the right thing. "They're going to suspect you." Rycroft was going to be pissed if he found out. Ty wasn't sure what would happen to Megan then.

She shrugged a shoulder, her expression mutinous. "I don't care. She's my sister."

Well, she should care. She could get into a shitload of trouble if anyone found out what she'd done. "Do you need to leave?" If so, he'd help her get out of the city and hide.

Her eyes lifted to his. "I'm not leaving. Not until you go."

I don't want to go at all.

He held the words back, not wanting to start another fight. Instead he smoothed a hand over the back of her hair. She looked exhausted and her arm had to be bothering her after what she'd just done. God, she was incredible. "Where will you go?"

"Back to Laidlaw Hall. I'll work with Trinity and Rycroft remotely from there until we get a lead from Amber."

He hoped that happened. He wanted to be there when it did. "Are you okay?"

She searched his eyes for a long moment. "I don't know," she murmured finally.

He gave a slow nod, his heart unraveling at her honesty. His beautiful, stubborn and brave Valkyrie. He'd do anything to help her. Anything to protect her, spare her pain. And yet she still refused to let him all the way in.

Pushing aside the ache in his chest, Tyler curved a hand around her nape. She wouldn't be an easy woman to win over, but she was worth the struggle. He was ready to give up his life in the States to make this work. All he had to do was get her to trust him—and herself.

"C'mere, sweetheart," he murmured, and drew her in for a kiss meant to imprint himself on her forever. He was going to win her heart tonight or die trying.

MEGAN'S HEART CLATTERED against her ribs as she gripped Tyler's wide shoulders and flattened her body against his, kissing him with all the longing and urgency inside her. He'd just protected her, risked everything by helping her free Amber. And in a matter of hours he would walk out that door.

Out of her life.

She ignored the dual blast of panic and grief that terrifying reality brought and poured herself into the kiss. Trying to show him without words what he meant to her. Every touch, every caress loaded with meaning.

Tyler growled deep in his chest and picked her up by the hips, holding her lower body tight to the bulge of his erection as he carried her over to the couch. She peeled her shirt off and tossed it aside as he set her down.

Cool, supple leather caressed her back and shoulders. She arched as he reached beneath her to unhook her bra, another shot of arousal punching through her at the way his eyes heated when they landed on her bare breasts.

"You're so damn gorgeous," he muttered, coming down on his elbows to rub his face against the tingling mounds.

Megan slid her hands into his hair, sunk her teeth into her bottom lip as his mouth closed around one aching nipple. Pleasure streaked through her, sizzling down to the heated throb between her legs. She rubbed against him, wishing they were naked so she could feel that hard length without anything in the way.

His hands closed around her ribcage. Pinning her. Adding to the heat, building the anticipation as he switched to the other nipple, teasing her. Her body was greedy, frantic.

She shifted until she could get hold of the hem of his shirt and tugged it upward, hungrily taking in the sculpted power of his torso as he shrugged out of it and dropped it to the floor.

She caught his face in her hands and they both stilled, staring at each other. *Don't go. I can't handle losing you. Please don't leave me.*

Something in her chest quivered. The words were right there, crowding her throat. Her mouth. But she was too scared to let them out. Afraid of what would happen if she did.

Equally afraid of what would happen if she didn't.

Asking him to stay was beyond selfish. Her life had no room for a real relationship, and Tyler deserved better. He deserved everything. That was something she could never give him.

"Don't," he whispered. "Don't pull back from me."

She wanted to. All her protective instincts were screaming at her to. But the way he was looking at her, with such need and a fierce tenderness that crushed her heart…

She gathered him closer, fusing their mouths together even as her throat tightened. A deep groan rumbled through his chest as he stretched out on top of her. The feel of his weight anchoring her eased the edge of the panic and pushed her arousal higher at the same time.

They stripped off the rest of their clothes in a rush and Megan moaned at the bliss of having that hot, hard body full-length on top of her once more. She curled her legs around his hips, rocking to rub him across her throbbing clit, the empty ache inside her intensifying. She wanted to go fast, yet she also wanted to slow this down and savor every single moment.

This is goodbye.

Pain splintered through her, dragging a cry from her. Tyler lifted his head to look down at her, his face strained. He covered her mouth with his, his tongue sinking between her lips to tangle with hers as his hands gripped the backs of her shoulders and turned them both over.

Megan came up on her knees to straddle him, the rigid length of his cock between her open folds. She set her hands on either side of his head and slid back and forth, rubbing the head of him right where she needed it, offering her breasts to him.

One big hand splayed across the middle of her back while the other cupped a breast, his mouth coming up to close around a hard nipple. She made a soft sound and closed her eyes, absorbing the sensations.

It was like she was melting, liquid heat pooling inside her. "More," she gasped out. "Need more."

"So take it," he rasped out, his voice so deep and dark

it made her shiver. "Put me inside you and ride me." He flashed out a hand to grab his pants, pulled a condom from his wallet and put it on.

When she shimmied back up to straddle Tyler's thighs, the sight before her stole her breath.

He was gorgeous laid out like that against the leather, his body latent, masculine power, contained as he waited for her to sink down on him. He was deceptively relaxed, but the molten hunger in his eyes and the hard length of his erection told her otherwise.

He wanted her. Badly. Enough to sacrifice his happiness to stay with her. It tore her up.

Holding his gaze, she slid forward into position and reached between his thighs to stand him up. His hands came up to close around her hips, his jaw taut.

She eased down a little, taking him just inside her. Eased down a little more and then back up, watching his face. Enjoying the fullness as he stretched her. The way his breathing sped up, the tension in his muscles.

His eyes seared her. Cut right through everything and straight into her heart, plunging deep.

The searing ache in her chest threatened to crush the pleasure. Eyes on his, she slipped a hand between her thighs to stroke her clit. Waited until her body sighed in enjoyment, the heat spreading through her pelvis, then slowly sank down, taking his full length inside her.

"Oh, God, Megan," he groaned, his hands tightening on her hips, the muscles in his chest and arms bunching as his face contorted.

I know. I feel it too. But she was too far-gone to say it aloud.

She rode him slowly, forcing them both to endure the excruciating rise in pressure. He let go of one hip to cup her breast, his fingers squeezing and rolling her nipple. Her eyes slid closed, her body rocking and swaying as it chased after the tantalizing glow of release looming at the edge of her consciousness.

"Tyler," she gasped out, lost in sensation, already starting the climb to the edge.

His hold on her hip tightened. He thrust upward, adding to the pressure, the delicious friction right over the hot glow behind her pubic bone.

She trembled, sucked in air as everything crashed together. Then she threw her head back and moaned, writhing in his grip as the orgasm hit.

His breathing sped up and he rolled his hips faster. Harder. She opened her eyes just in time to watch him arch beneath her in a long, lovely line of ecstasy, his eyes squeezed shut, that beautiful jawline taut as he shuddered.

Finally, he relaxed, his body sinking back into the leather. His eyes opened and found hers. The smile he gave her turned her inside out. And she wished…

She wished so many things. Impossible things.

"Shh. Come here," he murmured, sliding his arms around her and bringing her to his chest.

She tucked her knees up underneath her more and snuggled into place with her cheek resting between the rise of his pecs. She closed her stinging eyes, sighing at the way he stroked her hair, her back.

Don't think. Hold onto this and just enjoy.

But damn, she could stay here like this forever, wrapped up in his arms. Safe and content and…adored. Like something out of the books she loved.

Her throat tightened, the pain she'd managed to push aside suddenly drowning her. She had to tell him how she felt. Had to, or she would always regret it.

The doorbell rang.

Her eyes flew open and she jerked upright as the hollow peal echoed through the stillness of the room.

Time to pay the piper.

Chapter Twenty-Two

Tyler tensed beneath her, his hands tightening on her back. "Meg…"

Megan twisted around to fish the phone out of her pants pocket on the floor and swiped through to the security app to access the camera at the front door. "It's Trin."

Tyler groaned and hugged her close. "Maybe if we ignore her she'll go away." He kissed her cheek. "Or we can slip out the back window and take off."

"I wish." She slid off him and hurriedly dragged her clothes on while he dressed, pulling on her shirt on the way to the door. Then she flipped on the kitchen light on her way past and pulled the door open.

A stony, deep blue stare greeted her.

Megan stepped back. "Come on in."

Trinity walked in wearing another understated yet sexy wrap dress and heels. She brushed past Megan and perched on a stool at the kitchen island.

Megan tucked her hair behind her ear, dreading what was coming but ready to face it head on. She was a big girl. She could handle the consequences for her actions. "You want anything? Coffee maybe?"

"No. This won't take long," she answered, her tone ominous.

Tyler came up to stand beside her, wrapping a steadying arm around her waist. "Trin. What's up?"

Trinity crossed one elegant leg over the other and leveled her gaze at Megan. "There was an incident at the holding facility an hour ago."

She kept her expression blank. "Oh?"

"Yeah. Seems there was a corruption in the security system during a brief power outage. And when the power came back on, your sister was gone."

She put on a surprised expression. "That's crazy."

Trinity sighed. "Did you do it?"

"She's been in bed with me all night," Tyler answered, tugging her closer.

His willingness to cover for her after everything else he'd done stole the last ragged piece of her heart. "I appreciate that, Ty, but no." She faced Trinity and raised her chin. "Yeah, I helped her escape."

Tyler cut her a sharp, incredulous look but she kept her attention on Trin. She didn't want him taking any heat for this. He had nothing to do with it. Any fallout that came from her actions should fall directly on her and no one else.

Trinity shook her head in exasperation. "And just how did you two accomplish that?"

"I gave her my burner phone this afternoon. She used it to hack the system and shut the power down at eleven. I helped her get out."

"Through what? A sealed plate-glass window?"

"A heating duct," she answered, then shrugged. "The main air intake vent let out on the side of the building, so we just rappelled down."

A tremor ran through Tyler, as if he was suppressing a laugh.

Trinity sighed. "A burner phone. She shut down that entire system with a burner phone."

"Don't ask me how, because I don't know. That's out

of my area of expertise."

"But not the escaping part. That's definitely your area of expertise."

Another shrug. "I'm not bad at it."

Trinity cocked her head and gave her a fond what-am-I-going-to-do-with-you look. "You realize the potential consequences of your actions?"

"Yes. But I did the right thing. She's the only one who can find Hannah, and we both know it. She literally just hacked out of your high tech facility with a *phone*."

Trinity held her stare. "You think Amber's actually going to try and find her? Or did you just help her disappear on us again?"

Megan shook her head. "She's going after Hannah. She wants to help us."

"You sound pretty sure about that."

"I am sure." As sure as she could be, though a niggling worry persisted. *You'd better not screw me over, Amber.* "It's a sister thing. Did anyone else escape?"

"Thankfully, no. Only her cell door malfunctioned, it was so strange," Trinity said dryly. "Where is she now?"

"I have no idea," Megan answered honestly. "I asked where she was headed but she wouldn't tell me anything. She said she'll contact me once she's found Hannah. Then we can plan the extraction as a team."

To Megan's surprise, a smug smile curved Trinity's lips. "Perfect." She slid off the stool. Looked at Tyler. "Safe flight home, if you're still going." Her gaze shifted back to Megan. "I'm flying out tomorrow as well, but I'll be in touch soon."

"Sounds good."

She started for the door. Stopped. "Oh, and Megan?" Trinity turned to face her. "I was never here, and this conversation never happened. Not even if Rycroft asks." She reached for the doorknob. Smiled. "Have a good night."

Completely off-balance, Megan locked the door after her. Swinging around to face Tyler, she let out a little laugh. "What the hell just happened?" It was like Trinity—and maybe Rycroft, by extension—had expected her to try and break Amber out. Like they'd hoped she would, even.

"I have no freaking idea, but you Valkyries are all insane." He strode over and cupped her face between his hands. "What the hell, Meg? Why did you tell her?"

"Because Trin already knew the truth. She was testing me to see if I'd come clean to her." She regretted nothing. "I'm not sorry for what I did and if I'd lied, it would have eroded her trust in me."

Tyler didn't look convinced. "Rycroft's gonna want answers."

"She won't tell him anything that would get me in serious trouble—and I get the feeling he planned for this anyway." *Loyal Unto Death.* Exactly how it was supposed to work.

Tyler searched her eyes, so strong and sexy, his scent filling her lungs. "You really don't know where she's headed?"

"No. It's safer that way for all of us." But wherever Amber was going, Megan hoped she'd be safe.

Tyler dropped a slow, thorough kiss on her mouth then raised his head, his eyes heavy-lidded and full of heat. "Let's go to bed," he murmured, catching her hand to tug her away from the door.

"Ty, wait."

He stopped and faced her.

Under the intensity of that slate blue gaze, Megan fought the urge to fidget and shift her stance. "You covered for me."

"Yeah."

"And you helped me get Amber out even though it might have gotten you in a shitload of trouble."

His gaze never wavered. "I'd do anything for you."

The last vestiges of her protective walls came crashing down. *I think I'm in love with you.*

The words stuck in her throat, horror freezing them there. *Love? What do you know about love?*

"I don't want you to go," she said softly instead, her heart frozen in her chest. Saying the words aloud made her cringe inside.

He searched her eyes, his expression intent. "Then what do you want?"

"You."

"Then ask me to stay."

She swallowed at the verbal challenge. "I can't ask you that."

"Yeah, you really can."

"You know what staying would mean. You'd have to leave your life in the States behind, leave your family."

"It's not like I'd never talk to or see them again. And I also know you're worth it."

Oh, dammit, was he trying to make her freaking cry? She was a cautionary tale for as far as a relationship was concerned. He had to know that. She didn't know how to truly let someone in, but she was willing to try for him. He meant that much to her. She just prayed he wouldn't break her heart or make a fool of her.

"So ask me, dimples. I need to hear you say it."

Dimples. God, she loved it when he called her that. "Please stay," she whispered, her heartbeat thudding in her ears. Maybe there was a chance for them. Maybe...

"Why?" he pressed.

"Because I care about you. A lot. And I...don't want to lose you," she blurted, her heart about to explode.

He groaned and pulled her to him, his arms locking around her so tight they compressed her ribcage. "Okay. I'll stay."

She clamped her arms around him, overwhelmed

with joy and relief, then laughed when he swept her up and carried her to the stairs.

****

Standing at the bow of the ferry, Amber tugged the hood of her jacket tighter around her face to block the cool wind coming off the Channel. It was still dark out and she could see lights twinkling in the distance.

There was a safehouse in Paris she could use to start her hunt. It would take a couple days to generate any leads. The last intel Amber had gathered said Hannah was last seen in Turkey after escaping over the Syrian border. If she'd been captured, they'd likely taken her back into Syria. That's where Amber would begin her search.

The bag at her feet contained everything she needed to get underway. Megan had gathered everything for her, taken care of all the logistics while Amber planned the hack. Without her, Amber would still be languishing inside that cell, facing an uncertain future.

Her future was still uncertain, but at least it was back under her control again. She had a sister she'd once loved to death.

Amber still loved her now. She wanted more time with her. To repair the bond that had been cruelly severed. But before that could happen, Amber had a lot of sins to make up for. Beginning with what would hopefully be a rescue mission.

She stared out over the darkened waves at the tiny lights dancing on the far coastline in the distance. Whatever it took to find out the truth and make amends for her mistakes. This was her fault and she had to make it right, no matter what.

If you're still out there, Hannah, hang on. I'm coming for you.

Amber would find her and bring her back, or die trying.

Chapter Twenty-Three

There it was. Sneaky bastard.

Megan tightened her knees around the cantering horse's sides and pushed up in the stirrups as she drew the arrow back. The last target was low, notched between an old hedge and a log.

She loosed the arrow, tracking it as it flew. A surge of satisfaction washed through her when it hit a few inches off center.

She eased her weight back into the saddle and slowed the horse to a trot, posting in the stirrups to avoid the bumps in the animal's gait. "Well done, Rollo," she told the horse, patting its neck.

Rollo snorted and shook his head from side to side, seeming proud of himself.

Late afternoon sunlight filtered down through the canopy of leaves arching over the path as she rode along. Up ahead, two familiar figures stood near the old stone wall. Marcus and Karas.

"Well?" he called out, leaning slightly on his cane.

"I hit all but one. And only because I spotted it too late."

One side of his mouth lifted slightly. "I've got to keep you sharp."

"Yes, you do." She stopped Rollo in front of him. The horse stretched his neck to bump Marcus in the chest, earning a deep chuckle and a knuckle rub over the white blaze on its forehead. "So, what are you doing all the way out here?"

"Karas needed a run." The dog sat beside him, tongue lolling as she panted from her exertion, her favorite yellow ball lying at her front paws. "You finished for the day?"

"I think so. Why?"

"No reason. Except that your presence is requested back at the manor."

She frowned. "My presence? By whom?"

"Come and find out," he said with a mysterious smile, and started for his ancient Land Rover. Karas picked up her ball and trotted after him in a perfect embodiment of the translation of her name—devoted.

Megan turned Rollo around and rode at a sedate pace back over the hill and down into the valley. Laidlaw Hall glowed like warm honey in the summer sunshine, and beyond it, the smaller gatehouse where she and Tyler had moved in together last week.

She still couldn't believe it. It had taken some juggling on his part, but he'd willingly pulled up stakes from his life in the States and left his family behind to be here with her full time.

Every morning she woke up with him beside her, she was convinced she was dreaming. He'd given up so much for her. Was willing to stand by her through all the uncertainty and whatever else came, and ready to help if—when—they heard from Amber.

There had been no word from her sister over the past two weeks. Rycroft and his people had tried to locate her, to no avail. But Megan knew in her heart that her sister was searching for Hannah and doing everything to find the lost Valkyrie.

In the meantime, Megan was doing her part to help the others search for the four remaining Valkyries identified in the files Amber had given to Rycroft's analysts. She read intel reports and reviewed fresh data as it came in, sent to her electronically here at the manor. All four women were believed to be in hiding and safe for now, including Chloe. Whether they were still operating or not was unknown.

When she arrived at the barn, Marcus's vehicle was parked alongside it. She handed the now cooled-down Rollo off to the stableman to untack and brush out, then walked through the formal garden and across the lawn to enter the back of the main house.

The scent of something awesome and savory wafted through from the kitchen, making her stomach rumble. "What is that heavenly smell?" she called out, expecting the cook to answer.

"Come see for yourself," a deep voice replied instead.

She stopped and turned left with a smile. What was Ty doing in here? The stone floor was cool and smooth under her socked feet. "I thought you were going into town for—" Her voice dried up and she stopped in her tracks, everything inside her stilling when she came to the threshold of the formal dining room.

Ty stood at the head of the long, antique table, smiling at her as he gripped the back of his chair. Marcus sat to his left, grinning from ear to ear.

Trinity was next to him. A blown-up and cut out picture of Amber's face was taped to a broomstick and propped in the chair beside her. Pictures of Briar and Georgia each marked its own place in front of a table setting.

Megan looked back at Tyler in shock. "Is it my birthday?" Maybe they'd found out her real one, that had been in the files Amber had hacked?

"No, but I hope you'll like this anyway." He reached behind him and opened the door into the parlor, revealing a gorgeous, fully decorated tree. It stood in front of the window, glowing in the summer sunshine, strings of multicolored lights and ornaments covering its branches. "Surprise."

Megan put a hand to her mouth. "Oh my God, Tyler…"

He walked over to her, slung a strong arm around her waist and leaned in for a kiss. "Merry Christmas, dimples," he murmured.

She covered her face and leaned into him to hide the tears in her eyes. "I don't believe it," she whispered back, her voice thick.

He kissed the top of her head. "Come sit."

"Aye, we're all starvin'," Marcus put in.

Megan pulled it together and straightened to look up at Tyler. He smiled, drew a finger down the side of her face. "I didn't think you should have to wait until the end of December to have a real Christmas."

He remembered. All the things she'd told him. The things she'd asked him about Christmas with his own family. He'd done this to heal part of her.

Megan broke into a smile as she looked around the table, giggled when she took a better look at the enlarged pictures taped to the broomsticks, putting the faces at the right height. About the least flattering shots of the three women that Megan could imagine. "They'd kill you for putting those up. Where did you get them?"

He lifted a broad shoulder. "Snagged them from security camera footage from London. Come on." He tugged her over to the head of the table and put her in the seat of honor.

Megan gazed around the table at all the food laid out as Tyler took the chair to her right.

"Feast your eyes on this," the cook, Mrs. Biddington

announced as she came through carrying a platter containing a beautifully browned turkey. She placed it in front of Marcus, beaming with pride. "Christmas in August, how lovely. Here, you do the honors." She handed him a carving knife and fork.

Yes, it was lovely. Magical. Megan gave Tyler a smile, her heart trembling. "Thank you."

He stole another kiss. "You're welcome."

Trinity raised her glass. "A toast."

"Wait," Marcus said, dropping the carving knife. "You bloody Americans. No sense of tradition," he muttered, and grabbed the paper candy-shaped thing from his plate.

He glanced around, frowned at them all. "Christmas crackers. We open them first, then make the toast." He held his out, extending one end toward Megan, and waved it at her. "Grab the end. No, with your other arm," he said, exasperated. "You 'ave to cross arms when you do it. There's a little bit of cardboard inside. Grab it tight." He crossed his arms and reached toward Trinity, who quickly picked hers up and mimicked him.

Megan and Tyler crossed arms, sharing a grin.

"Ready? On the count of three," Marcus instructed. "Three—"

Megan and Tyler both pulled. A loud snapping sound cracked through the room.

"I said on three," Marcus groused, frowning at her. "As in, at the end of the countdown."

"You said on three, so that's when we pulled," she argued, peering inside the now open tube.

A little package fell out. A tiny set of screwdrivers. She held them up, grinning. "Cool. Wonder what trouble I can get into and out of with these babies?" She glanced at Tyler's. "What did you get?"

"The saddest little compass I've ever seen in my life," Tyler said, examining the sad tiny trinket in his palm. "Wouldn't trust this to find my way to the bathroom."

Megan chuckled and looked over at Marcus, who was putting a bright purple, paper crown on his head. "Hey, who made you king? How come you get a crown?" she complained.

His expression turned bland. "You've one too. Look inside. There's a joke, too."

Sure enough, she found a dark green paper crown. Smiling, she unfolded it and put in on. "How do I look?" she asked Tyler.

"Like a queen."

"Right, now we toast," Marcus said, lifting his wineglass and gesturing for Trinity to take over.

Wearing a neon-orange crown, Trinity raised her glass. "A toast to new beginnings and new friends." She smiled at Megan. "And to our family. Dysfunctional as it is."

"To family," Megan echoed, returning the smile. She stood to reach across the table and clink glasses with her, then Marcus, and finally Tyler, then tipped her glass at the awful taped-on pictures at the other end of the table. "One hell of an interesting family."

They might not be a traditional one in most ways, but Megan wouldn't have traded them for anything.

The entire meal was a thrill for her. She had three helpings while they chatted and joked, and Marcus even chuckled once at something Tyler said. After dinner they went into the sitting room and sat around the tree.

"I always got to play Santa at my house growing up," Tyler said, swapping out his paper crown for a fuzzy red Santa hat with a white pompom on the end. He reached under the tree for the first wrapped present. "Where's Karas?"

The dog, lying at Marcus's feet, popped her head up and cocked her ears.

"Here, girl. It says 'With love from Santa Paws'."

Karas came over, sniffed at it, then took it in her mouth and rushed back to lie at Marcus's feet before tearing open the loosely wrapped paper to reveal a large doggy bone. Marcus reached down to rub the dog's head, a half-smile on his scarred face. "There's a good lass," he murmured.

He and Trinity had presents too. Then Tyler handed Megan a small, wrapped box. "This one's for you," he said.

Megan unwrapped it, the grin fading from her face when she opened the lid and found the silver bracelet nestled inside. "My mother's bracelet," she whispered, pulling it out. Sure enough, her mother's initials were engraved on the back of it. She looked up at Tyler. "Where did you get this?"

"It arrived in the mail last week, so I hid it and wrapped it up for you."

Amber had sent it. But when? From where? "Did it have a return address?" Maybe Amber had left it as a clue?

His eyes twinkled with amusement. "No, but it was stamped in London. She must have sent it before she left."

Oh, damn. She would not cry. Would not.

"Put it on me," she whispered, biting the inside of her lip as Tyler clasped it around her wrist. It made her feel closer to her dead mother. Now Megan had a piece of her forever.

"I didn't get you anything," she said to Tyler, feeling bad.

"You've given me plenty," he answered, his expression so full of love it pushed her to the verge of tears.

Marcus cleared his throat. "I need to stretch my leg. Trinity, can I interest you in a brandy in the study?"

"You can," she answered, popping up and making a beeline for the door, Marcus and Karas following her.

Megan glanced at Tyler. "What's going on?"

Rather than answer, he kissed her. She grabbed his shoulders and gave in, the desire pooling hot and sweet in her lower belly.

Just when she was starting to get light-headed he lifted his head, searched her eyes for a moment, then reached back under the tree and came up with a small box.

She stared at it, her heart tripping. Part of her was terrified to take it, afraid of what she was pretty sure she'd find inside.

"Don't freak out on me, dimples," he said quietly.

Holding her breath, she took it and undid the red satin bow on top. Her normally nimble fingers were unsteady as she opened the box. "Oh, Tyler," she whispered, tears clogging her throat when she saw the ring inside. A simple band of white gold.

"It's a promise ring," he explained, watching her. "I didn't want to rush you, but I wanted you to know how serious I am about you. About us."

She blinked to clear her vision and looked up at him. "You've left everything behind and moved halfway around the world to be with me, and you're willing to risk your life to help find the others. I already knew you were serious."

He smiled and cupped the side of her face with one hand. "You're not going after the others without me. We're a team now."

She threw her arms around his neck and pressed her cheek to his, squeezing her eyes shut. "I love you. So much." And wow, it wasn't as scary to tell him as she'd thought it would be.

His deep chuckle made her heart turn over as he hugged her back. "I love you too, dimples. And that means I'm with you 'til the end."

No one in her life had ever stood by her before. No one had ever stuck around. But Tyler had. And he would stay with her through whatever came next.

With him at her side, together they could face anything.

—The End—

To read more about the original Valkyries, look for the following titles

BRIAR: *Disavowed* and *Guarded*
(Hostage Rescue Team Series #4 and #12)

GEORGIA: *Betrayed*
(Hostage Rescue Team Series #9)

TRINITY: *Brody's Vow*
(Colebrook Siblings Trilogy #1)

Dear reader,

Thank you for reading *Stealing Vengeance*. I hope you enjoyed it. If you'd like to stay in touch with me and be the first to learn about new releases you can:

Join my newsletter at:
http://kayleacross.com/v2/newsletter/

Find me on Facebook: https://www.facebook.com/KayleaCrossAuthor/

Follow me on Twitter: https://twitter.com/kayleacross

Follow me on Instagram: https://www.instagram.com/kaylea_cross_author/

Also, please consider leaving a review at your favorite online book retailer. It helps other readers discover new books.

Happy reading,
Kaylea

Excerpt from
Covert Vengeance
<u>Vengeance Series</u>

By Kaylea Cross
Copyright © 2019 Kaylea Cross

Chapter One

The bitterness of betrayal was still as fresh as the healing bullet scar on her side, but she had to overcome it if she was going to get this done. People were depending on her. Family, both by blood and creed. Having blood family was still a revelation.

Amber Brown pulled the edges of her headscarf tighter around her face and adjusted her sunglasses as she left the bus station on the outskirts of Damascus. Hot, arid air blasted her, the September sun beating down on her as she moved through the crowd of passengers toward the rental car facility.

The latest intel indicated that her target was here. Whether or not she was still alive, Amber wasn't sure. Given the people involved with the woman's capture several days ago, that chance dwindled with each passing hour. Amber had to act fast.

She stayed alert as she moved, on the lookout for any threat that might have managed to follow her here despite all her precautions. She was deep in enemy territory now. Her technological expertise was a double-edged sword. It allowed her to find those who wanted to stay hidden—and it also made her a target.

She was the hunter for now, but she was also prey. There were so many unknowns, and every time she made a move, she wore a target on her back.

Her rental vehicle was waiting for her, attained with fake ID under a new alias. She checked it with a critical eye, subtly looking for any signs of tampering before hiding her equipment in various spots in the interior and sliding behind the wheel to crank up the air conditioning. She'd managed to fly under the radar and evade everyone looking for her thus far. Now the most dangerous part of her journey began.

Amber prayed she wasn't too late. If she was responsible for the capture—and much worse—of an innocent fellow Valkyrie, then she was honor bound to do whatever it took to try to rescue her. Up to and including giving her own life. It was the only way she could clear her conscience.

The roads were crowded, especially on the approach to the city. Security was tight. She breezed through the first checkpoint in a matter of minutes. At the second, right on the edge of the old capital, the way the armed soldiers looked at her put her instantly on edge.

The soldier at her window checked her passport with the computer in his booth, then turned to stare at her for a moment too long. Unease crackled along her nerve endings.

"Get out of the car," he commanded in clipped Arabic, adjusting his grip on his rifle.

Did they know who she was? She kept her expression impassive. Running the checkpoint wasn't an option if she wanted to live. So she had no choice but to comply.

She stepped out into the midday heat, posture and expression relaxed but her hands ready to dive for the pistol or blade strapped to her ankles, hidden beneath the loose lower legs of her cargo pants. A few men watched with interest from outside a nearby café. The slight bulges beneath their shirts told her some of them were armed.

The first soldier stared at her while his partner searched her vehicle. She didn't move, didn't react even when the second tossed her bag into the dirt and began rifling through it. She'd come prepared for this. Anything sensitive or mission critical was hidden in the vehicle or on her person somewhere.

Not finding anything, the guard left her clothing and toiletries lying in the dust and shook his head at the first man. Amber held his stare as he approached, his expression hard. She tensed and shifted her stance slightly, mentally choosing an escape route that might allow her to flee on foot because if this asshole thought he was going to perform a body search, that wasn't happening.

The soldier stopped a foot from her, tall enough that she had to tilt her head back to meet his eyes. "What are you doing in Damascus?" he growled.

None of your fucking business. If her picture had triggered something in his database, he would have tried to arrest her by now. Key word, *tried.* Because she wasn't going to prison. "Visiting family." He was hassling her because she was a single female traveling alone and thought she was easy prey. But if he thought he and his friend might make a victim out of her, they wouldn't live long enough to see how wrong they were.

The soldier sneered at her before raking his cold, black gaze over the length of her and back up again. "You're lying."

Amber refused to cower or look away. Bullies thrived on fear and weakness. He would find neither in her.

Try me, asshole. She'd killed men a lot scarier than him.

Taking him out would cause major hassle because she'd have to kill the other soldier too, but if he tried to attack her it would almost be worth it to do the world a favor and put a bullet in his head.

Seeming frustrated that he hadn't elicited the reaction he'd hoped for, he stepped back with a disgusted sound. "Get out of here," he snarled.

With pleasure. She knelt to gather up her strewn belongings, aware of exactly where both men were positioned in case they tried anything. Even as she drove off she kept her eye on the first guard in her side mirror, prepared to react in case he decided to take a parting shot at her. He was on his radio, gaze locked on her vehicle as he spoke to someone.

They would have eyes on her now. Adding more pressure to this high-stakes mission.

Her shoulders relaxed a little when she put a safe distance between her and the checkpoint. Traffic was light, yet it was hard to say if anyone had followed her. She focused on her surroundings, heading for the apartment she had secured. This area of Damascus was still very much a warzone.

Several buildings were nothing but piles of rubble. Others were marked with scars from shells and bullets, windows blown out and several floors destroyed. Children ran through the streets chasing one another or playing soccer while mostly male adults stood around watching.

Curious, somewhat hostile stares followed Amber as she drove to the small apartment building and parked around back. Given the security situation at the moment, a single female traveling alone made her both a curiosity and a target.

It took time to ensure she wasn't being followed and get into the unit. Once she swept the interior, she set up a handful of micro cameras to give her a view of the hallway and streets below. Finally, she was able to get to work.

Her custom laptop allowed her to access what she needed, including CCTV footage from outside the old palace she was interested in. Word had it that the people she was looking for were using it as temporary headquarters.

This organization specialized in running weapons and people, and had ties to both the military and a powerful terrorist group also operating in Syria. They were also old school, preventing her from being able to remotely hack into their security systems, and everyone was afraid of them because they were ruthless and rich and powerful. They could buy off whoever they wanted, and kill anyone who wouldn't take the money or got in their way.

Her hacking and technological wizardry wasn't much of an advantage here, but Amber could do old school when necessary. On screen she watched the handful of armed men moving about the building, looking for familiar faces, patterns that would allow her to penetrate the target. She needed to get inside to see if there was any sign of Hannah.

Sitting around made her antsy. After several hours the need to keep moving pricked at her.

Time for some eyes-on recon.

She left the building on foot, a shopping bag over one shoulder as she made her way down the sidewalk and blended in with the locals on her route. Less than twenty paces in, a niggling awareness warned her she was being watched.

Her gaze snagged on someone across the street. A man. Around her height, but heavyset. He wore a full beard but the tops of his cheeks were exposed.

Showing the curved scar snaking down the right one.

Recognition hit. He'd been watching her from the cafe at the second checkpoint. The soldier must have sent him after her, either to keep tabs or...something worse.

She glanced away and kept walking, that warning buzz growing stronger in the pit of her stomach. Out of the corner of her eye she saw the scarred man step away from the building and follow.

She walked faster. Turned left at the next corner, using her mental map of the area to keep her bearings in the tangle of ancient streets. She needed to avoid a confrontation at all cost. There was enough heat on her already without adding more.

In her peripheral she caught the moment the man broke into a jog and crossed the street, coming after her.

Amber broke into a run, scanning for a place where she could lose him. Getting in a shootout in the middle of the street meant disaster for her and the mission.

She found an alley a block up and darted into it just as running footsteps sounded behind her. The old cobbled surface was narrow and deserted. The only cover was a wooden wagon near the other end, offering only partial concealment.

The heavy treads behind her kept coming, and the end of the alley was less than thirty yards away. She'd wanted to avoid this, but there was no other choice. If she was going to do this, it had to be here and now. The wagon would have to do.

She crawled under it, stretched out on her belly and reached down to grab the pistol from her ankle holster. Then she waited, weapon ready.

The man raced around the corner of the alley. Stopped, then ran toward her, a pistol in his grip.

Amber fired two rapid shots.

Surprise and pain twisted the man's features as the bullets struck his legs. He dropped to his knees, blood spreading across the cobbles, and raised his arm to fire at her.

Amber fired twice more, this time center mass.

The man toppled sideways with a painful groan and arched his back, his weapon now lying on the shadowy ground as he tore feebly at the front of his shirt. He would be dead in moments.

Glancing behind her to make sure no one else had seen her yet, she scooted out from beneath the wagon and hurried toward him, pistol aimed at his head this time. He lay unmoving, only his eyes moving, rolling toward her as she approached. She kicked his pistol out of reach, then crouched down and quickly went through his pockets. No ID, but she took his phone. Once she was safe she would use it to find out who he was and who he worked for.

She ran for the end of the alley, tucking her weapon in her waistband. The gunshots would bring unwanted attention. When someone came to investigate, she couldn't be anywhere near the body.

She scrapped her plan to conduct recon of the palace and headed back to the apartment, ready to go back on the offensive if someone else came after her. The dead man meant more danger for her. Everything was moving faster now, time slipping away too quickly and increasing the chance that she wouldn't live long enough to complete her mission.

It didn't frighten her. It came with the territory, and constantly watching her back was nothing new. She'd lived most of her life that way. Had learned long ago not to fear death, because death came for everyone eventually.

Except this time... This time she had something worth living for.

An image of her sister's face flashed in her mind. Eighteen months younger, taken from her when they'd been little, now a Valkyrie operative who specialized in stealing critical things from impossible places.

Megan was smiling at her as she handed Amber the small duffel of cash and other supplies she'd needed to leave the country after Megan had helped her escape the holding facility in London two weeks ago. "You're coming back, right?"

"If I can."

Megan scowled and shoved Amber's shoulder gently. "Well then make sure you can."

"I'll try."

She wanted to return to England and see Megan again. Wanted to spend time with her and help with the search for the other missing Valkyries. But the only way that was happening was if Amber completed this mission.

She shook her head. Wishing for things was dangerous. She couldn't afford to think about Megan, or dreams that would probably never come true. All that mattered was righting the wrong she'd done.

And if she was *really* lucky, one day she might even get to live a real life for a little while. Maybe even spend some of it getting to know her little sister again. Begin to heal the bond that had been severed by the people who had turned Amber and the others from young, frightened orphans into lethal weapons.

She pushed that from her mind and hurried toward the apartment where she could hack into the phone and dig into the dead man's identity. Rescuing Hannah was all that mattered right now.

Someone had sent that hired thug after her. She hoped it was the guard at the checkpoint and not a wider network aware of her presence.

One threat had been eliminated. God only knew how many more were coming.

—End Excerpt—

(***Covert Vengeance*** releases July 30, 2019)

About the Author

NY Times and USA Today Bestselling author Kaylea Cross writes edge-of-your-seat military romantic suspense. Her work has won many awards, including the Daphne du Maurier Award of Excellence, and has been nominated multiple times for the National Readers' Choice Awards. A Registered Massage Therapist by trade, Kaylea is also an avid gardener, artist, Civil War buff, Special Ops aficionado, belly dance enthusiast and former nationally-carded softball pitcher. She lives in Vancouver, BC with her husband and family.

You can visit Kaylea at www.kayleacross.com. If you would like to be notified of future releases, please join her newsletter: http://kayleacross.com/v2/newsletter/

Complete Booklist

ROMANTIC SUSPENSE

Vengeance Series
Stealing Vengeance
Covert Vengeance

Crimson Point Series
Fractured Honor
Buried Lies
Shattered Vows
Rocky Ground

DEA FAST Series
Falling Fast
Fast Kill
Stand Fast
Strike Fast
Fast Fury
Fast Justice
Fast Vengeance

Colebrook Siblings Trilogy
Brody's Vow
Wyatt's Stand
Easton's Claim

Hostage Rescue Team Series
Marked
Targeted
Hunted
Disavowed
Avenged
Exposed
Seized

Wanted
Betrayed
Reclaimed
Shattered
Guarded

Titanium Security Series
Ignited
Singed
Burned
Extinguished
Rekindled
Blindsided: A Titanium Christmas novella

Bagram Special Ops Series
Deadly Descent
Tactical Strike
Lethal Pursuit
Danger Close
Collateral Damage
Never Surrender (a MacKenzie Family novella)

Suspense Series
Out of Her League
Cover of Darkness
No Turning Back
Relentless
Absolution

PARANORMAL ROMANCE
Empowered Series
Darkest Caress

HISTORICAL ROMANCE

46483205R00161

Made in the USA
Middletown, DE
28 May 2019